CODY WAS HERE

and other stories

D.W. HITZ

Cody Was Here
and Other Stories
D.W. Hitz

Fedowar Press, LLC

www.FedowarPress.com

ISBN-13 (Digital): 978-1-956492-46-0
ISBN-13 (Paperback): 978-1-956492-47-7

"The Ancestors", "The Gate", "Love is Cold", "It Stretches", "Cody Was Here", and "On the Run" were edited by Heather Ann Larson

"Chester's Cave" was first published in Fedowar Holiday Horrors Volume One, November 15, 2021, by Fedowar Press, LLC, edited by Richard T. Ryan

"The Trophy" was first published in Fear Forge Anthology: Winter Quarter 2022, October 24, 2022, by Horrorsmith Publishing, edited by Lyndsey Smith

Cover Art by Don Noble of Rooster Republic Press

Interior Design by D.W. Hitz

Also By D.W. Hitz

Adult Fiction

Judith's Prophecy (Big Sky Terror Book 1)
Judith's Blood (Big Sky Terror Book 2)
Judith's Fall (Big Sky Terror Book 3)
Gods are Born
Brady: A Novella
Bloodtooth
Cody Was Here and Other Stories

Extreme Horror

Larval Seeds
Stay Out Of The Tub
You're Going to Die In Here
Santa vs. Satan

Middle Grade Fiction

They Stole the Earth!
The Curse of Grohl

Contents

Foreword   IX

Chester's Cave   1

The Ancestors   63

The Gate   87

Love Is Cold   121

It Stretches   135

Cody Was Here   153

The Trophy   179

On The Run   201

Foreword

One of the things I've always loved about horror, and have grown more and more conscious of over the years, is its ability to encapsulate genres. Horror is not just the thing that scared you or the thing that made you dread getting up in the dark to use the bathroom in the middle of the night. Horror is anything that provides you with a feeling of unease. Splatter, dread, revulsion, nervousness and anxiety, and, of course, fear are all expressions of horror. And so, too, are the tentacles it weaves into fellow genres.

Horror can exist in any type of tale. Romance can include the horror of newly found lovers being struck by a car, where the fear of their being torn apart is imminent. An honorable space-faring mission can turn to horror when an unknown beast sneaks aboard a ship. A cowboy can discover a cave where ancient evils corrupt his ranch and animals. All these things contain elements of other genres but also bring horror to light because horror is innately within the human condition, making it easily a part of any story.

When it came to putting together this book, I thought there was no better way to create it than playing around with various avenues of horror. So, within these pages, you'll find a ghost story (Love is Cold), sci-fi stories (The Gate & The Trophy), folk horror (The Ancestors), crime horror (On the Run), and a few I'll leave you to discover. It's a blend of some of the genres that fill me with giddiness to play in.

I hope you enjoy them, and I thank you for reading.

-- D.W. Hitz November 14, 2023

Chester's Cave
1

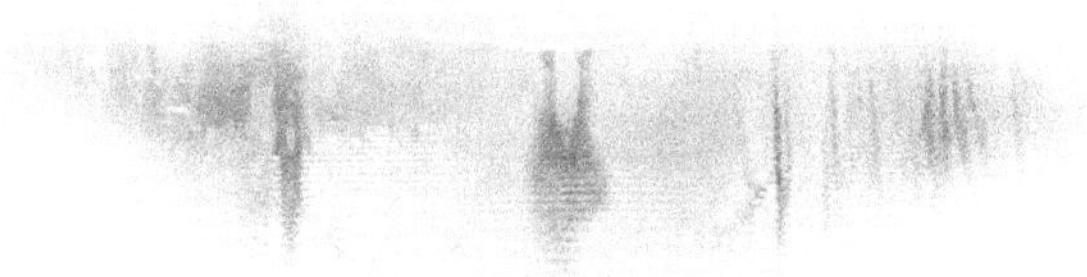

CHESTER COLEFIELD AND BILLY Bryant looked down from the roof of Chester's mid-century split-level home. He wasn't supposed to go up there. Wasn't supposed to take his friends up there either. But who could really stop a couple of teenagers when they had a really good bad idea in mind?

It was that time of Halloween night when the little kids had finished their trick-or-treating, and the teens were the only ones out. It was that time of Halloween night when the electricity in the air warned: *Only bad things are yet to come tonight.*

"You sure they're coming?" Billy asked. His gaze ran up and down the darkened neighborhood from their perch.

"Molly said she was sure," Chess said. A smirk crept up both sides of his mouth. "Matt and Doug were so pissed. She said they spent all of algebra planning it."

Molly Higgins was right, though the truth was the entire school was aware of how pissed Matt Axley and Doug Palin were.

It had been a week since Chess's images went viral among the student body and a month since the event inciting those images had taken place.

In late August, once school had started back up, Matt and Doug had been on hate patrol through the lunchroom when they found their target. It was Randy Myers. The kid had been homeschooled since birth, and it was his first day in a real school. His hair was long, and his face narrow and feminine, much like many freshmen, but to Matt and Doug, his image was a thread they could pull. He sat alone at a table when Matt and Doug moved in and started up with every gay slur they could muster. In less than ten minutes, Randy was in tears and running from the lunchroom. In two weeks, he was dead by his own hands.

Chess had no love for Randy Myers specifically. He didn't shed a tear when the kid had died. What he did feel was a sense of injustice. Matt and Doug were questioned by the police and the vice principal, but nothing came of it other than a few assemblies about the dangers of cyberbullying. Those assholes essentially got away with murder.

It was at the second assembly that the school was forced to sit through when Chester got the idea. There he was, bored out of his mind, eyes scanning the bleachers, and his gaze fell upon Matt and Doug. They were huddled together, pointing, laughing at the presentation. And the smiles on their faces filled Chess with such a rage he could barely stop himself from standing and screaming—until a second later, when their positions sparked a thought. They were shoulder to shoulder, left knee against right. They were so close that if you didn't know it was an assembly, know that they were trying to hide their conversation and keep out of the teachers' sights, you might just think they were cuddling together—like lovers.

When Chess got home that day, he raced to his computer. He searched through every app he had access to: Facebook, Twitter, Instagram, Tik-Tok. He pored over Matt's and Doug's accounts, downloading every image of them he could find until he found the magic three; three images of them at the mall.

Chess fired up Photoshop and began slicing and dicing. He was no pro, but he had done plenty of tutorials and knew his way around. He took his time and worked for hours. By night, he had something he liked, but it wasn't quite good enough. The next day, he tried again. Better, but still not there. On the third day, he got it. He ended his night by creating a new, fake Facebook account, liking the school's page, and posting the images. He went to sleep that night happier than he'd been in quite a while, longer than he could remember. He'd found the one thing that Matt and Doug hated the most and turned them into it. Tomorrow was going to be a good day.

Chess woke up with a smile on his face. He was so sure his stunt had worked that he didn't even check Facebook that morning. He had decided that he would rather have the surprise and the thrill of showing up at school as if he knew nothing and simply watch it unfold.

Walking into the school building that crisp October morning, Chess was warm inside his baggy black hoodie. His backpack was snug against his back, and his shoes swept over the floor as if he were floating. The hallways were as loud as any other day, but today, Chess didn't try to block any of it out or focus on his music as he usually did. Instead, he eavesdropped on every conversation he passed.

Lisa Collighan and Megan Towers were wide-eyed on his right. "Can you believe it?"

"Oh, my god!"

"They were French kissing in the mall!"

On Chester's left, four members of the football team joked. "Funniest thing, dude!"

"No wonder they act like they hate gays!"

"They're totally gay!"

The jokes flooded the hallway, the homeroom, the lunchroom. Someone at the school removed the post, but it was too late—half the school had already downloaded the images and posted them to each and every social media site in existence. It had gone viral. Matt and Doug hid for days. And Chess wished he could have taken credit for it publicly.

But Chess did tell three people before the week was up: Billy Bryant, Molly Higgins, and Jeff Patterson. Both Billy and Molly swore to Chess that they didn't share the secret. Jeff did too, but it had to be one of the three. Chess's suspicion settled on Jeff. At that point, it didn't matter, though. Matt and Doug had found out, and from what Molly had heard, they were coming to Chess's house tonight for a little payback.

"Let them bring it," Chester said.

"I still can't believe you did that," Billy said. "I mean, that was some next-level shit."

Chess smirked. "Yeah, it was pretty badass."

"I mean, those assholes had it coming." Billy leaned left, knocking the bucket beside him on edge. It wobbled, and Billy had to grab it before the thing tipped and rolled down the incline.

Chess shook his head. He looked west along the street again. Then east. The morning's light snowfall had completely melted. Most of that had evaporated, though small sheets of thin ice resided in patches along the road. The shaded grass below the front yard's blue spruce held dotted clumps of slush. The wind blew and a chill passed over his skin, even below his thick hoodie and long sleeve shirt. That was when he heard them.

Footfalls echoed up Chess's street. They were light, muted, as if held above the ground, and only allowed to touch for seconds at a time. But he heard them. It was the sound of sneaking through his neighborhood, and he was very familiar with that sound.

"What do you—" Billy stared to speak but was cut off when Chess grabbed his arm.

Chess pointed to the left, west, with a finger over his lips. Billy squinted and strained to see.

The view was blocked by the neighbor's trees, but as the footfalls continued and the sibilance of whispers rose, Billy showed an expression of recognition. His hand went into his bucket—so did Chester's.

Matt clutched the grocery bag tightly in his right hand. Doug held his in the left. They had rested their bikes at the corner and were creeping as quietly as they could.

Matt grinned with eagerness. He thought about the impact of eggs against a house, a car, a window and wondered how they would sound, how they would dent, smash. Because they weren't regular eggs. They had been regular before he stacked them in his father's meat freezer in the garage yesterday. Now, they were as hard as stone and ready to rock.

Doug's expression was frozen in a sneer. The muscular tension had latched on when they had left Matt's garage and wasn't going to leave for another ten minutes—not until Matt was dead.

Matt and Doug reached the edge of Chester Colefield's yard and surveyed the scene. A skeleton lay on the porch. Plastic graves with cotton spider webs stood in the yard. The lights were out inside.

"Are they here?" Doug whispered.

"One way to find out," Matt said. He marched halfway across the yard, about even with the headstones, and Doug trailed along. He reached into his grocery bag, where three dozen frozen eggs clacked against each other. He selected the first one he touched. The shell bulged, a thin crack ran from one pole to another. He wound back his arm and pitched the thing as hard as his arm would allow.

An image crossed Matt's mind as the ovoid ice slipped free. He saw himself on the pitcher's mound during the World Series, though at the plate wasn't a rival batter; kneeling at home was Chester Colefield, his face dead center of the batter's box, ready to have some teeth shattered.

The egg shone as it crossed the yard from moonlight into the darkness of shadow that surrounded the house. There was a second of complete silence as it flew, and then the world of soundlessness was brought to life with the crash of egg against the dining room window, and a firm, rubbery object smacked Matt across his face.

There wasn't enough time for Matt to register that something had hit him or that he knew this feeling, regardless of whether he was ready to recognize it yet. His next thought would have been to question if the impact had come from Doug. There was no one else there. Instead, wetness drenched his face along with the sting of popping latex, and his face, shirt, sweatshirt, and pants were cold and moist.

Matt looked down at his chest as the dampness encroached. He turned to Doug as another thing hit the side of his face, and he watched a red water balloon explode against his friend's nose, cheek, and forehead.

"Fuck!" Doug shouted.

Matt scanned the yard frantically and saw nothing. Another balloon hit his shoulder. The sound of laughter trickled down from somewhere high. A splash wet his legs as another hit the ground.

"There!" Doug pointed at Chess's roof. The shithead and his asshole friend Billy were perched on the edge of the roof and lobbing wave after wave of balloons downward.

Doug leaned back, winding up. A projectile exploded against his chest as he swung and released. His egg soared upward.

Billy was raising his hand to pitch as an egg that felt like stone caught the back of his wrist. He yelled and dropped the balloon. It burst against the shingles and splashed his shoes. Billy cupped one hand inside the other.

Chess fired again. It collided with Matt's shoulder as Doug released another shot. The frozen egg hit Chess in his right cheekbone. The pain was hot. It sent him rocking backward. He stepped forward to settle himself, and his foot landed on Billy's broken balloon. Only that wasn't all. In the blackness of the night, they had failed to see a patch of stubborn ice that had survived the overcast day. Now covered with water, it was as slick as an ice rink.

Chess's foot slipped forward and up. His other tried to catch him, but it was too slow, too weak. He fell back against the roof and slid.

"No!" He shouted.

Billy was frozen beside him. His eyes were wide and unbelieving. Matt and Doug were motionless below. They watched with bated breath to see what would happen next.

Chess felt himself moving down the incline. His legs went over the edge. His hands grabbed at the rough, sandy surface of his home. They found his water balloon bucket. He took it in his grip, panicked for anything to hold onto. It slid forward with him as his waist came over the edge. Chess grabbed the last shingle. It slid through his hand and scraped the skin from his fingers as he drifted downward.

Matt watched Chess sail downward. His leg hit the ground first and folded sideways as if it were meant to bend that way. His hips hit next. He crumpled down, his head crashing last into the lawn.

"Holy shit," Matt said.

Billy stared at his friend. Tears streamed down his face.

"Come on," Doug said. He grabbed at Matt's arm.

"What?" Matt wasn't sure why Doug was pulling at him. He wanted to see more. He wanted to know if Chess was going to get up. If Chess was going to do anything. Matt had never seen anyone fall like that. His eyes were fixed, not believing what they had just seen.

"Come on, asshole!" Doug said. "I threw that—they're going to blame me—blame us."

It clicked inside Matt's head. They could get in trouble for this. They could even go to jail. Maybe for a long time if Chess were dead. Chills ran through him. "Shit."

The bag of eggs slipped through Matt's fingers. He turned to Doug, but Doug was already running away, back toward the bikes.

"Wait." Matt ran. The cold night wind blew across him as he fled. It penetrated his clothes through each and every drop of water that soaked him. Colder and colder as he moved, and the air crossed him. He reached his bike and climbed on, feeling as though he were layered in ice.

Doug peddled north, toward the back of the neighborhood. Matt followed, not sure where his friend was going. They flew past street after street, their names and their houses blurred. Halloween lights and inflatable scares blended into a singular blob. Matt's legs burned as he peddled faster and faster, struggling to keep up with Doug.

They passed the last street, and the road dead-ended at the edge of Custer National Forrest. A dirt trail vanished into the darkness of the woods beside a parking area used for county snowplows in the winter. Doug hopped the curb and rode full bore inside.

Chills enclosed Matt's chest, arms, and legs. They told him to stop—that this wasn't the way. He didn't listen. He followed his friend.

Billy peered over the edge of the roof. The world below zoomed away and faded back, numbing the back of his head and turning his legs to jelly. He shuffled backward.

Fear gripped his chest. He had to look, had to help. His friend had gone over, and he had no idea what had happened at the bottom. He had to see. Had to help. Had to *get* help.

Billy dropped to his hands and knees and crept forward, avoiding the wet spot where Chess had slipped. The wet spot Billy had made. And it raced through him—*he* had done this. It was his fault that his friend might be dead.

"Oh, God." Billy's head edged out over the precipice.

At first, Billy couldn't tell where Chester was. He didn't see anything body-shaped. As his eyes adjusted to the view, he began to make out the different textures and subtle differences in shadowed tones. He still saw nothing that looked human. What he saw was a pile of something. A mound that was not quite as dark as the late-night grass with an arm stretched out toward the house.

Billy scurried backward and raced to the window they had used to get out onto the roof.

"911," he huffed. "911, 911."

It was a path Matt faintly recognized. He'd been this way before. Once, he, Doug, and Paul Neddles had *borrowed* his father's pistol and come back here for target practice. He had almost suckered Sally Thompson into coming this way with him on another occasion and regretted that he wasn't able to seal that deal. But each of those times had been during the daytime. This was different. This was night, a dark night, a Halloween night.

Matt wasn't generally superstitious about things. He used to have a lucky rabbit's foot that he had stolen from another kid in middle school. He took it because it was soft, and he liked how it felt when the kid showed it off. He had no notions of it actually being lucky, though. It wasn't lucky for that kid—Matt stole it without a problem. It surely wasn't lucky for the rabbit. But there was something strange about this night, this Halloween night that made Matt feel off—hesitant about coming back into these woods.

His night had started with rage as they went to Chester's house. But then Chester fell... was the kid even alive? The chills that Matt felt across his limbs still hadn't relented. He wanted to chalk it up to how wet those assholes had gotten him, but he could tell there was more to the sensation. There was something more in the air. Something more resonating against the hairs on the back of his neck and telling him: *This is bad. Get out of here.*

Doug turned, taking a trail to the left. It branched from the main path under the boughs of century-old pines and spruces. Matt didn't know this deviation, but he turned anyway. He had never seen Doug like this. He had to assume he knew where he was going.

The night became darker and gloomier as they passed under older and denser forest. The scent from the woods was heavier as well, thick with the tart smell of sap and rank with the aroma of musty fungus. The little light provided by the moon and stars faded into nearly nothing. The trees on either side of the trail seemed to disappear into blackness, and Matt was overwhelmed by a presence. There was someone here, watching, hidden in the unseen.

"Wait up!" Matt shouted. He squinted and peddled. Only the barely visible dirt below his bike and the red reflector under Doug's seat showed Matt where to go.

"It's not far," Doug shouted back. After another short distance, he vanished from view.

Matt's heart jumped inside his frozen chest.

"Doug!" Where did he go? Did he speed up to where Matt could no longer see him? Matt forced his legs to move faster. Pushed his feet harder into the pedals, making sure his grip was tight, that no ounce of pressure was wasted.

The path below disappeared. Pain raced through Matt's chest. A wall cracked against Matt's forehead. Something wet and hot was in his nose and scraped down his face. His bike was ripped backward from beneath him, and Matt found himself on his back.

Matt tried to sit up, and his right side screamed. His fingers didn't work. Wouldn't brace him against the ground. Wouldn't respond to his direction. He opened his eyes to see what had happened, but the navy and black world of the forest only appeared through his left side. He couldn't see from his right. Was something on his face? It was wet and felt suppressed by something.

A strange sound vibrated Matt's chest and rang through his ears. He ignored it and felt his face with his good hand. Whatever was on him, he had to clear it away.

His fingers walked along the skin of his right side and found what was on him. A stick bulged from his right eye. Blood seeped over and down, drenching his cheeks, his nose, his lips, his chin.

Matt tried to scream and realized he already was. He heard a screech that sounded like a madman, and a blunt crack rocked his head from behind.

Doug dragged his friend by the feet. Down a small hill and into the mouth of a waiting cave. He watched Matt's head bobble back and forth as they moved. He cursed Chester the entire way. When Matt was inside, he went back for Matt's bike.

Doug dropped Matt's bike on top of his own just inside the cave's entrance. He glanced around the inside of the cavity, amazed that he was able to find this place. He had no idea there were caves in these woods. He had only been hoping to find a clearing or boulder to rest behind, away from the cops he knew would be coming. A place to stop and think. Then Matt had to be an idiot and ram himself into those trees.

But either way, Doug had found a place. He had a feeling it was a good place. It was warm and welcoming inside his gut and only felt warmer the longer he stayed.

Doug pulled his phone from his pocket and shook it. The flashlight came on and lit the cave so brightly he had to squint to see.

It was a small cave, maybe the size of a two-car garage. There was writing on the walls, but it was hard to make out. Faded drawings decorated two of the granite sides. Mold grew in various shades of green and yellow on the stacked boulders that created the opposite walls, and the strange layers of boulder on boulder made Doug wonder if this cave were somehow man-made. He brushed away the thought as soon as it came to him. The size and weight of those rocks were way too much—no one could have done that. But the idea would not fully recede.

Doug took a step toward the wall with the largest script. It seemed to be calling him over, whispering just below the whine of the night's increasingly cold wind. He took another step, and Matt began to moan.

Doug glanced at his friend, shined the light on him. He looked even worse than Doug had thought he would. His entire face was dark red. Not only was his right eye destroyed, his nose was split. A gash tore across his cheek from the cheekbone down to his jaw. His moan turned into a wail. Into a scream.

"Stop it," Doug hissed. "They'll hear you."

Matt didn't stop. He got louder. "Help! I need help!"

"Stop it!" Doug's eyes shifted from his broken friend to the cave entrance. Why was he doing this? They had found a perfect hiding spot to figure this all out. Why was he trying to ruin it? "Quiet."

Matt grew louder.

"No. No, no, no," Doug paced the cave. Distant whispers grew in his ears. The cave walls began to glow with faint orange illumination. The words stood up from the granite, strange words that Doug could now see but not understand. "No, no, no. Quiet!"

"Help!" Matt shouted.

The whispers became stronger. Their words unintelligible, but their meaning was clear.

Doug ran his light over the cave floor, searching for something—what, he didn't know—something to help, to help quiet his friend. His beam stopped on a rock. It was large, a foot wide, six inches around, like a massive stone football.

Yes, something said in Doug's ear.

"Yes," Doug agreed.

Doug picked up the football. He felt wetness on his face. He carried it over to Matt and realized he was crying. Salty liquid ran into his mouth.

"Please stop," Doug said.

"Help!" Matt screamed again. "My eye! My face!"

Doug raised the football over his head. His lip trembled. His hands trembled. His legs trembled.

"Help!" Matt's good eye fell upon his friend. "Wha—"

The stone rocketed down at the teenager's skull. His shrieks became gurgles. Hot frothy blood ran down his head to the cave floor. The stone raised and came down again. Blood ran to the center of the room and pooled. The ground began to vibrate.

Doug dropped the stone and watched the room quake. It was amazing, and he knew that somehow, he was a part of it. Wind raced around the cavern. It was a warm wind. It invited him to step closer to the walls of words, through the pool of his friend's blood. Doug smiled. He stared into his reflection on the floor and began to laugh at his face. The face laughed back. It laughed as he walked through and raised his hands, reaching for the inscribed wall.

Doug touched the glowing words. He caressed the wall. Warmth enveloped him. The walls shook, and the stacked boulder wall moved. It closed the cave's entrance.

"Wait," Doug said. Something was wrong with this.

He raised a foot to step toward the closed door, and a clawed red hand reached from the granite wall. Its long thin fingers and sharp black claws dug into Doug's leg and pulled.

He screamed. The hand, its claws, they were cold, frozen, as if they had been carved from ice.

The alien hand yanked harder, tearing into Doug's leg. It vanished into the wall and dragged Doug with it. His foot. His calf.

"No!" Doug shouted.

He watched as another clawed hand came out and seized his other leg. Pain shot like lightning up his limb, and the thing dragged his second foot inside.

Doug couldn't scream anymore. He cried and whimpered as his knees went in. His hips. His waist. His chest. He tasted the salty iron of Matt's blood which was spattered across his face. His eyes fell on his friend, and everything became red.

2

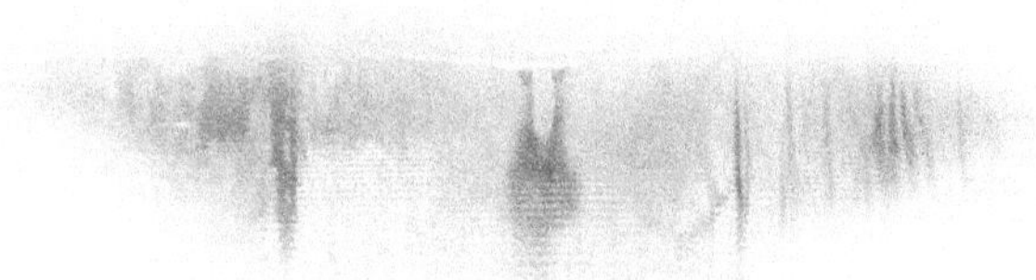

I T WAS THREE WEEKS into November before Chess began to feel like life was returning to something near normal. He'd been released from the hospital with a cast on his arm and another on his opposite leg. The bruises were finally starting to fade from purple to pink. He was getting used to his crutches and was going to start back at school if Mom would let him.

It took a dozen hours of Chess pleading and nagging and explaining to Mom that without getting some social exposure, his mental health was going to deteriorate right along with his physical health. But she finally relented. He had shown off his skills at manipulating the crutches, getting up and down from seats—albeit extremely slowly—and he had to promise that she could drop him off and pick him up for the next few weeks. The last one wasn't too bad, as he didn't like riding the bus anyway, and the next two weeks were really only a week and a half with Thanksgiving coming up. So with Mom's blessings, Chess showed up at the drop-off lane at school on a chilly Monday morning.

Inside, the noise, the movement, the people—the exposure rushed Chess's senses at once. He'd been so bored the last two weeks, he was now more excited to be at school than he would ever admit.

With a lean and a swing, again and again, he worked his crutches to his homeroom. Nods followed him down the hallways, along with a series of comments: "Welcome back." "You're alive!" and "Holy shit."

The exception to the warm reception was Paul Neddles, Matt and Doug's third wheel, who had been grounded on Halloween night and unable to join his friends' attack on Chess's house. He scowled as Chess passed, offering his own nod—this one more ominous, this one saying, "Yeah, I'll catch up to you later."

Other than Paul, the rest of the school was relatively unbothered by the disappearances of Matt and Doug. No one had seen them since Halloween, and after the trouble at Chess's house, most people assumed they had run away, afraid of being arrested. Nonetheless, every asshole has a mother, and Doug's raised hell at the police station until Deputy Harrison agreed to form a search party. They walked the streets and woods for ten miles around the Colefield home and found nothing. Not their bikes, not their blood, not the hole they had vanished into.

The missing persons' cases remained open for both Matt and Doug, but at this point, little was being done to find them. With nothing having been found on any of the grid searches, the assumption that they had run away became the prevailing theory around town.

The bell sounded with Chess ten feet from his destination. Mrs. Irons stood in the doorway of the classroom, watching him and waiting. She held a pleasant smile on her face. Chess couldn't tell if it was from pity or genuine happiness at his return. He guessed happiness. Chess was wrong.

Behind Jennifer Irons' thoughts was the image of her brother, Jeremy, who had drowned in the Missouri river when she was ten. He had just gotten a cast removed from his leg the week before, and instead of the picture of him going under the water over and over, his hands surging upward for help, the image Mrs. Irons always forced to the surface when she thought of Jeremy was him with that damned cast and an effervescent smile aimed at her.

In almost the dead center of the room, Chess plopped down into his seat. Billy held out his palm, and Chess gave it a slap.

The majority of homeroom was a blur for Chess. There were announcements from the speakers overhead and from Mrs. Irons, then she let the room quietly talk until the next bell rang. There was gossip to catch up on from Billy about everything Chess had missed in the past two weeks, but most of it was uninteresting to him. What he had wanted to know was what everyone was saying about Matt and Doug. What they had said about that night. Billy opened his mouth to answer, and the bell rang.

"Dammit," Billy said.

"Hold on," Chess said. As the rest of the class stood and rushed at the door, he raised his hand.

Mrs. Irons leaned in from beyond the front row of desks.

"Mrs. Irons," Chess said, "can Billy carry my books to my next class for me? It would really help."

Her pitiful smile returned, and she nodded. "Go on." Jeremy needed some help, too, in those last few weeks.

Chess and Billy had only gotten a few feet from their homeroom when the first period bell rang. They plodded down the empty hall, and Billy continued. He told Chess about the search party and the general consensus from most of their schoolmates that they were better off with Matt and Doug gone. As far as Billy knew, most people were of the opinion that life would be better off without them. That was with the exception of Paul Neddles.

"I'm sure," Chess said. "I saw Paul this morning."

Billy's eyes widened. "What did he say?"

"Nothing. He just gave me an *eat-shit* look and took off."

"Good—I mean, I'm glad that was all. I've been trying to stay out of his way. I think you should too."

"I'll do my best, but it's not like I can run away from the guy." Chester glanced down at his leg.

"Yeah," Billy chuckled.

They reached Chess's math class, and after he took his seat, Billy handed him his backpack and headed to science.

Molly Higgins watched with a sour pang in her belly as Chester climbed into his mother's minivan. People rushed past her in nearly every direction, grabbing books, papers, and backpacks from their lockers and running to catch their buses. They were a haze in her peripheral vision compared to her focus on Chess.

It was she who had told Chess that Matt and Doug were coming on Halloween night, a conversation that thankfully had not been repeated to anyone else since that fateful day. She would have been blamed for it all, she was sure. Blamed by the parents, the school, the police. If she hadn't told him about that conversation, there might have been some damage to Chess's house, but that would have been it—wouldn't it?

The self-punishing part of her brain wanted to think so, even if she had no proof. Matt and Doug could have just as easily bumped into Chess and Billy on the street and had a fight there. It might not have ended with property damage; there might have been welts and whatever else solidly frozen eggs could do. But that would have been better than Chess falling off a roof and the other two going missing.

As much as she wanted to blame herself, though, she watched Chess and realized she could have done nothing else. She was in love with him after all, and there was nothing anyone could do about that. Nothing she could deny him if he asked. Even if he had no clue of her feelings.

The Colefield minivan accelerated from the drop-off lane, and Molly turned away. The hallway had become barren beyond scraps of trash on the floor and the odors of disinfectant and teenage bodies.

She began her walk to the western side of the school—its exit was the closest for her walk home. She thought about her conversation with Chess in history class. He had said it would be four more weeks before his arm cast could come off and six for his leg. That would be by Christmas, New Year's Eve at the latest, she thought. Time enough for him to go to Floyd Munsen's New Year's Eve party. And this time, she wasn't going to hold back. She was going to get Chess alone in Floyd's parents' room and show him what he'd been missing.

The thought warmed Molly's insides, even against the rush of cold wind that hit her when she opened the western exit. A sly smile cracked her lips, and her thoughts made her eyes roll. They came back as she turned onto Fourth Avenue and stepped face to face with Paul Neddles.

The air rushed from Molly's lungs, and she felt her feet leave the Earth. She was floating, she thought, not falling. Paul seemed to grow taller, and she realized the ground must be coming ever closer. She was over concrete. This was going to hurt. She moved her hand, trying to wedge it behind her head before she hit the sidewalk. She made it as far as her ear when she felt a solid thunk against the back of her head and the burning of her fingers against the rough walk.

Molly squealed, and Paul smirked.

"What the hell?" Molly belted out.

Paul stepped forward and leaned over Molly's head. His eyes shone, and she winced. He held a pocketknife in his hand, and Molly gasped. Her mind raced for input from her chest, her stomach. Had he stabbed her as he pushed her down? She felt only a swelling soreness from the center of her chest.

Paul leaned closer and pressed the tip of his blade against Molly's side. She shrank away, and he spoke in a low dry tone, "Be still."

Molly froze. Her eyes darted up and down the street. One of the busiest thoroughfares in Custer Falls was dead, motionless. No cars, no trucks, no pedestrians. The storefronts and shop faces were empty. She shrieked inside herself, "How?"

"I'm going to say this once," Paul said. "I'm telling you because I know you were the one who warned that dipshit *Chess*. You tell him I'm coming for him. He won't know when or where, but I'm going to get him after what he did to Matt and Doug."

"They ran away—"

"Bullshit!" The blade pressed harder. "I know he did something. Him and baby Billy. And I'm going to get him, too. Now you go deliver that message, and maybe after I'm done with them, I'll forget about you. Or, maybe I'll find you when you don't expect it and give you something better." His eyes traced her chest and moved down to her hips.

Paul stood. "You can do it. You're good at sending messages." He swung his leg forward and planted a foot in Molly's hip.

She groaned and rolled to her side.

"Go!" Paul kicked again, slamming the toe of his boot into her ribs.

Molly scrambled to her knees, grabbed her bag, and ran.

Chess worked his way up the stairs, his mother trailing behind him, carrying his backpack. Once in his room, he sat at his desk in front of his computer and leaned his crutch against the wall. Mom set his bag on the floor by his feet.

"You sure you want to do homework right now?" Mom said. "I really think you should rest first. It's been a long day."

"Yeah, Mom." Chess flipped open his laptop. "I want to get it done and not think about it again 'til tomorrow."

She shook her head and took a step toward the door. "Okay. Let me know if you need anything."

"Okay, Mom." He turned to his computer.

She had barely left the room when his phone dinged. The screen read, *New message from Molly*.

It was more than a message. It was an invite, "Can I call you? It's important."

Chess replied, "Yup" His phone immediately rang with a video call.

Molly was in her room. Chess had never been there, but he'd seen it a time or two before when on the phone with her, also in posts from her Instagram feed. Posters of The Weekend and Ed Sheeran decorated pink walls between scattershot collages of Molly's friends and family. White Christmas lights circled the ceiling above and lit Molly in more festive light than her expression implied.

"What's up?" Chess asked.

Molly's eyebrow twitched. Her lips clenched together.

"Molly?" He wondered if they were lagging out or buffering or something. "You there?"

"Yeah." She closed her eyes and sighed. When they opened, they had glossed over and she appeared as if she were about to cry. But she didn't. "I saw Paul Neddles on the way home, Chess."

Chess leaned in. He felt anger starting to burn in his stomach. Not that Molly was his girlfriend or anything, but she was his friend. And that kid was nothing but bad news. "What did that asshole want?"

She gulped, and Chester could hear the click in her throat. "He said he's coming for *you*. He's going to get you."

"What the hell is that supposed to mean?"

Molly took a deep breath and recounted the entire interaction. Two tears made it through her wall and streamed down her cheeks. She was exhausted, and Chess could see it.

"I'll kill that fucker," Chess said.

Molly smiled through a wary gaze. "You're down to one arm and one leg, Chess."

"I'll figure it out." His voice was a low grumble.

"Just stay away from him?"

He shook his head and ground his teeth.

"I gotta go." She didn't, but she wanted to. She wanted to sleep and forget the entire day.

"Okay. I'll see you at school tomorrow." He tried to give her a pleasant nod goodbye. It came out as forced. It was the last time he'd say anything to her.

The call with Chess cut to black, and the screen went blank. Molly wondered for a moment if she had hit the power button by mistake, putting her phone to sleep. Her fingers hadn't been anywhere near there—it had been sitting up on the little leg that popped out from the rear of its case—but stranger things had happened.

She was lying on her belly in the center of her bed and reached over the linens to check her phone. Tapping the power button did nothing. She tried again, nothing.

"Shit." She pressed the button and held it. Had it turned off?

The device became warm under her touch, and the room's brightness seemed to dip. The strands of lights circling the ceiling flickered, and a chill walked up Molly's forearm. She glanced up at the strobe, and a painful pop sounded from her hand. Her fingers shot apart in a hot burst and went numb.

"Fuck!" Molly's eyes shot back to her hand. Her phone was on her bed, on fire; her fingers were scorched black.

Molly jumped up to her knees at the head of her bed. What to do? She searched for something, she didn't know what. Something to put the fire out.

My bed—my sheets, her mind raced. *Water? Fire extinguisher?* Neither was in her room. She ran to the door. Smoke from the rising flames gathered against the ceiling.

Molly's hands gripped the door. The knob wouldn't turn. She yanked on it. "Open, goddammit!"

The door rattled in its frame. It didn't open. The fire alarm outside Molly's room shrieked.

Molly turned back to her bed. Smoke was descending from the ceiling. Thick white waves floated down. She coughed. Her eyes bulged. Her heart pounded, and her lungs wanted better air. They pulled in only smoke, and she coughed more.

Molly dropped to her knees, her thoughts dizzying.

"I have to—" She studied her room again. She had to have something that would help. Her brain ached. Her vision blurred. The blaze seemed to be spreading so fast. Her entire bed was a wall of flames. The ceiling above was black. Flames seemed to be coming down from above and crawling across the once-white surface. Tendrils were getting closer to her with every second, and she could feel their desire. They wanted her. Wanted to get to her and climb all over her. The entire conflagration did—it wanted to eat her alive.

Molly felt the eyes of a strange thing upon her. Her thoughts dimmed. Sleep was coming. Her heart pounded, and her lungs fought, but the tiredness was overwhelming, and sleep seemed inescapable.

On hands and knees, Molly dragged herself to her closet. She opened the accordion doors and yanked down clothes. Dresses, shirts, sweaters. Maybe she could smother the fire? Put it out that way?

She tossed one after another, every garment she could force her fingers to bring down. They all went onto the bed. And the bed fed. The mounting flames burst with colors of reds and greens as they engulfed synthetic fabrics and belched black smoke.

"No!" Molly cried. The ceiling of smoke moved downward. Closer. The heat scraped against her skin. Burning.

Molly dragged her entire body inside the closet and closed the door. A whisper resonated inside her mind as her consciousness fell away. It blamed her. Derided her. It was all her fault.

It was just before lunch when Chess realized that he hadn't seen Molly all day. He was walking with Billy and filling Billy in on the call he'd received the previous afternoon.

"Jesus," Billy said. "I hope she's okay."

"She was when we hung up."

"Yeah, but... she isn't here today."

They breached the doors into the lunchroom, and Chess's eyes searched for her. Molly wasn't there. But he did spot Mary Fratelli, her best friend. She sat at a table not far away, eating a salad and chatting with

Sarah Collins and Jill Swanson.

Chess pointed. "Let's ask Mary."

He swung himself forward and made his way toward the girls, Billy just behind him. When he got there, Chess saw he was wrong. She had a salad, but she wasn't eating it. She wasn't talking either. Mary and her friends were simply staring into their food. Chess looked down curiously. As his eyes met the bowl of greens, they seemed to lose their color. Leaf after leaf was drained of its green, becoming more and more pale. The folded and stacked layers of lettuce withered, one leaf at a time. Brown stains crept along the edges of the girl's lunch, and a putrid-smelling juice leaked from the plant into the bowl.

Mary's head spun toward Chess. He shuddered. She swung away from the bench and rose, face to face with him. Her eyes were wide and bloodshot. Her lips spread, revealing grinding teeth. Her skin was pale, except for dark red and blue veins that swelled just below her skin. And, a muffled, demented laugh found its way through her clamped dental pillars.

"Mary?" Chess asked. A dark, cold sensation penetrated his chest. He glanced at Billy and saw Mary's hand was gripped around Billy's mouth. Her fingers pressed into his flesh, bulging the skin around her digits. His skin was pinkish red around the indentations. Her fingers were blackened at their tips, each nail coated in dirt and jagged.

"Mary?" Chess repeated.

Her face refused to move, but her eyes—her eyes jerked back and forth. They began to glow yellow. Her hair had changed from a short reddish bob to a long black matted mop.

"Chester," A growl of a voice spoke in the back of Chess's mind. "I'm coming for you."

Chess shouted and stumbled backward. He pressed his cast against the ground for traction, and pain blinded him from the lunchroom.

He jerked his foot away from the ache, spun, and crashed to the floor. He rolled onto his belly and crawled. One good hand and one good leg pushed him forward, and he was grateful for them both. He pushed harder, faster. He had to get away. She would follow him; he was sure of it.

"Chess?" A voice said from behind him. It was Billy. "Chess?"

Chess turned, smacking his broken arm into the floor. He groaned and looked up. Billy's head was tilted, wondering. Mary, Sarah, Jill, and half the lunchroom were staring at him. Some pointed. Some squinted. Some laughed uncontrollably. But Mary sat right where she had been when he entered the room, at her table, a fork in her hand with fresh, bright greens in its tines.

Chess felt his face flush with embarrassment and put on a fake smile. He was panting. His heart was pounding. Billy approached with Chess's spilled crutches and helped him to his feet.

"You okay?" Billy said. His face was drenched in concern.

"Yeah." Chess took the crutches and waved him off. "Just slipped."

Billy nodded, his eyes showing his disbelief. He left Chess and took a seat next to Mary.

Mary said she had talked to Molly's mom. Molly had started some kind of fire in her room yesterday and was now in Custer Falls Memorial Hospital—in a coma.

"No shit?" Chess said. His lungs and heart had slowed, but his face remained red.

"Yup," Mary nodded. Sarah and Jill nodded in agreement.

But how? Or, when? Chess had just talked to her. He figured it must have happened right after their call and told Billy so as they went through the lunch line.

"Weird, right?" Billy said. He carried both his own and Chess's food to a table, and they sat.

Chester was starting to wonder if his vision of Mary and Molly's fire could be related. He told Billy what he had seen and watched Billy's face go white.

"I saw the same thing," Billy said. "Not Mary—a girl in my shop class. She crawled across the floor at me with yellow eyes and black fingernails—and not like the cute goth chicks wear—they were black like... decay."

"What..." Chess felt himself at a loss for words.

"I thought I was just sick or something—maybe I had dozed off," Billy said. "I know that's not so, now."

Billy's face hung loose and grim. As he stared at Chess, Chess couldn't help but think that his friend looked older, like something was draining the youth from his face.

"Billy," Chess said, "I don't think we should be alone right now. Not until we figure out what's happening to us."

"Or to Molly."

"Yeah."

3

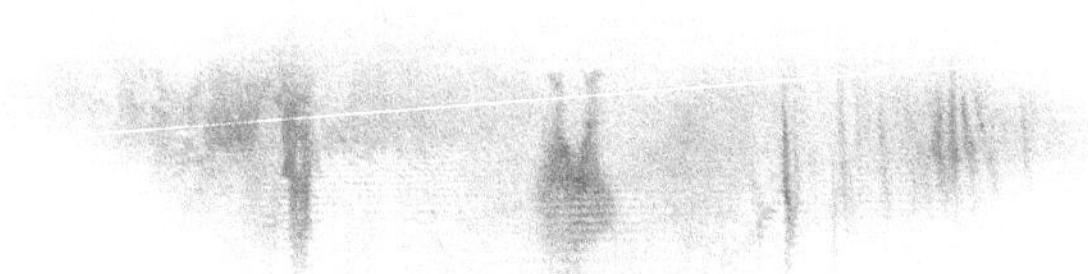

B ETWEEN SMALL LIES ABOUT homework and a whopper about a supposed joint science fair project, Chester and Billy had been able to convince their parents to allow Billy to practically live at Chess's house for a week. There had been no other occurrences of the weirdness that had brought them to the conclusion that something was out to get them, and both Chess and Billy were starting to think that maybe they had overreacted about the whole thing. Except Molly was still in the hospital.

When Thanksgiving Eve came, and Billy's parents were adamant that he spend the holiday with them, Chess and Billy decided maybe that was a good idea—a trial. Maybe whatever had happened, if it had really happened, had passed. Maybe this was a good time to separate and see if everything was okay now? Not a hundred percent convinced, they made plans for Billy to return in the afternoon, after his family had eaten their Thanksgiving Day feast, and his dad had started to fall asleep in his recliner to the Cowboys game. The experiment seemed to have worked until Billy was on his way back.

The early afternoon sun was shy in the western sky, already pulling its heat back from the Earth. Clouds had threatened a typical Thanksgiving Day snow shower earlier, but threats ended up being all they were. Now, only long strands of cirrus clouds stretched from north to south, and a swelling wind warned Billy that he should move a bit faster toward Chess's house because colder winds were coming.

Billy crossed White Pine, a stretch of road that separated his neighborhood from Chester's. It was deserted now that all the holiday travelers were at their destinations, either stuffing their faces with turkey or pie, or guzzling beer and watching Dallas's offense struggle. He passed the large boulder formation that signified the entrance to Custer Estates and walked toward his friend's street.

While thirty years ago, the Estates was the most desirable neighborhood in Custer Falls, it quickly fell from grace after the murders happened. Billy didn't know much about them, other than there had been a lot of them, and a lot of people went to jail. And even though they had technically been spread all over town, so many were located in this sixteen square block section of town that it was sometimes teased as the Murder Estates. That clashed with the selling points of beautiful views of the mountains and being backed up against thousands of acres of public lands.

The cold wind ripped through Billy's jacket, and he shivered. He passed the old Miller place—stop number four if there were ever a murder tour of the subdivision—and he thought he heard his name being called.

Billy turned left. There was no one there. The garage was open, and gusts of air swirled oak and aspen leaves into the vast empty space of the two-car garage's center. The interior was dark, but Billy could make out pegboards of tools against the far wall along with power tools and what looked like a chainsaw on a workbench on the right.

"Billy," someone said. A male voice.

He still didn't see anyone, but he was sure the voice had come from inside that garage.

"Hello?" Billy said. "Who's there?"

"Come on, Billy," a new voice said, this one a girl. "Inside. Come on in."

Billy backed away from the house. It was the thing, the thing that he had faced in school—it was back.

He took another step and felt something cold touch his ankle. He kicked his foot forward, trying to rip himself away from whatever was there. But he was caught. His leg had moved only a little, and whatever had grabbed onto him firmed into stone.

Billy's heart jumped. He spun to see what it was, and his legs soared out from under him. Weightlessness lightened his body, and in the garage, the chainsaw started. His thoughts went to that moment in school. A jolt tore through Billy's mind as the engine roared. Another jolt rocked the back of his head.

Billy had been standing in front of the bandsaw, a chunk of two-by-four in his hands. It was a free-build day, where they could make whatever they wanted with the wood in the scrap bin. He had decided to make a clawed stick, something like a Chuck-It, to throw the ball for his golden retriever, Bruce.

He'd drawn the outline in pencil on the hunk of pine. It looked as if it were going to be too small, but he figured he'd try anyway. Why not? It was free wood, after all, and he had to do something for the next thirty minutes. And if it didn't work out, he'd still have a really cool, industrial-strength backscratcher.

He slid his goggles over his eyes and flipped the switch to start the saw.

The band began to whirl, its motor whining up to speed. Then the lights went out.

Billy's gaze circled the room. The entire space was dark. He could see no one. Nothing. Did a circuit-breaker trip? That happened sometimes at his house. He'd watched his dad lose power to the garage before, when he got a piece of wood stuck in the circular saw after the blade went dull, and Dad had refused to put in a new one. "It'll be fine," he had said, then clunk.

But this was different. It was dark, but the machines were still running. The bandsaw behind him, the jigsaw a few yards away, something else that Billy wasn't sure about. A drill, maybe?

"Mr. Swanson?" Billy called. The teacher would have to fix this.

There was no answer from Mr. Swanson, or anyone. Beyond the noise of the roaring cutting devices, Billy expected to hear other voices, other kids who wanted to know what was going on, but there was nothing.

"Hello?" Billy asked.

A chill ran over Billy's limbs, first his arms, then his legs. Near the door into the hallway, a fluorescent light flickered. It twitched as if trying to turn on. For a brief second, Billy could see the door, the desks by the entryway, and then nothing.

"Mr. Swanson?"

The light flickered again, but this time Billy saw a girl. He didn't recognize her and cocked his head left, trying to think who she might be. He looked her over, and the more he saw, the more he didn't want to recognize her.

Her hair was dirty—not just unclean but filled with dirt. The soil clung to the strands of her long flowing hair, clumping it together and confusing its color. It could have been black, red, even blond; Billy couldn't tell through the grime. Her face was pale, near china-white, aside from smears of the same dirt. The weirdest thing, though, was the color of her eyes. They radiated a deep and dingy yellow, dark but seeming to glow in the dim light of the shop room. A tattered dress hung from her shoulders like a doll might wear, white and flowing but stained and torn.

"Uh," Billy fought for words. Should he ask if she was okay? If she needed a bath? And the lights went out again.

The roar of the machinery was all Billy could hear. The overwhelming darkness and the sight of that girl, that strange girl, made him move. He didn't even realize he was doing it until his back met the edge of the bandsaw's frame.

The saw's touch sent a shock through Billy's system. He spun and jumped away and froze. It occurred to him that he was surrounded by thousands of racing metal teeth. He had to be extremely careful. If he tripped and fell into one of these things, anything could happen. He could lose a finger like Mr. Swanson's pinky, or if he face-planted into it, much, much worse.

The light behind the bandsaw flickered, and Billy's eyes shot to it. There was the girl. One of her hands rested on its side, her fingers caressing its gray, metal frame. Her nails were pure black.

Billy took a step back. She took a step forward, and the lights went out again. They flashed, and she was on the floor, crawling toward him on hands and knees. Her mouth was open, and her tongue moved lustfully across her lips. As the last flicker of light faded, a shine rose from her green, rotted teeth.

"No!" Billy backed up. Something struck the back of his heel. It was cold. Whatever it was, it sucked the heat from his leg, and he tripped. He felt the air rushing past the sides of his face. He pictured the back of his head slamming into the jigsaw and splitting open or smacking into the cement floor and his skull cracking. Then he imagined *her* catching up to him. What was she going to do when she caught him? That skin, those teeth, they reminded him of zombies. Was she going to eat him? Tear him apart with her dirty black fingernails?

His back slammed into the floor with a thud. His head crashed into the cement, and bright spots filled the darkness of his sight. Dull pain seeped through his skull and into his brain.

A hand grasped Billy's foot. It was hard and cold. It sucked the heat through his shoe, and his foot went numb. Another hand grabbed his shin. It felt like a claw made of ice and burned the skin through his jeans. The first hand moved up to his hip, and he felt his skin shrivel away, burning, freezing, poisoned.

"Get off! Get off! *Get off!*" Billy shouted.

The lights above him flickered, and her face was right in front of his. Her lips dripped with black sludge, and her breath was Death.

"No!" Billy shrieked and closed his eyes. He expected the next cold burn would be on his face, or his neck would get ripped open. But it didn't come.

Billy opened his eyes to find the lights on. His shop class stood around him, staring, some laughing. Mr. Swanson shook his head and grimaced.

Billy was late, and Chess began to wonder. It usually took only twenty minutes to reach his house from Billy's, but it had been thirty. Maybe he'd gotten caught up on the way? What if he'd run into Paul Neddles?

Chess had to go see. Billy might need his help.

He hopped on one leg to the front door, balancing himself every few feet on a crutch. Turkey and potatoes weighed on his gut, nauseating him. He slid on his coat and headed past the hanging, golden wreath on the door. He thought he heard his mother's voice as the door shut, and he ignored it.

Chess wobbled across the yard and onto the sidewalk, then turned left. He scanned the street as he went, taking the path that Billy should have been using. But there was no Billy.

At the end of his road, where Billy would typically be coming from, Chess heard a noise. It traveled as a dim echo from within the woods, out from a path in the public lands, out from the trails that seemed to be swallowed by the darkness of the forest.

"He wouldn't be in there," Chess said. "Why would he be in there?"

"Chess," a whisper called. It was Billy's voice, Billy's whisper.

"Shit." Chess looked left and right and started across the street. "Billy! What are you doing in there?"

Billy didn't answer at first. There was only the sound of Chess's step, swing, step, and the crunch of leaves and pine needles under his foot and rubber-tipped crutch.

"Billy!"

"Here!" Billy's whisper was louder but strained. It sounded as if Billy were in pain. It came from the left, and Chester fought through a juniper bush to find another trail, smaller, hiding in a darkened section of the path.

"Chess, help," Billy called.

Chess saw a cave on his right. Its entrance was small, and he almost missed it. Grooves were raked in the dirt, making a path inside, and Chess followed.

"Jesus. Paul, if you hurt Billy!" He put a hand on the side of the cave entrance and peered into blackness.

Something shoved Chess from behind and threw him off balance. He tumbled forward into the cave, his crutch falling away from his hand.

Chess landed on his face. Dirt and pebbles scraped across his cheeks.

His hand fell on something cloth. As he lifted his head, his eyes adjusting to the light, he recognized it was Billy beside him, asleep. He touched Billy's head; it was wet, bloody.

"What the fuck!" Chess shouted. He turned to the cave entrance and saw the silhouette of someone in the doorway. Then someone else. Then someone smaller—a girl?

Chess heard the sound of rock grinding, and the gray light of fall shrunk to a sliver and vanished.

Molly had been dreaming for what felt like an eternity. She knew she was dreaming, but she didn't know why she wouldn't wake up. The longer it went on, the more she began to wonder if maybe this dreamland were actually some kind of afterlife—maybe she had died.

She had a vague notion of being in a fire. She remembered her room and flames, but none of it made any sense. It seemed the more she thought about it, the more it turned to a peripheral mush that hung around her mind like a pestering gnat.

Even so, she felt that she had talked to Chess, but the conversation wasn't finished. She had something else to tell him. Something important. But she couldn't remember what it was and why she needed to tell him. If only she could wake up and see it all clearly.

Molly shook the urges from her thoughts and found that she was overlooking a meadow. It was a place she had seen before, but she couldn't place it. The gentle rise and fall of the land and the mountains in the distance; there was something here she knew—and then it hit her. She was standing in the park in the rear of Custer Estates. She'd been there a dozen times over the years when visiting friends in the neighborhood, but it looked different from the way she remembered it. Molly gazed at the landscape. None of the homes was there. None of the roads was there. Instead, in one direction, the land was a sprawling grassland. In another, there was a deep, dark forest, one that looked ancient, primordial even.

Between herself and the trees, Molly spotted a cottage. It reminded her of an old trapper cabin, the kind she had seen hundreds of times all over Montana, a tribute to the hermitage of the state. It couldn't have been more than fifteen feet square and made of rough timber. There were no windows, and she guessed the door on the front was the only way in or out. From the roof, plumed gray smoke which came out of a stubby stone chimney. It rose and met the gray autumn sky, and Molly couldn't help but feel awed, as if she were seeing something important, though she had no idea what it was just yet.

As Molly watched the tiny home, she felt a pull inside herself. Something was drawing her in, asking her to come to the cabin. She looked down and saw her feet were moving. She didn't realize she was walking, but she was.

The closer Molly came, the more she knew what was going on inside. She was right. It was a trapper's cabin, but the trapper wasn't alone. He'd come out for the summer and brought his wife and daughter along with him. That was a mistake. The trapper knew that now, but it was too late. He'd gotten sick, and they didn't leave when they were supposed to. Winter was as close as a few days away, and their summer supplies were used up, bare. If they tried to go back to town now, they wouldn't make it. The snow would fall, and they'd die on the way. If they tried to last through the winter here, they'd run out of food before the season was halfway over. They had two choices: Stay and starve or go and freeze.

As Molly drew closer and closer to the cabin, she felt the world move faster around her. Nights, days, weeks passed her. The sun, the moon, the stars streaked overhead in cycles of day and night. When she reached the front door, it was night, and the patchwork of splintery wood swung open on its own as if it wanted to show her its insides.

The father had recovered from his sickness, but he was far from well. His face was long and gaunt. His hair hung as a greasy black mop from his head, blending with his beard in a wide bushy cloud. Gripped in his hand was his hunting knife. His eyes were stone, piercing into the cabin's single bed in front of him. And laying on the bed were two sleeping women: his wife and his daughter.

Molly's heart jumped inside her chest. She saw through the man, saw his hunger. It wasn't a physical hunger, though that was there too. What drove him was a hunger in his soul. A hunger that commanded him from some other place. It radiated from him in waves, invisible energy that collided with Molly and made her stomach cramp in disgust.

The man plunged his knife downward. It sank into the mother's chest. Her eyes flew open, and blood bubbled up from between her lips. It pumped from her chest onto her daughter. She retched, trying to scream, but her lips only produced heaving gags.

The girl opened her eyes, warm wetness flooding over her delicate white dress. Red droplets stained her face, cast from her mother's cough.

She could scream. She bellowed a terror-filled screech as her father tore his knife sideways, opening a chasm in her mother's chest. Blood gushed from the hole, running out along ribs and cartilage.

The father pulled back his blade, his eyes fixating on the child.

"No!" Molly screamed.

The child looked up at her. Her onyx pupils dug into Molly's thoughts. They burrowed inside her, transmitting the fear and shame the little one felt directly into Molly's soul.

"Run!" Molly said.

The girl jumped from her bed and sprinted from her home. Small, dark red footprints trailed behind her. They followed through the tall grasses and wet the tips of the swaying green stalks. She ran into the woods.

The father groaned and shambled from the cabin. He lumbered at a stiff uneven pace and followed her into the trees.

"Come back, Darla," he called.

The wind picked up. It howled through the boughs of the forest canopy, masking the snap and crack of twigs and needles under the girl's feet. Her father still heard her. He still followed her.

Darla ran down a game trail, turning back every few seconds. Tears ran down her cheeks. Her mother's blood had been wiped clean from her feet but now her own left tracks, her bare soles torn open against the rough forest floor.

Something called her from the left. Not a sound, but a feeling. It told her it was a place to hide. Fear gripped her mind and told her not to go, but fear also told her to run, get away from Father. She turned and followed another, smaller trail.

It was barely a few feet when she found the cave. She would have missed it without the feeling itching at her, turning her head right toward the entrance. She ran inside, spun around, and clung to the wall.

She heard her father's footsteps. They were hard against the ground, irregular. He panted like a winded madman, air raging in and out of his lungs with wheeze and rumble.

He stopped outside the cave, and she prayed, *Please God, save me. Let him keep going. Let him never find me again.*

It was as if her father heard every word. His breath lightened and he turned into the dark earthen room. He walked past Darla. He took a step toward the middle, bringing his empty hand to his face, cupping it around his eyes as they adjusted.

Darla had to do something. She could turn and run, but he'd be right behind her. She did the only thing that came to her mind and surged forward.

With both hands spread, she shoved her father, using everything inside her. He tipped forward, lost his balance, and tumbled to the floor. He tried to stop his fall, placing his hands against the cave floor. When his tumble reached the ground, his hunting knife thrust into his chest, stabbing him in the center of his heart. His blood drenched the ground.

Darla screamed and turned. She bolted for the cave opening. The rock entrance sealed shut in front of her.

Molly stared into the blackened space. She could see nothing, but she got the feeling that time was passing. The stone door opened, and a pair of men entered. They wore old-fashioned dungarees and sleeveless undershirts. One looked around the cave, studying markings on the walls. Darla's form floated in the shadows next to her father, and the other newcomer raised an ax and brought it down on his friend's head. The door shut.

Time went by once again. The door opened, but this time light only trickled in. It was night. Then, in came Matt and Doug.

"Holy shit," Molly whispered to herself.

The next gap in time lasted only seconds, and then there was Chess.

"No!" Molly shouted. She moved to the door and pushed against the rock.

Chess tumbled to the floor and rolled into something. He was shaking. He found Billy. He screamed, "What the fuck!"

The door closed, and Molly felt the others nearby. The father, Darla, the dungaree brothers, Matt and Doug, and something else, something she couldn't put her finger on, other than knowing it was old and it was in charge. She pushed as hard as she could against the wall and felt it shift.

A hiss fluttered through the darkness, and Molly felt a sharp pain in her shoulder. She turned and searched herself. A knife was in the meat of her shoulder. It was the father's knife.

Twinkles of light gleamed in the darkness in front of Molly's eyes.

"Hello?" Chess shouted. "Someone? I need help!" His voice was trembling.

Molly smelled rot. She smelled Death, and she knew the twinkle she saw was the girl, Darla. Her presence shook. Molly reached to her shoulder and ripped the knife free. It burned with a pain she could have only previously imagined. She thrust it forward into the darkness in front of her. Darla shrieked and faded, but Molly knew she'd be back.

Molly spun and pushed against the wall. She ground her teeth and thrust herself into it. She had to get Chess out. *She* had to get out. Darla would be back. Something worse might be coming back.

Rocks rubbed against each other, and the sound of grinding stone echoed. A streak of light stabbed the darkness, and Chess raced to the entrance. He pressed alongside Molly, blinded to her presence. They pushed together, and a crack appeared near the floor the size of a pumpkin.

"Yes!" Chess rocked Billy. "Wake up. Let's go." But Billy didn't wake.

"Go, Chess," Molly pleaded. "You have to go."

Chess didn't hear her. Or, more precisely, he didn't know he heard her.

"I have to go," Chess told the sleeping Billy. "I'm going to get help." He dropped down and began crawling through the opening. His head went through. His shoulders.

The rocks shifted. Molly saw a glimmer of light, and then Darla's father. His hands were on the wall, pressing it back closed.

"No!" Molly pushed the other way, holding the gap open. Another sharp, burning pain ran through Molly's body, this time in her lower back. Chess pulled his hips through, and Molly spun to see Darla in front of her. Her mouth was rotten, hanging wide. Her once youthful, beautiful face was stretched and terrifying. Her eyes, dry and clouded. Her lips were wet with black sludge, and Death came from her breath.

Molly found the knife in her back and tried to pull it free. Pain ripped through her so hard, all she could do was release the blade and drop to her knees.

Chess's feet slid through the hole, and the room turned black once again.

Molly felt the knife ripped from her back and had the sensation they were all standing in front of her now: Father, Darla, the dungaree men, and several others. They all had things in their hands and were leaning back and readying them. She only felt the first thing that hit her, the one that stopped her heart from beating back in Custer Falls Memorial Hospital and caused the nurses and doctors to race into her room.

4

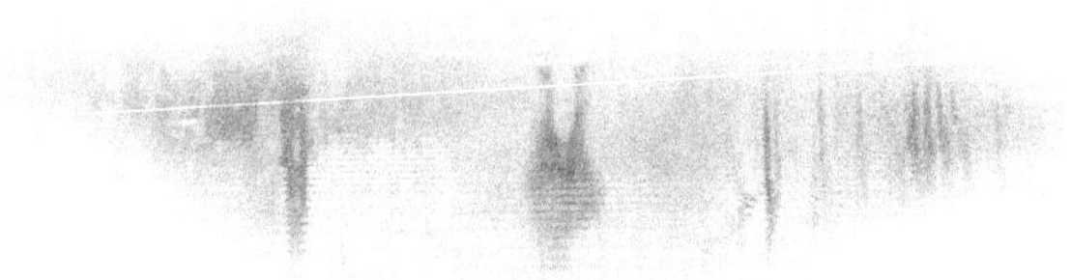

DECEMBER BEGAN WITH A gloom that predicted a long and frigid winter. Snow fell in a deluge that seemed never-ending from the first until three weeks in. It was a quiet yet maddening fall. It would stop one morning, and the clouds would thin, only to rush back in by the afternoon and drape the world in hours of white.

Chess and Billy had found each other late that Thanksgiving Day, neither knowing how they stumbled to safety. They merely met along the street, both in a daze, both unsure of what had happened. By the time night came and Billy had to head home, they both had a feeling that things could be getting better—that there could be an end in sight. It seemed so; with the snow came calm. Their hopes sank at the news of Molly's death, and they went to the funeral. It was sad, but since then, everything had seemed quieter. The school, the entire town seemed subdued.

Eventually, Chess's casts were removed. He wasn't sure it would come, but he was actually getting excited for Christmas. With that came plans with family and friends. The excitement lasted until the twenty-second, the last day of school for the year.

A City of Custer Falls' School System bus stopped where the road met

Custer Estates. Giant red bows that had been tied to the subdivision's bouldered entrance fluttered in the wind. Out of the bus came Chess, along with three other high schoolers and Billy, who was going to stay at Chess's house overnight.

The latest snow had crystallized, melted, and frozen again overnight, and now crunched under the thick soles of their snow boots. The wind ripped past Chess's nose and instantly numbed it. He shivered and took a step toward home.

The bus rumbled and rattled as it drove on. The students of Custer Estates fanned out toward their houses. And Chess was flooded with a feeling of dread that gripped his spine like a frozen claw.

"What is it?" Billy said.

Chess had stopped in the middle of the sidewalk. "I—I don't know." It was a marked change from the past few weeks. His sense of optimism, of hope, had left him. Ice was running through his veins. Worry gripped his chest, and breathing became harder.

Billy took a step, and the feeling took hold of him as well. It was a dark, grimy feeling, like Death buried in the snow. It said that bad things were coming while making the skin on his palms and the back of his neck feel wet, cold, and oily.

"I don't like it," Billy said.

"You feel it too?" Chess asked.

"Yeah."

Chess nodded nervously. "Let's... just get to my house."

Billy nodded back, and they set off at a hastened pace.

The rest of the afternoon passed without incident. They played on Chess's Xbox and pigged out on snacks from the pantry. The kitchen was more stocked than usual because it was Christmas, or almost was, and they expected family to come in that night. It was a challenge for Chess to convince his mother to let Billy stay over because of it, but he won out in the end.

At around six in the evening, the doorbell rang. Chess got up and nudged Billy to come along. He knew Billy would want to see this.

Chess's mom and dad were at the front door, ducking under the silver garland that festooned the entry. Outside were Chess's Uncle Jim, Aunt Carrie, and his cousin of the same age, Amy.

Billy stopped in his tracks as soon as his eyes fell on Amy. The blonde girl stood in her winter wear, looking like a youth model for ski clothes. His only thoughts were of what she would look like once she came inside and removed all that unnecessary clothing.

"I knew you'd want to meet her," Chess whispered and elbowed his friend.

The hugging slowly worked its way inside along with their bags. Chess's dad asked Chess and Billy to help with the luggage. Jim and Carrie's belonged in the guest bedroom upstairs. Amy's went to the basement, where the pullout sofa was.

Chess's arm and leg both still ached from their breaks, but doing what was asked was the easiest thing right now. It wasn't too late for Mom to rescind her approval of Billy staying over.

He caught a glimpse through the narrow window beside the front door as he leaned to pick up Amy's bag. Night had come, and the festive lights on houses and trees up and down his street twinkled. They lit the neighborhood in that way that only Christmas lights can: inviting, cushioning the senses with hopeful expectations of family bonds and joy to come. Only this time, it felt hollow. The felling seemed to slip over Chess as soon as it came, and what was left was a cold chasm of trepidation. Something bad was coming.

Amy's bag was cold to the touch. The handle gave Chess a chill, and she saw the shiver as he lifted it.

"You okay, cuz?" She slid off her coat and hung it on one of the brass hooks on the wall.

"Yeah." Something drew Chess's eyes back to the window. This time, across his snow-covered yard, beyond the giant, lighted blue spruce, he saw a person. For a moment, he froze. They stood where Matt and Doug had stood. Was Matt back? Doug? Their hands were in their pockets, hood over their darkened head, and they looked directly through Chess.

Chess stared back at the stranger, wondering, and he felt their eyes meet his own. Whoever this was, they weren't just looking at his house or toward him; they were looking at him, his face, his eyes. It was bad. Chess wasn't sure why, but it was bad.

"What the hell?" Chess said.

"What?" Amy asked.

Chess looked at his cousin. "There's someone..." He glanced back at the window. They were gone. "There was someone there."

Amy looked through the little window. "Well, they're gone now." She smirked and turned and followed the adults into the kitchen.

Billy joined Chess and gazed out. "What did you see?"

"Doesn't matter," Chess said. He lugged Amy's bag toward the basement door. He knew that it did, but without proof, he found himself somewhat embarrassed to say how the sight made him feel. How he imagined Matt or Doug standing in the road. For what? Revenge or something? He hadn't done anything wrong. "You got those?" He nodded at his aunt's and uncle's bags, a large suitcase and a smaller one.

"No problem." Billy took one in each hand and headed up the stairs.

"No problem," Chess muttered and headed down.

At dinner, Chess couldn't help but feel he was in some kind of '90s holiday film, *Home Alone*, maybe. He sat at the kitchen counter with Billy and Amy. They each had sodas and slices of pizza in front of them, pieces from one of the take-and-bake monstrosities that Mom had picked up on the way home from work. The adults ate the same awful stuff in the dining room, only they had wine with theirs.

Billy spent most of the meal glancing from his food to Amy and trying to pretend he wasn't falling in love. Amy tried her best to keep up the small talk with Chess and ignore Billy. Chess fought to use any words at all. His mind rotated between the dread that had followed him since getting off the bus and the eerie darkness that had clamped into him at the entryway window.

"So, does it hurt?" Amy asked.

"What?" Chess said. This time he had completely zoned out.

"Your limbs, dummy." She furrowed her brow and grinned. It was the same grin she used when they were eight, and he had fallen out of her playset while pretending to be Jake the Neverland Pirate. She had been playing a life-sized Tinkerbell and twitched her nose disapprovingly—she was not one to drop character under heavy play. "You have your casts off now—does it still hurt?"

"Oh, no," he lied. They still ached almost constantly. "Well, maybe a little. If I'm lifting something heavy."

"Like when you took my bag downstairs?"

Yes, that did hurt. And Amy's question seemed to make her grin grow. Was she happy about that? Did she get some sort of kick out of him hurting? Of course, she did. And he'd usually dish back the ball-busting on any other occasion. But not tonight. He just couldn't summon it, couldn't lift the haze of doom around his thoughts.

"Yeah, a little." Chess frowned at her as he said it, followed by a *what-the-fuck* face that he couldn't hold back.

"Cool." Her grin dropped. She nodded and took a bite out of her pizza. She chewed and swallowed without pleasure, the food going down like a job, a duty instead of the delight that pizza should be.

"So, uh," Billy seemed to find some courage and stepped into the conversation. "Amy, do you play Xbox? Chess and I were going to play some Call of Duty later on."

She raised her eyebrows and refused to look at Billy.

"Chester?" Mom called from the dining room.

Chess was for once relieved to have his mom call him. He would have accepted much worse to get out of watching the train wreck of whatever Billy was trying to do. He dropped his slice of cheese-covered cardboard on his plate and walked into the dining room.

Mom had an ear-to-ear smile across her face. Her plate had two untouched slices, and her wine glass had the marks of having been emptied and refilled a few times. It sloshed in her hand as she turned to Chess.

"Yeah, Mom?"

"Your aunt and uncle have presents in their trunk. Can you and Billy please go out and get them? Put them under the tree?"

"Sure." Why not? He didn't think he could eat any more *dinner,* so he may as well.

Chess passed through the kitchen and pulled Billy away before he embarrassed himself any more. He grabbed Uncle Jim's keys from the counter, and the boys headed toward the front door.

Chess's hand raised to the doorknob and stopped an inch away. The feeling of dread surged. Something was out there. Something that felt like the cave from Thanksgiving. Something that could peer through him as that person beyond the yard had earlier.

He leaned and looked through the tiny window. His yard was lit in the golden rays of the incandescent bulbs strung around the yard's landmark spruce. He could see the tail of Uncle Jim's BMW, and a cold memory struck. A memory of being six years old and hitting his bedroom's light switch before darting across the space and into bed. A memory of fear contracting around him, because if he didn't hurry, something from the darkness would grab him. Something would reach from under the bed and pull him under if he hesitated or took too long near its deep, dark abyss.

He tried to shake off the feeling. *There's nothing out there to worry about.* He knew that was a lie. He had to go out there, just like he had to hit that light switch. He had to go out and get those presents and get them inside before something from the darkness, something from the black abyss grabbed him and pulled him under.

"What're you doing?" Billy said.

Chess jumped. How long had he been standing there, not moving? "Nothing. Let's go."

He pulled open the door, and cold air chilled his face. By the instant freeze, he guessed it was ten degrees or less. He realized he wasn't wearing a coat. But the car was right there; they'd get the gifts and be right back. He'd be fine.

His gaze circled the lawn, glanced past it, across the street. He saw the Mendlesons' foot-tall glowing Santa and his eight tiny reindeer. He saw the Canoles' manger scene, with baby Jesus sleeping so tender and mild.

Chess stepped outside and crept down the three stairs to his sidewalk. Green salt shone on the walk, leading the way like a crystal trail. He couldn't stop his gaze from pivoting side to side: the yard, the street, the side of the house. There was something out there; he knew it. The dread swelling inside him told him so. He might not be able to prove it, but something was coming.

Billy followed, slamming the door behind them, and Chess jumped.

"Dammit, Billy!" Chess shouted.

Billy's face scrunched up. Chess took a breath and tapped the button on his uncle's keys to pop the trunk. It clicked and rose as they neared.

They moved in on the car, and Chess got the overwhelming sensation that something bad was in that trunk—that he shouldn't get any closer; he shouldn't even look inside. But he couldn't stop. He was told to get the presents. He had to.

"What—" Billy's words stopped short.

Chess turned back to his friend. He had stopped walking too. "What is it?"

"You feel that?" Billy said. "There's something wrong over there. I—I don't want anything to do with that car."

Chess turned back to the Beamer. He agreed. He didn't want anything to do with it either, but what choice did he have? "Let's just get it over with."

He made himself move, strode on to the car. He heard Billy walking behind him. They'd get there, get this done, and be back inside playing Xbox in just a few minutes. He needed to treat this as a Band-Aid and rip it right off.

Chess reached the car and walked to the back. He was overcome with a smell. It was profane, sour; it tightened his stomach, but there was also something sickly-sweet attached. An image of a rotting candied apple formed in his mind.

Inside the trunk, illuminated by the vehicle's interior, were presents. But they were off. They were red and shiny. They were misformed and irregular. Chess tried to reconcile what he was seeing, but it didn't make sense.

Billy stepped beside his friend and screamed. There was a thunk, and Billy stopped. There was another thunk, and it all made sense. The image was clear. Each box, a hunk of meat, cut square, shining and rotting. Bows were strips of skin, lengths of intestine. And everything seemed to be coated with a layer of something Chess couldn't place, though his mind made him think of a fly and the way it vomits on its food, digesting it before eating.

Pain gripped Chess's skull, and the sound he heard now made sense as well. Someone had hit him. He sank beside the car and looked up. As his lights went out, he saw Paul Neddles picking him up and loading him into the trunk. All Chess could think of was: *I don't want those presents.*

A heavy bang jerked Chess from his sleep. His head slammed into the roof of the trunk. Now he had pain on both sides. He wondered for a split-second where he was, then remembered. And he was cold. Freezing. Why didn't he grab a coat?

Chess noticed he was moving. He felt it, heard the engine. The entire vehicle rolled and thumped up and down as though they were traversing a horribly pot-holed dirt road.

He saw a glowing trunk release in front of him. He tried to move his hands to grab it, but they were bound behind him. By tape, maybe? He felt around. Something else was behind him.

Chess remembered the trunk being full of wet, disgusting meat, but that wasn't what he felt. They had gone out there for presents, but it wasn't that either. It was cloth and something—Billy. He and Billy were both in this trunk.

"Billy?" Chess called. His voice was muffled. Something was in his mouth and tied around his head, something plastic. His throat was dry, and what voice came out was more like a squeak than anything he recognized.

Thunk. The entire car shook. He hit the ceiling and then the floor. Rocks squeaked under the tires. They flicked up into the bottom of the car and rattled the undercarriage.

The car stopped. The engine turned off. A door opened, and footsteps crunched against stone and earth. He was coming. Paul was coming. Chess trembled all over, partly from the cold, partly from fear.

Jesus. Why would Paul do this? I know Matt and Doug were his friends but—

The trunk clicked and whined as it raised.

He saw a coat, a red one. He saw red gloves running back and forth over each other. Chess saw Paul, a hood over his head and eyes that gleamed like embers of a fire. His face gleamed. The corners of his mouth were ratcheted all the way up to his cheekbones. Behind his face, Chess could tell there was another one. Terror engulfed Chess's body as no other emotion ever had.

Paul seized Chess by the arm and dragged him over the lip of the trunk. The frozen weatherstripping scraped Chess's arm and felt as hard as stone. He turned in a half somersault, smashing his face into the snow and dirt below.

Chess felt a bright pain as his nose cracked against the ground. Warm wetness flooded over his lips and stained the snow. He cried out. Only muffled shrieks came through.

Paul dragged Chess to the side.

"Let me go!" Chess tried to say. Only muffled consonants came out.

He looked around. Praying to see someone who could help. He didn't. He saw trees, only trees. They were on a dirt path in the middle of a forest. And judging by Paul's face and everything that had happened so far, they'd been dragged into the middle of nowhere to be murdered.

The word *No* repeated in Chess's mind.

Paul reached into the trunk again and pulled out Billy. Billy's eyes were open, but he was as docile as a doll. His mouth was sealed with bright red ribbon. As Paul threw him on the ground, Chess saw that Billy's hands were bound with the same.

Chess wondered: Was that what was binding him too? Red ribbon meant for a special Christmas gift? The kind Mom and Dad would put on his final present on Christmas morning, the big one that was the surprise, the finale.

Oh, God. Chess began to pray.

Paul slammed the trunk. He grabbed Billy's arm with one hand and one of Chess's with the other. He dragged them both into the woods.

5

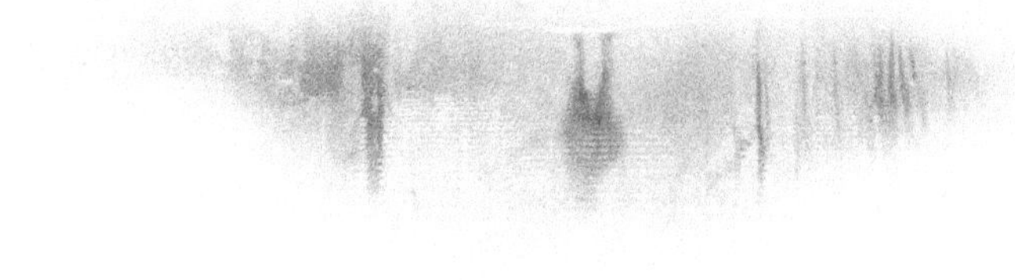

CHESS SHIVERED. HIS TEETH chattered over his gag. Sticks poked and scraped at his flesh as Paul dragged him through the darkness. *This is it,* was all Chess could think. His mind was permeated with fear. He saw his death looming. The only question was how. Did Paul have a gun? Was there a knife in his coat? Was he going to beat them with a rock? Or was he going to leave them out here in the cold to die from exposure? Part of him was hoping for a gun; that would be quick, stop him from freezing the way he was. His skin was painful, beyond numb, now burning. Part of Chess was hoping to be stabbed. He remembered the warm blood from his nose—that would be nice—more warm blood to flood over him. The pain from the blade couldn't be worse than this cold. As numb as some of his parts were, he might not have even felt it.

Chess looked up into the trees and rubbed his wrists together, trying to loosen his bindings. The snow in their piney boughs twinkled as if it were coated in silver tinsel. He saw things in the branches—he wasn't sure how he saw them in this darkness, but he did. Maybe ornaments? But there couldn't be ornaments up there. And the things he saw looked down with hunger. Glowing yellow eyes peered down, and he could feel their hunger, their starvation.

Paul released Chess and Billy, and they rocked in the snow. Chess crunched down on his hands and felt a sharp pain rip through the numbness of his left thumb. He screamed through his bow. Dear God, was it broken?

Paul leaned over Chess. His face was as grotesque as the things Chess knew were in the trees. His eyes were turning yellow, faintly glowing. His fist darted down and crashed into Chess's nose. It gushed warm blood, coating his lips, chin, neck. It rode the ribbon to his ears and lightly hung from his earlobes. Fresh pain radiated around Chess's entire skull.

Paul turned and walked out of sight. Chess rolled to his belly and saw him enter a cave.

Was that the same cave? The one from Thanksgiving? What was he doing in there?

Then Chess saw what couldn't be real. He must have been knocked out or delirious from pain. Maybe the frostbite had sent him into shock. One by one, people emerged from the cave. First, a black-haired girl. She looked exactly as Billy had described her, mirroring the horrible visage that Mary's face had distorted into; only this was worse. Her presence radiated Death, and Chess trembled harder. She stepped to the side, and a man came through. He was broad, his face bushy, but his bare chest was emaciated, bones pressing his skin outward. His eyes glowed as yellow as hers. He stood beside her.

Next through the cave entrance came a pair of men in dirty, sleeveless shirts. One held an axe; the other's head was split from the top of his skull to his nose, but his dangling eyes twinkled yellow. His body was coated in black blood, dried and molded. They stood and gazed at Chess and Billy.

Chess gasped as he saw two more bodies step from the blackness: Matt and Doug. They smirked in the same evil glare he'd always seen from them. But Matt was missing an eye; the one that worked glowed like the others. So did Doug's.

Lastly, from the cave came Molly. Chess's heart sank. She was burned all over, even worse than he had heard. Charred flakes of flesh hung from her skin as she walked. Her eyes were as the rest, and Chess felt pain in his heart.

"Molly?" Chess muttered.

The black-haired girl pointed at Billy. Her father and the axe man led the group toward him.

Billy stared through bulging eyes. He didn't make a sound.

The father kneeled over him, raised his knife, and plunged it into Billy's left shoulder.

Billy howled.

Chess fought against his bindings. One hand was numb, the other screeched in pain, but he wiggled them against each other. He dug his heels into the snow and pushed himself back from those yellow-eyed things—and his friend.

The father yanked his knife out with a slurping sound, and blood pulsated from Billy's shoulder. The ghostly shell of a man lowered his head over the wound. He sniffed at it. His eyes closed in ecstasy at the aroma. He stood and backed away.

The axe man came closer and glanced at the girl. She gave an approving nod, and his axe flew through the frozen night. It came down at Billy and dove into his chest. It made two sounds: the crunching of bone and a slap against wet meat. The axe dug into Billy's ribs and hooked into flesh as the axe man dragged Chess's friend across the ground toward the cave.

Chess screamed. He jerked at his hands and pushed himself backward. The girl's eyes fell upon him. He felt her stare, her hate, her hunger. He jerked and pushed. Jerked and pushed. He felt another wall of pain as his broken hand-squeezed through the joyous red ribbon.

Chess twisted himself onto his front, onto all fours. His broken hand collapsed into the snow, and he screamed. He crashed down to his face. But he didn't stop moving. He pushed himself up and onto his feet and darted into the woods. He grabbed and yanked at his gag with his good hand but couldn't break it free. It slid over his chin and then his neck.

Cold air clawed at Chess's face. His skin burned all over. Freezing air filled his lungs as they pumped in and out. He found himself smelling the piney scent of the forest through the veil of coppery blood.

Chess ducked under limbs and skirted around bushes. He looked back and saw eyes behind him, glowing yellow eyes in the tress he'd just passed. But not just a few; he saw hundreds, thousands, staring down at him. He jerked his head forward, looked for a path out. He knew that he had been in these woods before. If only he could find his bearings.

Nothing looked familiar. Everything was so dark. And then things changed.

Chess halted in his tracks. He heard the footfalls of things behind him, but he had to stop. The trees in front of him were now swaying. They reached toward him with their branches, hands made of stick and needle, claws made of bark. Yellow eyes watched from within the spruces, pines, and hemlocks, and blood seeped from the branches.

"No!" Chess scolded. Whatever this was, it wasn't fair. What had he done to deserve this? What had Molly done? Billy? This wasn't right.

Chess sensed something from behind. It burst through the bush and soared at him. Heat ran from Chess's arm and then pain. He looked down and saw the father's knife stuck in his bicep.

He screamed. He screamed at the father, screamed at himself to move, and then he did.

Chess ran left, skating between the descending claws of a ponderosa pines. He pushed his legs as hard as they would move, and he saw a trail ahead. It gleamed white, its snow shining like a beacon. He placed a foot on the path, and his other was snatched from below.

Icy points pierced Chess's leg. They ripped into him and yanked him back toward the brush. He felt it inside his flesh. He felt his blood leaking out. He toppled forward, slamming into the snow. The knife in his arm smacked the ground and sent a fresh jolt of pain through his whole body.

Was this it? Was this as far as he could go? Reaching this path that he was sure would lead home but no further?

He watched the snowy trail slip from his fingers and said, "Fuck you." The words wobbled inside a scream.

Chess gripped the handle of the knife as a string of hate flowed from his mind. Fuck Paul and Matt and Doug! Fuck that whole ghost family!

He jerked the handle, but his muscle fought to hold onto the steel. He jerked hard and felt his arm cut worse as the blade backed out. He pulled himself toward the icy hand on his leg, his good arm coming down, the knife in his grip—and he paused.

The hand was Molly's. She gazed at him, crouched against the ground under a bleeding spruce bough. For a moment, she was smiling sweetly. She was the friend who always wanted to help and whom he suspected had a crush on him. But the minute passed, and her eyes flashed yellow. Her teeth turned green and were coated in fresh blood, Billy's blood.

Chess's arm changed direction. He swung from the side and drove the steel blade deep into Molly's temple. It crashed into her with an almost soft thud, passing through bone that was weak and rotten. The wound released a putrid smell of decay, and her eyes rolled back into her head.

"Let go!" Chess grumbled.

He kicked away her hand and scrambled. He limped to his feet and then down the path. He stumbled ahead, finding the larger trail.

He knew where he was now, he could make it home. But should he?

Chess thought as he moved. He had left so much death behind. So many lives. But what could he do?

As he hobbled from the forest, Chess saw his street. He looked right and saw the parking area. It was occupied by two county snowplows. They were little more than old dump trucks fitted with massive blades, but Chess knew how they worked. His other uncle was a plow driver. Chess had gotten a lesson over the summer when they went and visited, and then spent an hour riding around his cousin's pasture with a grin on his face.

Chess opened the door of the closest truck and pulled himself inside. He looked at the ignition, *No keys*. He searched the cab. The drivers took shifts with these things, and he knew that often the keys were hidden in the vehicles so any one of the three-man team could jump in at any time if a flurry hit town.

He felt under the passenger seat. Deep in the back, he found it, a tiny tin which once held mints. And inside it was the magic key.

Chess thrust the key inside and started the beast. He turned on the heat and trembled at the sound of cold, blowing air. It would be warm soon, and he needed that warmth so much. But he didn't have time to wait. He put the monster in reverse and lined up the plow facing the trail.

Doubt rose in Chess's mind. Should he really do this? What if he got the thing stuck in a tree? What if those things pulled him out of the cab and—the thought of Billy filled his mind. The axe crashing down into his chest. The sound. The blood. Billy's eyes.

He flexed his good hand around the wheel and slammed his foot into the gas. As he entered the woods, he upshifted, using his knee to stabilize the wheel. The beast thrust forward.

Tree limbs battered the plow. Snapping wood and thrashing needles scraped the edges and tried to reach for Chess. It became a rhythm, a song of crashing and tearing, wood on steel. It vibrated the vehicle and goose flesh rose on Chess's numb exterior.

Chess approached the trail's turn and felt the plow's heater begin to blow warm. He yanked the wheel left. The truck crashed through a break in the limbs, rocking forward and back, left and right. Its suspension jumped and shook like a bull.

He tore down into the smaller trail, and as his skin began to warm, Chess thought, *Maybe I can die warm.*

The plow smashed apart boughs, crushed saplings that were growing into the trail, and Chess pictured his target: the half-hidden cave that jutted out from the side of a small hill.

Chess stomped on the gas. He upshifted again. Maybe he'd plow right into that opening and crash through the side of it. Maybe he'd open it so wide that nothing could ever hide inside it again. He'd crash the roof if he could. He didn't know exactly what would happen, but inside him grew the feeling that this was right. This was the thing he needed to do to end whatever was going on inside that cave, these woods, inside his friends.

The giant diesel heart roared inside the truck. It throttled up, and the massive beast rushed ahead.

Chess saw the end approaching. The nearly hidden cave now seemed to glow with a faint yellow light. The father appeared in front of the plow, and Chess rolled over him with a thunk and a slight hop of the right tire. The sleeveless things stepped out. The axe man jumped in the way and slammed his axe into the hood. Sparks flew from the dented orange steel, and the man was sucked under the plow's blade. The split-skull thing jumped on the side of the truck and yanked on the door. Chess veered left just a few inches and the being was crushed between the steel door and an ancient hemlock.

For a moment, Chess felt a swell of hope. Maybe he could do this and live. He'd taken out three of them now. He focused on the hole, the wall of stacked boulders that was the cave entrance, and he saw Billy step out.

Billy, he was alive. He was okay. There was no hole in his chest or arm. Had Chess been mistaken? Had he imaged or hallucinated that? He was in the way. He was going to be smashed like a bug, cut in half by the plow's blade.

Chess slammed on the brakes, but it was too late. The vehicle squealed as it barreled through the final saplings and decimated Billy. Chess began to tear. Billy's face paled with yellow eyes as his body was mashed into a pulp between the blade and the cave wall.

The impact sounded as loud as a bomb. Rocks shattered and flew in all directions. The cave ripped open, and the plow toppled inside.

Chess flew forward, shattering the windshield with his face. His body pushed him along, down the hood in a trail of his own blood, over the blade, and into the inner cave.

When Chess opened his eyes, he saw the granite walls. The truck's headlights flickered and sparked and illuminated the writing. It was black, and in a language Chess didn't understand, but he knew what it was. It was a prayer. It was a message to something beyond, and it was written in blood.

There was warmness over Chess's face. He touched it. His face was torn, shredded into strips of skin from the plow's windshield. He smelled it. The metallic smell was heavy, as was something else. Chess took it in. It was diesel fuel. The fuel was pouring from the plow and pooling onto the floor of the cave.

Chess realized he was going to die warm after all.

The diesel pool lit. The fire climbed onto the truck. A whoosh thrust from the vehicle, the start of an explosion. And a clawed hand reached from the wall and dragged Chess inside.

The Ancestors

W HEN HE WAS YOUNGER, Thomas spent much of the day staring at the wall. His eyes would follow the layers of boards, white-washed yearly to maintain the look of civility. He would wonder about the land beyond.

What kid didn't want to know what was in the wider world? He had imagined there were knights and dragons, spacemen and talking dogs, all the things that filled the crumbling, old books in the village library. They had told him those things weren't real—some never were, some weren't anymore—but who could tell for sure if no one went out there? Not unless they were banished.

A thought of Mother crossed his mind. She was over there now, an ancestor. She had joined him at the library, read him books about travel and dragons and rockets to the moon. She brushed his hair as they stared at the pages. Then the winter took her.

He stood from his rest at the end of the orchard and carried two baskets of apples along the path between the wall and the trees' edge. He wasn't supposed to go that way. They said it would tease the ancestors and everyone should always stay as close to the interior of the village as possible. He didn't believe that; many of those his age didn't. They had never seen an ancestor, only the oldest of bones that hung from the walls, the skulls that decorated the village.

He supposed it was possible that they were out there, roaming the wild on the other side of the wall, reclaiming the world that was once theirs. He'd heard leaves crunch and sticks break as he walked. But that could have been a deer, the wind, anything. He had seen no proof.

He turned right and walked to the grocery, setting his baskets by those of lettuce and carrots. The skulls stared down at him from the corners of the shed. Mrs. Withers said they protected the harvest. Thomas didn't see it. All he knew was with this job done, he was free until tomorrow's duties with Mr. Hodges, collecting eggs.

He gazed over the stores of vegetables and breads and pictured himself packing them in a bag and running off. It wasn't that he hated this place; it was his home. He'd lived here his whole life, but that was just the thing... he wanted to see more, not be told there was nothing out there and ordered to obey.

"Done already?" Maria's voice sang from behind him.

He couldn't stop himself from smiling as he turned to face her. She wore a purple wildflower behind her ear and a smudge of dirt under her sparkling, green eyes. The dusky sun cast soft shadows that highlighted the tenderness in her cheeks. She was more beautiful to him each day than in the previous fourteen years of their lives. She was the reason he hadn't packed a bag yet.

"Cat got your tongue?" She swung a basket of strawberries forward and back, probably the last pick of the year.

He snatched a berry before she could pull the basket away, or just in time to allow it. She grinned and spun and placed it inside the grocery.

He chewed and watched her move, his eyes captured as if by magic.

"Hey!" Mrs. Withers slapped Thomas on the back of the head. Her wrinkled face was red with anger, and she pointed at him with a stone finger. "That's not your lot. You know you don't eat from here unless it's part of your family lot."

He held the strawberry cap behind his back and swallowed quickly. "I'm not! I'm not!" His teeth were pink.

"Yeah, I seen it." She glowered at him up and down. If only she knew how many apples he'd eaten while picking in the orchard, she probably would have called for him to be banished long ago.

He backed away.

"I'll expect you at the coops tomorrow at dawn to help Mr. Hodges, Tommy. No more lateness or I'll have you reassigned to gathering manure."

The thought of spending days collecting shit again turned his stomach as the strawberry sank. "I'll be there, Mrs. Withers."

The old woman grumbled and shuffled into the grocery.

Maria came to his side, and they strolled toward the center of town and the setting sun. She slipped her arm through his and looked up at him.

He pretended to be occupied, looking ahead and relishing the attention.

Streamers made of corn husks and dandelions decorated the small square in the center of the village. They looped around the ancestors' skulls and hung from the long bones that crossed in the center.

Tables were already arranged for tomorrow's celebration, another finished harvest. The village matrons would hang a number from the streamers at the start of the meal to celebrate the number of successful harvests the village had collected since its founding, and they would drink and revel and sing until the sun set. They would never go past sunset, despite the few drunks that would insist when being told to go home.

We can't excite the ancestors.

"What's the number this year?" he asked, flexing his arm around hers.

"Ninety-three."

"Your father giving the speech again this year?"

"I don't know if they could stop him." Her gaze turned to the ground.

He knew what she wanted to say. They'd talked about it for weeks, and each time it ended in a fight. She wanted them to marry. He did, too, but her father would never allow it. The man wanted her to wed the mayor's son, the oafish Henry, whose skin always shined as if it were wet and, for some reason, persisted in smelling of cheese.

If they started, the conversation would repeat the pattern: Thomas would say they should just leave—take their chances among the ancestors and make a home outside. She would call him insane. He'd argue that just because no one had come back didn't mean they were dead. She would shut down, and he'd walk away feeling angry that she didn't believe in him.

It was better not to start.

They reached the edge of the square, a block from her cottage, and she stopped and pulled away. "Lunch tomorrow?" She glanced toward home, making sure her father couldn't see.

"How about tonight?" he whispered. "At the orchard barn?"

She shook her head. "Thomas, it's not allowed."

"No one's ever out. They won't know."

She shook her head again.

"I have a surprise for you. Come on?" He pleaded with his eyes, his smile.

She glanced toward home again then around to the square. Couples hurried home. She saw the mayor pass down the street. He eyed the youths sourly and carried on.

"Well?" He watched her eyes for any hint of weakness. She was going to say yes. He knew it.

"Okay. Just this once, though." She smiled, shyly staring into his eyes.

It was a look of *I trust you, so don't hurt me.*

"Just this once. Take this." He handed her the greenish, copper pocket watch his mother had given him long before she went to live with the ancestors. "Come when both the arms point at the twelve."

She clasped the watch in both hands then leaped and planted a kiss on his lips, pivoted, and ran. He watched her cross the street, scanning again to see if anyone saw. She turned at the pile of ancestor skulls on the corner of Mrs. Harwood's small garden and vanished from sight.

Thomas walked east toward home as his long shadow skated across the pits and rocks in the dirt road. Doors closed and windows shut. Curtains were drawn, and the town died the same death it brought upon itself each night. Quiet. Stillness. Abandoned from life.

Thomas had to wonder: *is this really what the ancestors want?*

He looked at the reminders, mounted to the neighbor Pembrokes' fence for as long as he'd walked this road. Bones tied to wood, bound with skin like the sinew-wrapped tools he used when farming for Mrs. Withers. They said it kept them away, helped to keep them quiet, keep them outside. Thomas pondered.

He tiptoed through Dad's garden, careful of the beets and grains, the last of the year. He eyed the mulch and the grinder, a long, thin bone standing up from its blades. He wondered how long they'd stay away if the elders continued to grind their bones into fertilizer.

The door to Thomas's cottage creaked as he pushed and let in the last of the day's rays. Father mumbled something from the table, some growl about the light and the noise. He was full and drunk, barely holding his head straight. Maybe that meant he'd sleep soon?

Thomas went to the cupboard, taking a muffin and a carrot. He walked to his bed and sat on the edge.

"Don't you eat any more," Father grumbled.

"I know."

"Just one muffin and one carrot."

"Yes, Father."

"You're not going to eat us out of our home like your brother used to."

Thomas ground his teeth. He wished he could forget that day. James was only nine. He had deserved better, no matter how sick he'd gotten. He deserved a chance to get better.

"No, Father," he muttered.

"Good." Father rested his head on his wrist then, as if he'd forgotten, he raised his head, drank from his mead, and put his head back down. It wouldn't be long now.

Once Father's snores were deep and heavy, Thomas went into his chest. He got out his knapsack, his two shirts, and his second pair of pants. He packed them along with a small, wooden man Father had carved for him when he was young, a container that held a lock of his mother's hair, and a compass from the old world.

The compass hadn't worked properly since before the village. He was told the North it used to point to was cold, where no man could live. Now it pointed to a new North that was hot, a place like Hell, where bugs the size of a boy's fist spread sickness and the ancestors roamed in congregations as large as the old cities. He didn't know if that was true, but maybe one day they would find out.

He drew the ties on his bag and slung it over his shoulder. He picked up Father's knapsack and dumped it out on the old man's bed.

Half-empty mead jugs clanked together, and a shock shot through Thomas's heart. He spun and glared at Father.

The man snorted and shook the table.

Thomas breathed lighter. He took Father's knife, slid it into his pocket, and went to the cupboard.

There were so many mead jugs, he shook his head. He hated the stuff, but he thought Maria might enjoy it. So he took one. He wrapped five muffins in cloth and laid it all gently in Father's sack. There were no more fruit or vegetables, no more eggs. Where had it all gone? He'd have to go by the grocery. It was early—he had time.

From the table near the door, he took two candles, his flint, and char cloth.

"Goodbye, Father," he whispered and slipped outside.

The night was still. It was the time of the dead, and the air carried their sour scent in streams, like sheer fabric on a breeze. The ground shimmered in moonlit trails of darkworm slime, reminding Thomas to watch his step.

He crept down the path to the grocery, soft with each pace and watchful for the sounds of pebbles beneath his footfalls. The grass would have been quieter, but fear of a darkworm bite kept him where he could see his feet.

Evergreen branches creaked beyond the wall. They rustled, the sounds of needles brushing needles in the wind. Scratching. Movements in the grass. The wet slurp of darkworm slime as they searched for their next meal. Each home was silent. Each house closed, unlit, asleep.

He opened the door to the grocery, careful of the squeak at the far end of its swing. He rested it gently against the wall and gazed at the village's stores.

There was so much. It could last Maria and him so long, months, but he had to restrain himself. By mid-morning, they'd know he was gone, and Father would be blamed for any perceived crime. He loaded a handful of strawberries, half a dozen potatoes, a dozen eggs, and a few tomatoes into Father's sack.

He shut the door gently and glanced at Mrs. Withers's cottage. Candles out, doors closed, quiet. The last thing he needed was that old bat raising alarms.

He headed for the orchard. It was early, but he could wait for Maria there. He could be sure he saw her as soon as she arrived, and they could be right on their way.

Some said the orchard barn was two hundred years old. Thomas had a hard time believing that, but it was definitely old. Dozens of farming tools lay scattered around the floor and leaning on posts. Rusted chains hung from pulleys in the high rafters. Mr. Douglas said they were for moving squares of grass, cow feed, back before darkworms poisoned their meat. Thomas had helped the farmer from time to time, using the chains to store harrows and harnesses, nothing too big, things that had to be put up for winter.

At least a dozen boards from the building's roof had fallen in over time, and Thomas could see the stars through the empty slots. They came and went, fading and showing themselves through the sky's green and blue glow. Thomas had read that those lights were millions of years old. It reminded him that even something as simple as light could survive beyond their home. He must be able to also.

He climbed the ladder to the loft, set his bags down, and sat against the inside wall where he could see through the open doors. He wanted to know the second she came.

He thought about her smile. It made him warm in the cool night. He thought about the softness of her lips and the brush of her hair against him when she hugged him. She was like a dream, brightening every day with her laugh and touch... and that kiss.

He had nearly fallen asleep when he heard footsteps on the path. A shadow crawled across the long patch of moonlight that reached through the doors onto the barn floor. A head, shoulders. They stepped inside slowly, cautiously.

"Thomas?" she whispered into the cavernous building.

His heart warmed inside his chest. "Here," he whispered back and moved to the loft's edge. He strained to see her but could barely make out her features. "This way." He turned to grab the bags when he heard more footsteps on the path.

Terror shot through him like lightning. Who was that? They couldn't find them. He couldn't let that happen. The elders would take her away and lock her in her house. They'd find the food and banish him, alone, with nothing.

"Come," he whispered sharply, "Up here. Hide with me."

She scurried over, her hands in front to feel in the darkness. She found the ladder and climbed. He pulled her closer, smelled her scent, and his flesh rose in goosebumps.

"Over here." He pulled her to the wall and huddled beside her. His chest pounded. He wondered if she could feel it.

"Thomas." Her breath was soft against his cheek.

"Shh." He could see her eyes glistening, reflecting the patch of moonlit floor. They were wet. Teared? Was she crying?

"Thomas..."

"Come on out, boy!" a man barked from below. Firelight flickered through the barn door. Then more. It leaked through the wood siding. Shadows danced as more came.

"Thomas, I had to," she whimpered.

"What?"

"Father found the watch. He... hurt me until I told."

Rage boiled inside Thomas's belly. "He did what?"

She didn't speak. She wept, pressing her head into his chest. It was warm, then wet.

He placed a hand on her back, drawn between anger and sadness. How dare they do this to her? All she wanted to do was come and see him. She didn't do anything wrong, and they... She glanced up at him, and her face became lit. Her left eye was swollen, barely able to open. Her lip was huge, cracked and bleeding. Blood outlined her face, dripped from her ear, down her jaw, and wet her neck. *Those monsters.*

One stepped inside. It was her father, the judge. His torch lit the barn from floor to rafter. He scanned downstairs, then the loft, until his gaze met Thomas's. Fire danced in his eyes like the Devil himself, the ancestors' maker.

"Get down here, boy!" He pointed at Thomas. "Time to pay for what you've done."

"What I've done? Look at Maria, you spineless bastard!" He stood, and Maria cowered back against the wall. "You beat a beautiful girl *for nothing!*"

"She's mine. I'll slice her whole face off if I think it's good for her. But what isn't good for her is you. Now, get down here and face your trial."

Trial. The last thing he wanted. As long as Thomas had lived, no man had ever gone through trial without being banished. It was fine if he could sneak his bags out and take Maria, but without them, going out there might have meant death. He didn't think the outside was as bad as they claimed, but without her, it might as well have been.

David Jeffrees and his father, John, stepped inside. Mayor Bloom and his son Henry stepped inside. So this was the group that would banish him? All despicable. All crude and corrupt. He wasn't surprised, just angry.

"Come on, son." The mayor waved Thomas closer. He squinted and looked Thomas over. "Don't make us come get you."

Thomas looked around the loft. There was nowhere to run. He looked at Maria. She buried her face in her knees. There was no way out of this. All he could hope for was that they didn't punish her. He'd have to take all the blame.

He caressed the back of her head, he figured for the last time. "I'm sorry. I love you."

She shook her head and refused to look up.

"Come on, boy," the mayor whined.

Thomas came down the ladder. John Jeffrees seized him by the shoulders and pulled him toward the entrance.

"Now your things..." the Judge insisted. "Henry, go get his bags and let's see what he stole from our community."

Henry climbed the ladder, and Maria pulled herself closer to the wall. He picked up Thomas's knapsacks and stared down at her.

"Leave her alone," Thomas shouted.

The judge spun and slapped him across the face. It burned.

"That is his betrothed," the judge snapped. "He can look at her whenever he chooses."

The mayor nodded.

Henry hung both bags over one arm, climbed down, and handed them to the judge.

The judge lifted them up and down, weighing them in his grip. "Feels like you stole quite a bit." He grinned, and Thomas could see the glee in his eyes. He cast his gaze up to the loft. "Now come on down, Maria."

She shuddered in place and came no closer.

"I said come down here. Now."

"Want me to get her?" Henry pointed up.

The judge shook his head. "No. She's not yours yet." He took hold of the ladder and climbed up to the loft. He grabbed her by the arm and yanked her from the wall.

"Let go!" She dropped to the loft floor like a doll. "No more!"

"You will do what I say, child." He grabbed and jerked her toward the ladder.

Her arm popped. She screamed.

"Now go on down."

She sobbed and collapsed beside the ladder's edge.

The judge wound his leg back and kicked her in the ribs. His foot thumped against her flesh. "Girl, you will do what I say." He kicked her again then bent down and grabbed her arm. "Go down."

He pulled her up to a sit and put her hand on the ladder, but she didn't move. He growled and kicked her a third time. She groaned and fell on her side, and he slammed his foot into her face.

"Move!"

Maria rolled, one hand grasping her face, the other her ribs. Her eyes were sealed with tears, and all she wanted was to get away from the man. She reached for something to grab, to lift herself and move, and all she found was air.

"Maria!" Thomas called out, but it was too late.

She slipped from the edge of the loft, her arms and legs flailing, searching for purchase, and finding nothing.

The world seemed to slow as Thomas watched her drop. Her gaze found him, and their eyes locked. There was a shared fear. She didn't know what would come next, and he could see what was underneath. He tried to move, to change her fall, but John Jeffrees held him in place.

Below Maria, leaned against the loft's beam, Mr. Douglas had sat upright a large, hook-bladed harrow in the midst of repair. Its foot-long rusted stakes pointed straight up as if waiting for something to hang on them.

"No," Thomas whispered.

The palm of her hand touched first, a spike ripping up and through its center. Another spike hooked through her ribs, plunging into her lungs and heart. A final one drove through the bottom of her chin, pinning it against her upper jaw before digging into her skull.

She stared with a helpless gaze at Thomas. Her lips moved a tremor. Her body convulsed. Blood bubbled from her mouth and nose, and then she was gone. Her eyes never left Thomas.

Thomas dropped to his knees. Jeffrees couldn't hold him up.

"Dammit," the judge roared. He pointed at Thomas. "This is your fault." He stormed down the ladder and kicked Thomas in the face.

Thomas didn't move, didn't look up. Blood streamed over his lips and chin.

"Goddammit!" The judge pointed at Henry, then David Jeffrees, then Maria. "Get her off of there. We have to deal with this right now." He went to the ladder and pulled it from the side of the loft. "Help me," he commanded the mayor.

A gurgling came from Maria's throat. Her arms twitched.

"Let's go." The judge and the mayor held the ladder from both ends and walked. Henry and David carried Maria. She dripped blood and jerked, more and more it seemed with each step. In the back, John Jeffrees shoved Thomas along.

Thomas watched the wall get closer, tears streaming down his face. He watched Maria squirm in their arms.

Was it true? Did the ancestors really live forever beyond the wall? It had been the last thing he cared about, but then he saw Maria die. And now she was moving. It couldn't be—could it?

The judge planted his end of the ladder on the ground beside the wall. The mayor pushed his end to the top.

"Go on," the mayor grunted. He and the judge held the sides, and Henry and David climbed, Maria dangling in their arms. Her hands reached for her father. They reached for the mayor. They swiped at Henry, and he tossed her over the top.

There was a soft thud, nearly inaudible, from the other side.

The boys climbed down, and Henry stared at the ground. A pair of gashes ran from his cheekbone to his chin.

The judge turned and stared at Thomas. He grumbled, "Now you."

Thomas sat, his back against the wall, Maria's head in his lap. He stroked her hair, and it stuck to his hands in bloody clumps. Her bones and muscles crackled. Her limbs spasmed every few minutes, stretching longer and longer. Her jaw extended, and he felt it swell against his leg. His tears stung his face.

The night wind pushed boughs to sway, reminding Thomas of a child in a swing crying to go higher and higher. He watched clouds pass in front of the moon and glimmers reflect from within branches. Footfalls, like pairs of running children, neared in the evergreens' shadows.

Thomas strained to see. Forms of blackness moved in the gloom. They leaned and jerked and pawed at the earth, and one stepped into the moonlight.

Thomas froze with fear. His heart raced below his stiffening chest. He wanted to scream and run, but his body didn't respond. He felt the chill of the night as if for the first time and could only scream inside his head, *God, what was I thinking?*

It was without clothes or hair, and skin hung from its muscles with non-bleeding rips and tears. Its arms, legs, fingers, and jaws were stretched, distorted, angular, and pointed like nothing Thomas could have imagined. Its pale, dry skin seemed fragile in the moonlight, while the tips of its elongated fingers were like claws, threatening to tear holes in the world itself.

Were these the ancestors? Were these those that came before? Was it—he looked down at Maria, the clumps of shed hair in his lap, her cracking and creaking limbs and fingers. His back pressed firmly against the wall.

Another came from the shadows, walking on three limbs like a wounded animal. It was missing an eye and jerked its head as if to take in the entirety of the scene. It marched toward Thomas, its legs and arms twitching with each movement, and its brother followed. Their mouths stretched wide, and a soft hiss sounded without lips or tongue.

Thomas glanced down at his love. Her skin paled. Her fingers extended. She was becoming one of them. It was true. He slid from beneath her head and jumped to his feet. He had to get away from them, from her, or—he didn't know what they would do, but it was bad, it had to be bad.

Thomas ran. His legs pumped and his arms swung. He followed the fence. There was no door back inside; even the gate had been sealed years ago, but on the other side was his home, his father, everything he had ever known—there had to be some way back.

Things pounded on the earth behind him. *Thump-thump, thump-thump. Thump-thump, thump-thump.* It was like the sprint of ancient animals he'd only read about: horses, dogs, deer. But it wasn't an animal—*they* were back there. He knew it. He ran harder.

His head was heavy. His legs burned. More pounding joined the pair. Was it three? Four? More of them? God, he didn't want to look back, but he had to.

He turned his head, refusing to slow. He saw rising limbs, bobbing heads. They tossed dirt and debris behind their beast-like strides. He saw angles in their heads that were inhuman, strangely-shaped bones and sharp ridges around their eyes. And the hiss. Hisses washed over him and chilled his insides.

He tried counting them. He got to three and had to stop. Their bobbing heads, their flailing limbs; it was a mob of monster parts, in-distinguishable as individual beings in the gloom. All he could do was push himself faster. There was no other choice.

His gaze moved forward just in time to spot a waist-high tree limb he was about to hit. He jerked toward the wall to squeeze between the limb and the hardwood boards. His back slammed against the wall. His chest scraped on the limb's edge. He felt a gash under his shirt, warm wetness, and a sting.

He groaned and kept running.

The beasts went under, losing a half-step but gaining on him. He felt their footsteps as they pounded. He sensed their teeth spreading behind him.

A thought occurred to Thomas. He had a knife. It wasn't much, smaller than the machete he used to trim branches in the orchard, but it was something.

He reached into his pocket and fished it out. It slowed him down, and the hiss grew louder in his ears. He unfolded it and held it firm in his hand. He was going to have to stop soon. His lungs burned, and there was no way he could keep this pace. He'd have to be ready to fight.

The choice was taken from him. Pain tore into his heel. He jerked his foot away, and searing heat raced up his calf. He put the foot back down, and his leg failed. He tumbled, chest, face, over, back, then rolled sideways. Something poked his eye. Something tore into his side. He felt his leg soak as his heel bled.

Air, like the stench of rotten meat, hovered over his face; it was one of them. Stretched jaws with blackened teeth jutted forward, then down, then up.

Thomas tried to push himself back but found himself against a tree. He searched his stinging hands for his knife. It was gone, lost in the roll. His eye was blurred. His side stung.

A second beast hovered over Thomas. It snared his shirt with the tip of its finger and ripped down, splitting his clothes and exposing his belly.

More pain was coming. He knew that as much as he knew calling these things his ancestors was a lie. These were not his relatives. They were beasts from another world, a Hell like the one he'd heard the librarian speak of. Any second, one was going to tear his stomach apart. The other one would chomp into his face. He trembled below them and closed his eyes.

He forced himself away from that place and thought of Maria instead. He thought of her laugh, her gentle breath on his skin, how much sweeter that was than the death and decay that hovered over his face. He thought of her touch. Her hugs. Her kiss.

He was ready to go. With her in mind, would death be that bad?

But it didn't come. No claw in his belly. No gouge into his face.

He opened his eyes, and the creature stared down at him. Its jaw continued rotating up, forward, down, and back, cracking as it moved, like rocks scraping between slabs of dried meat. Its hiss still rolled from its throat.

"Do it!" Thomas screamed. "If you're going to kill me, then do it!" His words hitched in his throat.

There was a moment. The fiend above him cocked its head and seemed to ponder. Then it seized Thomas's wrist, plunging its clawed fingers through his flesh. Their tips emerged from the other side, and it closed its hand around his bone.

Thomas screamed. Blood ran down his arm. It dripped from his fingers.

The thing took off once again in a gallop, this time dragging Thomas from the arm with two beasts behind them.

He slid on his back over brush and twigs. He slammed into rocks and felt things scrape down his back. "Stop!"

He screamed and howled. He thought his arm would snap and the thing would rip away the flesh in its grip.

They went deep into the woods. Night became darker. Growth thickened, and the pine scent of hundred-year-old evergreens fought through the stench of death and blood.

"Let me go," he yelled at his captor. He screamed at the followers. Before he knew it, his screams had become cries, and the forest faded from sight.

Thomas looked over a sea of glowing faces bathed in a bright white light.

He saw smiles and laughter. He felt love, real love, between everyone there. It was an overwhelming beauty that soaked him to the core. He saw his mother and father. He saw Maria, Mr. Douglas, Mrs. Withers, and so many others. There was a happiness beyond anything he had felt in the village or anywhere. He was in the place where they were supposed to be. He didn't know why he knew that, but he knew it.

He reached out and touched Maria's face. She reached toward him and embraced him. Her face was healed. His arms were healed. Her chest had no marks from the harrow, and her body was back to itself—how it was supposed to be.

Something grabbed his shoulders and yanked him back. The light faded, taking everyone with it. The joy, the love, the perfect sense of belonging were all ripped from his being, and it hurt with excruciating torment. It wasn't a pain of the flesh, it was a pain of the mind, but he felt it in every inch of his being.

He clawed against the air with nothing to grasp, and he cried. He looked to fight whoever was dragging him, and he found Maria. Not the perfect Maria that had been snatched from him, but the other.

Her head bore three clumps of hair, scattered across her skull in a sickening mockery of who she had been. Her brow and cheekbones pressed through her flesh, cracking the skin on the outermost edges. Her arms and legs were as bad as his attackers, long and thin and crackling like some demonic animal.

She glanced back at him, and he wanted to weep for the life she had lost, but the pain surged inside his arm.

He looked down at the hole through his forearm and clenched his teeth together. He wanted it back. His arm, the love, the joy, his perfect Maria, and the truth of what he had seen came through like the rise of dawn: they were waiting. All of them were waiting. The people in his village, the ancestors, they were the last ones, and they were all waiting to move on to that other place. It was why ancestors killed, to stop the waiting. Because once they were all finally gone, they could all go to that other place, that perfect place, together.

It was so simple that Thomas didn't understand why no one in the village had ever discovered it. They were not the survivors of the human race. They were the petulant children holding the rest of the species back from moving on.

Thomas looked up into Maria's eyes. They were filled with nothing. There seemed to be no recognition of who he was. He wondered if this was the biggest part of the trick. Humans didn't understand. Ancestors couldn't tell them.

"Stop."

She pulled him on.

"Let go, Maria." He squirmed and broke free of her grasp. He stood with a pained limp, and she opened her mouth and hissed. She flexed her fingers and reached for him.

"Easy." He threw up his hands and backed away. He wept and stared deeply into her eyes. "Do you remember me... at all?"

She swayed with the wind. Her jaw moved up and down.

"I love you."

She cocked her head just slightly and stared up at the lightening sky.

He had to wonder. Was she helping him from nothing but a vague memory of what they had been?

He looked at where they had come from. The other beasts crept toward him, studying, swaying, their mouths creaking as they chewed some invisible meal. There were more than a dozen reaching for him. He mourned his arm. They were going to tear him apart to end this.

"I'm going to help you." He put up his good hand. "Please."

They looked at him sideways, and Maria stepped between them. She hissed, and they backed away, but just a step.

Hour after hour, Thomas worked. He dragged dead saplings and limbs from the woods to the wall. He piled them beside it first; then, as the mountain grew, he laid them perpendicular, making a ramp from the ground to the crest of the wall.

His fingers ached. They were covered in blisters and sores from working all morning with only one hand. He climbed to the top of the wall regardless.

He peeked over and saw cottages, then the grocery in the distance. Beyond that was the square, where everyone would be gathering and drinking by now.

Thomas climbed back down to Maria. The others crouched under the trees, their gazes endlessly moving over him, gauging their chance to take him.

"There," he pointed at the ramp. He thought of the white light, the love, the happiness filling his mind and body. "It's time to end this."

He climbed up the ramp and waved for Maria to follow. She did, and the rest came behind her.

Mrs. Withers sat at the table with a slice of strawberry pie and a half-finished mug of mead. Mrs. Harwood sat beside her, a drunken smile on her face and strawberry jam across her upper lip. Thomas's father and

Mr. Douglas sat at the next table along with a half dozen farmworkers.

John Jeffrees, the mayor, and their boys sat at the table of prominence in the center of the square. Their wives and daughters sat at the neighboring table, and the rest of the village radiated out from there.

Thomas scanned over the festival, noting the only person that seemed to be missing was the judge. He watched his father, as drunk as always. The man drank and roared with his workmates, oblivious to his banished son. Thomas pressed the pain down deep inside.

He waved the ancestors forward.

No one noticed the gallop of long hands and contorted feet as they closed in on the square. They drank and ate and laughed until a pair of ancestors sunk their fingers into the spaces around Mrs. Withers collarbones and ripped her in half. Her mouth moved to scream, but as she fell, her lungs pushed no air.

Ancestors dragged five villagers down as others rose and howled and ran. Jugs of mead crashed to the ground. Tables flipped, pinning women and children, and teeth sank into flesh, soaking the square in blood.

Thomas watched as the one-eyed thing tackled and tore into Mrs. Harwood. He smiled as John and David Jeffrees stumbled in the dirt, bleeding and collapsing from gaping holes in their bellies. He saw the mayor and Henry run, leaving their wife and mother and sisters behind, then ancestors seized their heads and clawed into their throats.

Thomas closed his eyes and imagined them all within the white light to come. He saw the square in the light and himself sitting beside them, drinking, eating, celebrating the rest of their existence. It was going to be wonderful. He opened his eyes and saw Maria.

She walked at first, beyond the square and down her road. As she got closer to her house, she dropped onto all fours and galloped like a beast. She turned the corner where his gaze had always lost her, and he decided this time he should come.

He limped past the carnage, down the road, and around the corner. He saw her house, the place that was supposed to be safe for her, where she was supposed to have the love of a family. Yet she never did. He was more a part of her family than that judge. He was the one that brought joy and light into her life, and he was going to do it again.

She banged on the cottage door. Screams from the inside, "Go away! Leave me alone!"

"I'll help you," he whispered and picked up a rock from the garden. He walked to the judge's window and smashed it.

"No!" the judge screamed.

Maria grabbed the sill and raised her leg to climb inside. The judge flipped his table on end and blocked the hole.

Thomas nodded. He walked to the other window. His head was getting heavy again. He had been all day with no food or water, his blood dripping everywhere he went. He didn't know how he was still moving other than his drive toward that vision, the white light.

He lifted the rock and smashed the window. He leaned in and saw the judge. The man was pressing all his weight into the table to keep Maria out, to keep his daughter out of her own home.

Thomas growled. He climbed through and walked toward the judge. He gripped the rock as tightly as his weak hand and blistered fingers would allow. He raised the rock.

"Let her in!" Thomas shouted. His voice sounded shallow, like an old man.

The judge stared at him with wild eyes. At his wounds. Thomas's flesh was as white as the ancestors. He stumbled like the dying.

"Get away!" The judge charged Thomas. He swung up, and Thomas swung down.

The table crashed to the floor. The judge plunged a knife deep into Thomas's gut. Thomas's rock slammed into the judge's head. They both crumpled.

Maria crawled across the floor on all fours.

The judge watched her, dazed, unknowing what he was even seeing. She leaned over him and looked into his eyes, studying his face.

"Don't," he muttered. A flash of recognition sparked in his eyes. "I'm—your father."

Her hand swiped across his throat, tearing his Adam's apple and half his windpipe from his neck. She watched as he clutched with bloody fingers. He covered the wound and held it. His jaw waved up and down, but the only sound he made was the slap of his lips against one another.

Maria backed away from her father and crawled over to Thomas. She studied the blade in his gut and laid down beside him. He gasped and coughed, blood rolling over his lips and down his sides. She rested her head on his chest as his heart beat slower and slower.

Thomas caressed her head and smiled.

The Gate

1

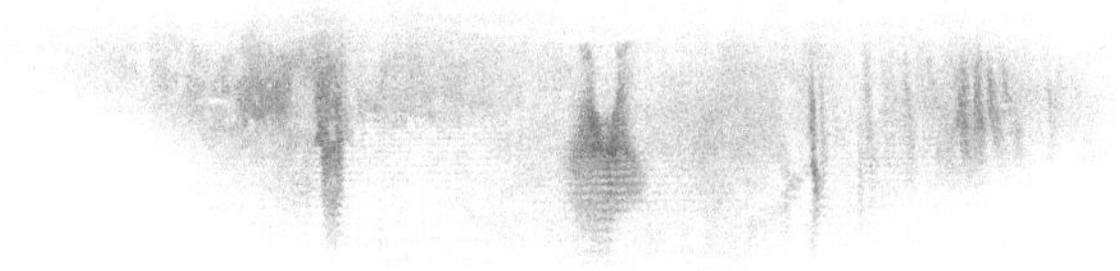

"**P**UNCH IT." CAPTAIN STONE'S voice was as calm as ever. If you didn't know any better, you'd think the crew was headed down the street to get a batch of lattes, not thrusting through a wormhole with no idea what was on the other side—or if the shields would keep them from stretching into meat strips as thin as needles.

Jones glanced back at the captain, only as briefly as he thought he could get away with, then at the other three crew members. He knew what he heard, but if there was any chance he was mistaken, he wanted to see it on Stone's face before he engaged the Crow's thrusters.

There was no hesitation in the captain's face, no sign of worry on Diaz, Samuels, or Hendrix. Jones rotated back and aimed the small craft at the mouth of the red, kilometer wide object.

It reminded him of a blood cell of some cosmic beast, flowing from light red to dark crimson in its center. The endless color shift gave him chills.

"Thrusters full." Jones tapped the console, and the ship hummed as it raced forward from the formation of USSF ships surrounding the portal.

In the three months since the garish, red wormhole had been pinpointed as the source of the Scourge attacks, this was the first manned exploration inside. They'd sent probes, none of which returned—none of which transmitted back. If humanity was going to get to the bottom of where these alien monstrosities were coming from and how to stop them, Jones's team needed to return with some worthwhile intelligence.

The red mass filled the front viewscreen as they shot forward.

Jones's chills seemed to invade every inch of his being. He had been in combat with the Scourge, the large slime-drenched ones, and the smaller, muscular beasts, but this mission was going into their home turf. This was going where they may find thousands, maybe millions of them, not the hundreds at a time that had been expelled from the blood-colored portal and volleyed at the Union's nearby colonies.

"Two hundred meters to contact." Jones's chills turned to ice in his veins. He felt it creep from chest to limbs to digits. It tickled the insides of his guts with a nagging hesitation. It told him this was a bad idea. He wanted to listen. But he had orders.

"One hundred."

They were right on top of it. The nose of the craft was about to touch, and dread washed over Jones. It was a strange knowledge of his imminent death, cranking the tickle in his belly into a painful twist. He wanted to puke.

"This is it."

Red, glowing energy invaded the small ship's control room as a webbed wall of light. Jones's eyes shot wide. The edge of the wormhole traveled through their titanium, their steel, and their air. As each inch of ship overlapped the strange substance, it stretched and warped out of existence while its vision hung imprinted in their eyes. Their ship was being stretched below the atomic level while visually frozen in the event horizon of this beautifully terrifying thing.

Jones prayed inside his mind to some higher power he'd never met. His muscles tensed, his fingers restrained but wanting to act. He wanted to stop, to switch the thrusters to reverse. He tried to lift his hand in case the captain came to his senses and ordered the action. He found his body moved slower than the creeping wormhole wall as if time itself had reduced to a crawl.

Red wiped over the front of the console, then his legs. He felt a warmth then frozen numbness, and all he could think was they had made a terrible mistake. Could it have all been a trap? Something sent by the Scourge to trick them into going inside and being wiped from reality?

God, please, ran through his mind as the scarlet wall froze his face and sucked him in.

Jones blinked inside a black void. He saw no control room, no crew, no viewscreen. There was no sound, no engine, nothing but him, naked, floating in a barren space.

"Hello?" His voice was flat, without reverberation. He wondered if it could be a dream, but as he touched his body and tested his mind, he decided it couldn't be. He tried calling again, "Hello?"

An immense pressure seized onto his head from every direction. It squeezed inward as if trying to pop his skull like a pimple.

Jones grabbed himself and searched, trying to isolate his attacker. He felt no one.

The wide, curved bones around his head creaked and squealed. He felt them shift. His flesh burned. It was wet, bloody. His hands shook. His heart raced. His fingers slid across the squiggly joints, and he knew in another few seconds his brains would be pasty globs leaking through the cracks in his skull.

Then, the feeling descended, surrounding his entire body, compressing him.

"Stop!"

Pain from every inch of his skin. It was like wearing something too tight over his whole body, and it was shrinking by the second. He knew his blood vessels were bursting, bruising him, flooding his insides with an ocean of internal bleeding. The strain on his chest made it hard to breathe. His skull popped as if it may crush inward at any moment.

Blackness faded to red, and a crimson fog encircled him. It crossed over his flesh, leaving a thick wetness. He tried to wipe it off, but as he swept his hand over his skin, just as much remained.

He felt dampness between his fingers. It shined red inside the fog. Was it water, red from the strange light?

He held it under his nose and smelled it. Blood. He was drenched in blood. Floating in a cloud of blood. It stuck to his skin, stinking of iron and salt, and as the pressure cranked harder on his body, it turned darker, and the stench of decay invaded his nostrils.

His skull cracked loudly. The vibration traveled down his bones, down his spine, as if warning, *It's coming for you next*. He screamed into the cloud, "Help me!"

His ribs cracked. Air rushed out of his lungs, but he couldn't pull it back in—the pressure, the pain, it was too much to fight. Sharpened, broken rib bones lacerated his lungs. He wanted to howl. His diaphragm flexed to push out a wail and failed.

Jones's vision faded to dots, then black, and sounds of screaming came from the void. The fog grew thick, harsh like heavy smoke, then wiped over him like hot slime.

"No!" He forced out a burst of defiance.

Crack. His skull collapsed inward. He saw blood, then bone. His eyes sunk inside, and he glimpsed his own pinkish-gray brain.

Sirens screamed.

"Jones!" Someone was calling his name.

Jones opened his eyes. Sparks showered the control room. Lights flashed. The viewscreen flickered. He reached for his console, and his fingers slid across it. It was covered in thick, red slime. His hands were drenched in it. He looked around the control room— everything was.

He wiped his hand sideways over the console, splashing the floor with slime. He pressed a series of buttons, and the viewscreen woke up.

"What the hell?" Hendrix muttered.

Ahead was a glowing, red ball, a red giant star surrounded by a ring of millions of asteroids. They crashed into each other like a never-ending game of pool, propelling massive hunks of rock toward the sun. And it was all getting bigger with each second that passed.

"Turn us around, Jones!" the captain shouted.

Jones punched frantically at the console. The ship turned, the thrusters fired, and a boom rocked the entire vessel.

"What the hell was that?" Diaz screamed.

Red lights flashed on the console's corner.

"Impact!" Jones shouted.

The ship bucked upward. Jones's face slammed into the console as sparks erupted. The control surface cracked and sliced his cheek, and his blood swirled within the red slime.

"Dammit." Jones lifted his face.

A blue light blinked. It was the ship's emergency artificial intelligence system begging to be activated. He tapped the light, and another boom rocked the ship.

The viewscreen went black. The console off.

"What's going on, Jones?" the captain shouted.

"It's all dead, sir. Have to trust in the autopilot now."

The ship rocked from every side. Each crew member yanked on their harnesses, checking their tension.

Diaz pulled out a cigarette and tried to light it, but the red slime had ruined her lighter. She tossed the pack on the floor, wiped the slime from the pendant around her neck, and gave it a kiss.

Hendrix glared at Jones, and as if their upcoming deaths were the navigator's fault, he ground his teeth and clenched his fists.

Samuels leaned his head back and closed his eyes. He was ready to die any day, if that's what was coming. He'd rather do it rested, though.

Stone gripped the sides of his seat and said a prayer.

The hull howled. Metal scraped on metal. Things crunched within the walls. Thrusters fired on each side of the ship. The deep-space engines roared, vibrating the crew's seats. The world around them grew quiet for a moment until crash foam shot from every corner of the control room and hardened around them.

Jones felt a final boom from below, and his mind went black.

Even through the semi-translucent foam, the control room was dark. So dark that Jones wondered if he was still inside the ship. But he had to be. Crash foam was designed to stick in place and hold you there. The room, though, had no illumination, no consoles lit, no floor lights. He didn't think he had ever seen a starship without at least a dozen lights on, even during night mode.

As the foam melted away, it became clear he was indeed on the ship. And strangely, there was no sound. Were the engines off?

He laid on the control room floor, a foot of foam between himself and the deck, and he slowly sank as it degraded. There were, in fact, no lights. Each ceiling, floor, console, and display was off. The little light that existed in the room seemed to have no source. It was an ambient red hue that hung in the air with no root and casting no shadows.

"Jones!" The captain's voice was muffled through foam.

"Sir?"

"Report."

He surveyed the room again. How was he supposed to report with no electronics? No computer? No lights? "Sir, I..."

"Where are we?" Diaz snapped.

"Through the wormhole. Something hit us, or we hit something. I think the autopilot crashed us on some planet or large asteroid."

"You think?" Captain Stone was clearer now; only his chest and legs remained insulated.

"All instruments are down, sir. It's my best guess from memory."

A large crack rocked the room from above. The ceiling hissed.

"Sir," Hendrix said. "I think the hull's breached."

"Shit." The captain tore his feet free. "Everyone, environmental helmets on. Double time."

Hendrix led the way to the starboard storage bays. Diaz took the port side. They passed out helmets and couplers to seal the crews' jumpsuits.

The ceiling cracked again. Metal plates crashed onto the control room floor. Wires hung from a gap in the roof.

Five couplers slid over heads. Five helmets snapped into place. Respiration systems whirred, and Heads Up Displays lit on each helmet.

Jones braced himself, expecting the air to rush out of the ship as they became exposed to a vacuum. It didn't. A red mist came in.

"What the fuck is that?" Samuels asked.

2

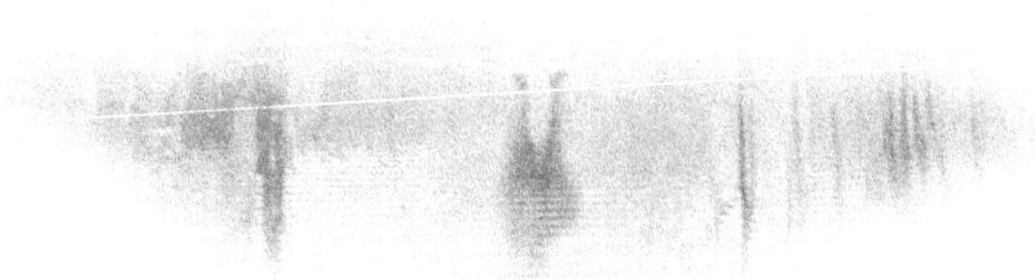

"Not good," Diaz read from her HUD. "That air leaking in is thirty percent cyanide. It also has a high concentration of acidic gases."

Jones read from his own HUD. His oxygen tanks were ninety-nine percent full with an Expected Depletion Time of twelve hours.

The captain's eyes scanned the readout in his HUD then stared at the breach in the control room ceiling. "That means we have twelve hours to repair that hole and get this bucket of bolts making air—or we die. I don't know about you, but neither carbon dioxide poisoning nor burning from acid while inhaling cyanide sound like acceptable ways to go."

"Worse than that," Diaz chimed in. "Our suits weren't made to deal with acidic environments. If we can't seal that or confine ourselves to habitable portions of the ship, we have... maybe... half that amount of time."

"Okay, people. You heard the lady. That means teams.

"Jones, Diaz, work on getting the computers back online. No computers, no life support.

"Hendrix, Samuels, head outside. Inspect the hull breach and determine a repair schedule.

"I'm going to inspect the rest of the interior then meet up with Hendrix and Samuels to assist.

"Everyone clear?"

Yessirs broadcasted through the comms inside each helmet. Hendrix opened the service compartment beside the control room door and cranked the emergency lever to pry open the hatch. He, Samuels, and Stone went through and cranked it closed from the other side.

"Start simple," Diaz said. "Inspect the power relays on the port side, and I'll take a look at the starboard."

Captain Stone ignored the growing churn in his gut as he watched Hendrix and Samuels check their sidearms and crank open the inner airlock. The lights on the sides of their helmets brightened their paths beyond the strange, red, ambient hue.

Stone kept the feeling to himself. There was no need to spook the crew, even if his gut was screaming at him that they needed to hurry the fuck up and get out of there as soon as they could. He'd see dozens of alien planets, killed more aliens than he could count, but for some reason, this place felt like none of those. It had a ringing to it, not an audible one, but one that chimed inside his mind. It rang at a high pitch within that lizard part of the brain that reached out when there was something wrong—something the modern, logical thought centers were too obtuse to pick up on. And as the seconds ticked by, the warning bells from his old lizard boy were starting to wear on him.

He went to the crew's rack room, studying the floors, walls, corners, while glancing back and forth at his HUD. The air in this part of the ship only contained trace amounts of the planet's gases. That was good. It pointed to no leaks, or at least small ones in this part of the starship.

He ducked and looked below the pair of bunks. Nudie mags under Samuels's. A shoebox of contraband snacks under Diaz's. Photos were taped to the walls beside each mattress: loved ones and kids. Dust specs floated past Stone's helmet beams, but there were no cracks in the inner hull. He noticed scratching sounds drifting down from above. They gave him chills.

Rats? he wondered as he stood. The air in this section may still be fine between the inner and outer hulls. There had been cases of rats being found in the crawl spaces and conduit tracks before.

He moved on to his own quarters, a cabin the size of a bathroom, having a bed and a small desk where he could hold private communications with upper brass. Floor, ceiling, a cupboard-sized closet. He pushed his uniforms back, watching the closet's corners. It looked good. His HUD read the same: only trace gases—but something felt off. As he walked, he sensed it. The air may have checked out, but this place just *felt wrong*.

He glanced at the photo of Stara taped to the mirror behind his desk. She held the stuffed animal he'd brought her three missions back, an Arthurian Slug, which, for some reason, all the kids thought was the cutest thing since the race was discovered three decades ago. He wished he was with her now, even if that meant having to deal with the ex-wife. He'd deal.

More scratching, this time from under the floor.

"I hope that's rats." His voice was high, and he surprised himself with its nervous pitch.

"Sir?" Jones came through the comm.

He didn't realize his comm was still open to the team. He hoped they hadn't caught the nature of his tone. "There are sounds coming from the ceilings and floors. I think we may have a rat problem."

"Possible," Diaz chimed in. "We usually wouldn't hear that when the ship's in operation." She grunted, and Stone heard the sound of metal scraping through her comm.

"Okay. Well, keep an eye out as you dig through the wiring."

"Yessir," Jones responded.

Stone tapped the button on his wrist to mute his microphone and headed to the mess. He opened each compartment, checked the walls, floor, seals, HUD. He moved to the Armory and checked behind the rifles and munitions. No leaks. More scratches. More chills. More screams from his lizard brain to hurry the fuck up.

He unmuted his comm. "The interior visually checks out. I'm headed outside. Hendrix, Samuels, coming your way."

He expected a response. None came.

Red mist rushed inside as Hendrix rocked the outer airlock lever back and forth. He wanted to jump out of the way as it neared him, but he held still. He let the chills in his neck be.

Samuels peered through the widening crack. "Fuck, this place sucks." Their comms were on peer-to-peer, a closed conversation, isolated from the rest of the crew's network.

When the airlock had opened enough for both men to fit through, Hendrix stopped. He stared alongside Samuels.

Beyond the door was a rocky surface of orange and crimson stone. Strange, organic shapes grew from the ground like black, leafless trees. Red, orange, and black clouds scattered across the sky, mirroring the ground's tri-tone palette. A gap in the clouds revealed a large, red sun surrounded by what looked like millions of rocks.

"Where the fuck are we?" Hendrix said.

"Looks like Hell to me."

"Yeah," Hendrix muttered. His thoughts passed through a dozen things he wasn't proud of: the man he nearly beat to death in that bar in the Ryzon system; Salima, who he dumped after she got pregnant and wouldn't abort; the face of his mother as he told her to go fuck herself on his way out the door five years ago. Did he belong here?

"Let's get to work so we can get the fuck out of here."

Samuels stepped down from the airlock and popped the cover for the outer crank loose. Hendrix followed him through and waited for the door to seal, letting his eyes scan over the alien landscape. He looked for life—the chills told him there was someone out there. Maybe it was the Scourge. Maybe it was wildlife. He didn't know, but his hand went to his sidearm, and he wished they had brought rifles instead.

No large, slimy beasts. No small, tentacle-wielding things. But there had to be somewhere in this system, that was for sure. If this was the region of space the Scourge came from, there had to be some on this planet, even as a way station if nothing else.

Samuels grunted as the door sealed. "Let's go before acid eats its way into our asses."

"Yeah."

Samuels pointed at the starboard ladder. "I'll head up and get a look at the control room breach. You take a lap and look for any others."

Hendrix nodded. As his gaze moved from the alien trees to the ship, he thought he saw something move. He looked back. Nothing. Must have been nerves. "Yeah. Let's get it done."

Samuels climbed. Hendrix walked.

He examined the titanium plates, seams, bolts, then shot a glance back to his surroundings. Something was moving out there; he knew it. He could feel it. It was watching him too. He saw nothing new. Where was it hiding? What was it?

He moved to the front. One of those black trees was crushed under the ship. Hendrix kneeled and looked closer. Its limbs had no texture. They were as smooth as skin, and only at their tips did they appear hard. There, they narrowed to points as if they were massive claws.

Hendrix took a step back. "We squished one of those trees." He expected to hear from Samuels. Maybe a laugh. Maybe, *Good*. Maybe, *One less fucking alien thing to worry about*. But all he heard was silence.

A trickle down his spine made him spin. Something told him there was someone behind him. He felt a thousand eyes on him but saw none.

"What the fuck?" He wanted out of there. He wasn't one to shy away from a fight, but as his adrenaline rose and his trigger finger itched, there was no one to aim at. It was a disconnect he couldn't resolve, and it tickled his insides with a strange type of fear utterly alien to him. "Fuck this."

He moved on to the next side and scanned the hull. Limbs of the black tree stretched from beneath the ship, and violet liquid seeped from cracks in its skin, or bark, or whatever it was. The liquid was splattered up the side of the vessel, and despite making no sense, it seemed to be dripping upward.

It was weird, but the hull seemed okay. He walked to the rear of the ship.

There were dents in the two lower exhaust shrouds, but they looked functional. The titanium skin appeared fine there as well.

"Looks pretty good overall. I'm coming up." He walked to the starboard ladder and climbed the inset rungs to the roof of the craft.

Samuels stood at the most forward plate, gazing off into the crimson landscape. In the center of the control section, a black tree was implanted in the hull. Hendrix knew there was a rupture there but couldn't see it at all. It was completely concealed.

"Sammy, what are you doing? Why aren't you getting this thing out of the way?"

Samuels moved—only enough to shift a wrinkle in his suit.

"Come on, man." Hendrix bent down and lifted one of the branches. It slipped from his grasp and dropped, then clanked as if clamping down on a titanium seam. He shook his head and pulled at it again. It was stiff this time, unmoving. "I think we may need some tools. A plasma cutter? Angle grinder, maybe?"

The ship creaked below the black thing, a wail of warping metal.

He grabbed one of the higher limbs, thinking he could rock it loose. This one was flexible, bending and curling in his grip. "Give me a hand with this. Let's pull and see if it'll budge."

Hendrix yanked. The mass of the thing didn't alter, but a hiss came from the limb. The pointed tip shot up and plunged into his forearm.

Hendrix's suit popped then shrieked as the atmosphere mixed with his respiration mixture. Blood rimmed the fabric around the black thing, and his mind stuttered for what to do next.

He screamed and let go, but the thing didn't let go of him. It detached from the trunk of the tree and dove into his flesh. He felt it move within his arm and puncture the opposite side. It squirmed inside his muscle, climbing through his suit, through his body, like he was nothing. It weaved through him like a seamstress with needle and thread.

He grabbed the black limb with his other hand and pulled. It drilled into his bicep and popped out the other side.

Blood seeped from Hendrix's suit. It ran down his arm and spattered on the hull. His HUD read *EVA Breach*. His arm screamed from the pain and burned where incoming gases met his tissue.

"Sammy! Help!"

He felt the thing slither behind him and slice into his back. His lungs burned as acidic gas found its way into his helmet. His eyes teared. In his mind, he heard them sizzle.

"Sammy!" He gasped. His throat was on fire. Each breath burned his lungs more. Each particle of toxic air melted his insides.

The black thing's end wriggled into his suit. Was it some fucked up alien snake? Was the tree like its mother? None of it made any sense.

Hendrix dropped to his knees as it punctured his lung and dug through his chest. Its muscles flexed as it turned and wormed through him. Each agonizing move, each twitch the creature performed felt like a new stab, a new hole for death to sink into.

He stared at Samuels. His partner turned toward him. Sammy looked down on Hendrix with dead eyes. A black limb was wrapped around his neck, and punctures decorated his chest. He walked toward Hendrix like a marionette directed by a jittery puppeteer.

"Sammy?" Hendrix gagged as the thing climbed up his throat. He convulsed. What was left of his lungs ached and flexed, trying desperately to suck in air. He clutched at his face from the outside of his helmet as the thing came out of his mouth and encircled his head.

Stone's voice crackled through the comm: "The interior visually checks out. I'm headed outside. Hendrix, Samuels, coming your way."

Hendrix tasted blood and bitterness. His skin burned all over his body. He bit down on the slithering thing, and it drilled into the side of his head.

"You see anything?" Jones said to Diaz over the P2P comm.

"A bunch of fried conduit, but these systems were built to handle that.

We should still have power."

"Same. I've seen these ships run under much worse conditions."

Stone spoke through the comm, causing both to stop and listen: "The interior visually checks out. I'm headed outside. Hendrix, Samuels, coming your way."

Jones looked up at the dangling wires. None of those should have caused this situation either. Those were either exterior lights or viewscreen data connections—also, they were all redundant systems. But there was something else hanging. Something that wasn't a wire.

"What is that?" The words made his mouth cold as he said them. Whatever it was, like so much else that was happening, wasn't supposed to be. Nothing natural was supposed to be able to breach a six-inch titanium hull. Nothing was supposed to cause this kind of red, ambient light.

"What?" Diaz lifted her head and followed his gesture. "The cables?" Then she saw them: dangling black things, like snakes with pointed heads. "What are those?"

She stood and walked to the center of the room, examining the bulbous, hanging strands. She pushed away color-coded electrical cables, moving them to the side to get a better look at the black things.

"They go up through the hull." She leaned in, almost touching it with her helmet.

"Diaz!"

She turned toward Jones. One of the black things had lifted its pointed end. It aimed its sharp tip at Diaz's leg.

"Back away."

She put one hand up and grabbed her sidearm with her other. Jones drew his.

The hanging thing swayed its pointed head like a cobra then shot toward her.

Diaz fired. The floor sparked. She fired again. The round ripped the hard point in two, shredding the thing in half. It hung limp then shook as if it was having a seizure.

"Fuck!" she backed away. "What the hell?" She studied the dangling creature. She stared at the others and counted. Five other alien black things.

Jones slid with his back along the wall toward the control room door. The urge to flee was tight inside his chest. Each step made him wonder if it was the right move, the right time to step without triggering another of those hanging things to attack.

The split-headed creature lifted its end back up. Its two wounds folded in on themselves, forming a two-headed beast. It lowered itself to the floor and slithered toward Diaz.

"Fuck you!" She fired at the thing. The metal floor blossomed in flowers of sparks as rounds ricocheted across the control room.

Jones drew his pistol and aimed at the thing. Then, from the corner of his eye, he saw another black limb drop to the floor. It followed the other toward Diaz.

"Diaz, there's two now. We need to fall back, get bigger guns."

"Screw that." She paused and aimed and put a round through one of the creature's two heads.

It exploded into a black shell and dark purple goo. It kept moving toward her, leaving a red trail below.

She fired again. The second head exploded. "Take that, fucker." But the creature kept coming.

"Diaz, come on!" He was cranking on the door. It was almost wide enough.

"Why is it still moving?" Her gun swayed to the second one. She fired. Its point shattered into hunks of hard, black debris.

"Look." The door was open. He paused beside it, pointing at the formerly two-headed thing. Its neck bubbled and gushed, and from its center, a shiny, new, black claw erupted and sped toward Diaz. "Get out of there!"

"That can't be." She fired as she backed toward Jones. One shot soared past the newly-clawed beast. The next sliced through it, splitting it with a black and purple canyon down its right side. "Die!"

The other wounded thing grew a new claw and followed her. Another limb dropped from above and slithered toward Jones.

"Get the fuck over here!" He stepped out and held the lever in his hand. His fingers twitched, ready to crank it.

Diaz slid through. She fired as Jones cranked. The door moved. It was the slowest closing Jones had ever seen. He pumped his arm forward and back. Black goo spurted through the gap. Bullets flew into the control room. The door thumped into place.

3

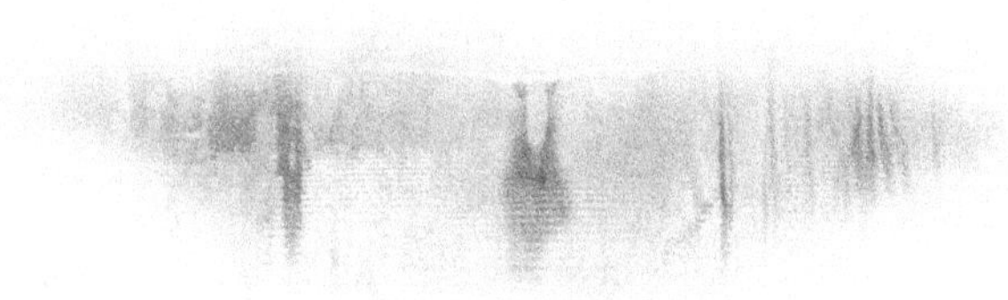

"**S**TONE, THIS IS JONES." He spoke over the crew channel. "Acknowledge, please?"

"Give it up," Diaz said. "It's been an hour. No one's replied. No one's come back in. They're dead out there."

Scraping continued on the far side of the control room door. It was the squeal of claw on metal that would have grated on the inside of your ears on a normal day. On this planet, on this ship, it was as if the claw was digging through Jones's brain. More than that, it was a reminder that those things were going nowhere, just like him and his crewmate.

She pointed at the armory. "I still say we need to try the flamethrowers."

"There's no oxygen. They won't work here."

"Then the plasma rifles."

"You saw it regrow itself. You're just as likely to turn one creature into five."

She ground her teeth together and shook her head. "Then what's your plan?"

"Still working on it."

She threw her hands up and marched away.

The scratching continued. Then a hiss.

Jones looked at the door. A single hole poked through the metal. A black claw shimmered inside it.

"Diaz, they're getting through."

"No, that's bullshit."

A second hole, another claw. They hooked into the steel door, and the door's motor began to squeal.

"They're..." Jones couldn't say it.

"The fuckers are prying it open." She aimed the plasma rifle at the holes.

"No!"

She fired. The claws sizzled away, and the holes smoked red with hot steel. New claws moved in, easily peeling the heated metal back into the control room.

"You gave them a way in," Jones shouted.

"We have to get out of here." She fired again. "Grab a rifle and some grenades."

"We'll die out there." He read from his HUD: ten hours of oxygen, four hours of suit integrity under this planet's atmosphere.

"We'll die in here if those things get through."

Jones's mind raced. The captain was outside. Samuels and Hendrix. Maybe their comms just weren't working out there? Some interference, some magnetism on this strange world? Maybe he and Diaz could find them and regroup?

"Okay." He slung a rifle on his back and hooked a grenade on his hip. "I'll open the door."

"Quickly."

He cranked the lever on the inner airlock. It was stiffer than the control room door, but he moved the thing as fast as it would go.

He watched the black claws poke through and then melt away as Diaz slammed them with a fresh blast of plasma. He wondered how bad the ship would smell after this was all over and the scent of burned alien flesh was plastered onto the inner walls. If they lived.

He focused on the crank. God, it was stiff. He dreaded that once this door was free, there was an outer door to fight.

"Move it, Jones," she shouted into the comm.

"Almost there." He could see the inner lock. He could see... the light inside the airlock was a different color than the ship's ambient glow. It was red but brighter, almost like pictures he'd seen of sunsets back on Earth. Was the outer airlock open?

Diaz glanced at Jones, at the airlock. Her face went blank, and her trigger finger relaxed. The door behind her creaked, and claws stretched steel.

"Sammy?" she muttered.

Samuels stood in the airlock, halfway between the inner door and the outer one. His eyes were white, and purple sludge ran from their corners. His skin seemed to be melting as they watched, and black limbs hung from his chest, arms, and neck like he had grown pairs of beastly tentacles. There were at least a dozen, and they reached for Jones.

Jones stumbled backward and tripped over his own feet. Terror consumed his thoughts as he fell. Would this Samuels-thing get him before he could recover? Would the demon snakes get through the door and take him from behind? Shock teased his nerves like jolts of electricity, and his back slammed into the floor. His head rocked back, and pain crisscrossed his skull. He scrambled up and scurried away like a crab, panicking, fumbling for his rifle.

Tears rolled down Diaz's face. She had been okay thinking Samuels had been taken or was dead and out of sight—she could have held that thought in the corner of her mind and waited to grieve later. But this? A mentor, a man she'd secretly loved and told no one in the world about, even him—standing dead and... what the hell else?

Two creatures stabbed into Diaz's legs. They dug into her calves, and she dropped to her knees. She screamed and grabbed one, digging her fingers in as hard as possible. It seemed to break in half in her grip, and she was left holding only the tail. She tossed it aside and went to grab the other. It slurped into her suit, and her legs burned.

Jones wrestled his rifle around to the front. He aimed at Samuels and fired.

Diaz howled and pounded on the floor. "Oh, God! It's in my gut!" Blood gushed from her mouth, over her chin, and onto her helmet's inner glass.

The plasma bolt hit Samuels in the helmet. It tore through glass and steel and melted half his neck. His head slumped right, leaning on the inside of the helmet.

He kept moving forward.

"Agh!" Diaz distorted the comm. She shouted so loudly Jones could hear her through his head protection.

Jones looked at her just in time to see her point her sidearm at her skull and squeeze the trigger. Blood and brain erupted inside her helmet, and she thudded against the ship's steel floor. Her body jerked and spasmed, and a thick black claw burst through her cheek.

"Oh, God." Jones jerked to his feet and backed toward the rack room. His eyes darted from Diaz and the hole in the control room door to Samuels. He thought about the rack room. No good. They'd claw inside just like they did through the control room door. He glanced at the Armory. Same thing, they'd get in, but he'd have more weapons. No, eventually they'd get him. His eyes went to the airlock. It was his only choice.

Jones aimed at Samuels. The rifle jittered in his hands. This had to work. He was never a good shot, but this time he needed it; his life depended on it.

He fired.

Samuels's right leg ripped in two. Jones fired again before Samuels could fall, searing off the second leg.

It was now or never. He could feel his heart in his throat, pounding, screaming at him not to fuck this up.

He ran toward the airlock, unclipped the grenade from his belt, and flipped off the safety. He dropped it into Samuel's grasping hands and leaped over his old crewmate.

In his mind, Jones counted down.

4

He ran through the airlock.

3

He ran around the starboard side of the ship.

2

He passed the forward hull.

1

He froze, staring at the rocky planetscape filled with black limbed things.

"What the fuck did I do?"

Behind Jones, there was a thump, quickly followed by a deafening crack. He felt it vibrate his chest, and he ran. His heart slammed against his ribs. His breath hit the inside of his helmet and washed back over his face. His EVA HUD flashed red: *Body Stress Detected, Heartrate: 157 BPM.*

He ran blindly for some time, unaware of where he was going or what he was doing. All he knew was he needed to move. He needed to get away from those things. Images flashed in his mind: Samuel's dead eyes; his melting flesh; black limbs digging through Diaz's legs; the terror on her face; the gaping hole in Samuels's neck from the plasma bolt.

His stomach clenched. He was going to vomit inside his suit. Something grabbed his foot, and Jones toppled forward. His hands thrust out, stopping his helmet from crashing into the rocky ground, and his knees slammed into huge hunks of red stone.

"Gah!" He spun, searching in every direction.

His ankle throbbed. He had caught his foot between two rocks and twisted it in his panic. His knees burned from where he'd slammed them as he fell. He realized these things as his gaze took in the hellish alien world for what seemed like the first time.

He saw tens then, as he turned, hundreds of black-tentacled trees. He saw jagged red mountains and a red sun. He saw things floating through the air that at first looked like clouds, but then changed directions against the wind and altered their shapes in ways that had to be intentional. With the acidic nature of the air, he could only imagine what creatures could live up there.

He searched for somewhere to go. He needed a place with oxygen, a place without this acid air. He saw only the same rocky ruin wherever he looked.

His thoughts went to the Scourge. Where had they gone? He'd seen none since landing, heard of none from the other crew. Scientists had dissected the corpses of dead Scourge from battles and ruled them as oxygen breathers. They may have looked like monsters to humans, but Jones had to question if even those things could have lived on this planet.

His HUD illuminated his fate in the top right corner: nine hours of oxygen, three hours of suit integrity.

His flesh tingled as he acknowledged his doom. There was nowhere to go.

He was going to run out of oxygen, and that would be the best way to die. If he couldn't get out of this air, he was going to burn alive. That was if he lasted that long and didn't fall prey to another gang of those snake things. He was a dead man already. There was no way around it.

A black tree waved in the breeze two dozen feet away. Its arms lowered to the ground.

"Shit." Jones climbed to his feet. His ankle howled in pain and failed him. He sunk back down, slamming his knees into the rocks. He groaned and pushed himself up on his good leg. He hopped and then limped as his knee would allow.

A large chunk of asteroid floated in front of the sun, dimming the world into a near twilight. Shadows deepened across the hilly path ahead, but Jones saw something shine in the distance.

He stopped, glancing back at the closest trees, then squinted at the shine. It was there. It was real, whatever it was. He had no way of knowing what it was or if it would be helpful, but it was the only thing on the godforsaken planet that looked the slightest bit different. He had to investigate.

He climbed one hill, went down, and could tell the strange shine was inside a cave. And not only was it shining, but it also appeared to be blinking. Blinking was good. It meant technology, maybe even air. The idea was far-fetched, but it could have been true.

Jones glanced back. Four tentacles slithered over and around rocks. He looked toward his ship. Black smoke rose into the darkening sky. The giant sun was moving behind clouds and closer to the horizon.

His pace increased, and he had to slow himself. Every other step sent pain shooting up his leg. What was he doing? This was hopeless. There was no way there was breathable air in there. There was no chance of getting out of this acid.

He paused and took a breath. It may have been hopeless, but he had to try. He raised his rifle to his shoulder and aimed at his slithering pursuers. Four shots. Purple globs of tentacle guts rained backward onto the rocks. He started moving again before they could regrow heads.

Jones crossed the small valley, wobbling over loose boulders, barely catching himself from falling over and over again. He reached the edge of the cave, and his shadow stretched deep inside. The red sun was cresting the horizon, casting the weakest rays of the day, and his suit's headlamps switched on.

Jones spotted the blinking light. It was about twenty feet inside the cave. He stared into the dark interior, then back at the oncoming snakes. They were only fifty yards back, threatening with each curve and crawl. They wanted to dig into him and walk him around like a puppet, the same as they had done to Samuels. But this cave—it had hope. What if it was false hope? What if that blinking light was nothing and, once he was inside, those things had him cornered? He patted on the rifle. He had to take that chance.

2 Hours of EVA Suit Integrity Remaining, blinked in orange lettering. Did the O$_2$ timer even matter?

He limped inside, watching the ground for rocks, cracks, or anything else he might trip over. As he neared the blinking light, he noticed it looked like a button. He stepped hesitantly closer. It *was* a button, a red one, standing out from a panel painted to look like the surrounding rock.

"A button?" Did it make something happen? Was it a door? Would it release some other terrible creature upon him? Did he have a choice?

He raised his hand to press the button and stopped. He glanced back at the slithering creatures. They had stopped. They waited at the cave's threshold, the hard, black claws swaying in the air like alien pit vipers. Why weren't they coming in?

He pressed his palm into the panel, and the button clicked. A second later, the wall to the left showered small rocks and dust downward. Gusts of air shot out from cracks in the stone. It pivoted inward as if a six-foot-by-six-foot section of the cave was actually a door.

Rock ground against rock, and after a few seconds, a hidden space lay ahead. His headlamps shined off the floor, the walls, the ceiling. It was red rock like the cave, but it seemed to be polished as smooth as glass. It reminded Jones of red dinnerware his mother owned when he was a kid. He had broken one, dropping it on the floor while clearing the table, and she had spanked his butt nearly as red as those plates.

The sight, the memory, both compounded his dread. He was going to die in there.

He checked on the tentacle things—still there—and he went inside.

Jones held his rifle to his shoulder. He scanned as far ahead as his EVA suit's lights would shine, but it wasn't nearly far enough. He limped five or six paces, and the rock door groaned and slid shut.

He cursed under his breath, hoping to God this was the right call, then realized it hardly mattered anymore.

Limp after limp he moved deeper into the stone hallway. He had hoped his HUD would display better news, but it didn't. He had one hour until his suit was compromised. The air inside this thing was just as toxic as the air outside. But now he was trapped with only forward to go.

Something rumbled under his feet, and a boom shook the entire mountain. Jones braced himself on his good foot, and a blast of wind rushed past him. More than just the alien location, this didn't make sense. The door had shut—where could that air have come from?

He pivoted toward where he'd come in, and as his head turned, he knew he didn't want to see what he would find. The sides of the corridor had opened, and thousands of small creatures were climbing out, down the walls, across the floor. They moved in lines toward him that swelled as more and more creatures joined.

In the dim, ambient red beyond his suit's light, they looked like some kind of bug, only larger. Not quite spiders, but eight- or ten-legged things that slapped the smooth stone as they walked, making a squeal and racing closer. The sound became louder as more and more poured from the walls and joined the swarm. They neared his light, and he saw they were red and slimy with double sets of pincers on their faces and stingers on their rears. Their legs flopped like tentacles but gouged the glossy floor with some unseen sharpness.

Jones had no idea what to do. They were a mass of things that his mind could not comprehend. He saw the creatures grabbing hold of his suit and ripping it to shreds. He saw their stingers plunging into his flesh and some alien poison destroying him from the inside.

He trembled. What kind of trap did he wander into?

He forced his finger to squeeze. Blue blobs of plasma shot down the hall. They crashed into the oncoming swarm, frying hundreds of creatures at a time. But they kept pouring out. He fired again and again. He couldn't fire fast enough to keep their ranks down. They just kept coming.

He turned and staggered away. He pushed his good leg as fast as it would go and put more and more weight on the bad one. Pain pulsed with every heartbeat. His HUD flashed red writing in his face like a taunting child: *45 Minutes Remaining.* And in the darkness ahead, something opened on each side of the hallway.

The walls moved back like sliding doors, letting orange light cascade into the corridor's gloom. Two beings stepped into the light, making silhouettes of men.

"Help," Jones cried. "Help me, please." He could feel the squid-things closing in on his heels. As he neared the shadowed shapes, they began to take form. It was Hendrix on the left, Stone on the right. Their faces had melted almost to skulls. Pink, putrid goo layered their bones and dripped onto the insides of their helmets. Black tentacles swayed from their suits.

He froze in place.

They shambled toward him.

Not you too? Captain? He raised the rifle to his shoulder and aimed at Hendrix. A dozen black claws stretched from his chest and whipped through the air. Jones aimed at the center of Hendrix's helmet and squeezed.

A sizzling, blue bolt lit the corridor as it traveled the few paces between the former crewmates. It crushed through Hendrix's helmet, burned through his face, and then the rear. He dropped to his knees then slammed onto his chest. Each black arm writhed below his body.

Jones moved his aim to his captain. He struggled to sight the weapon.

Stone had welcomed him aboard three years ago with a sincere heart and a firm handshake. *Give me your all, and I'll give you mine, and we may just make it through this assignment,* the man had said. Now he stumbled toward Jones like some kind of octopus zombie with pale eyes and purple slime bubbling over his jaw.

"I'll give you my all." He lined up his sights on the center of Stone's forehead. He rested his finger on the trigger, and a sharp pinch seized the back of Jones's good ankle.

He screamed and jerked his foot away from the pain. His wounded ankle buckled, and he dropped onto the ground. Scratches against the hard floor flooded his ears. The squids were all around him. His only option was moving toward his captain.

Jones crawled on hands and knees, glancing back at the growing army. He looked forward. Stone's tentacles reached in his direction, waving, seething, hungry.

He held his rifle in one hand, aimed with nothing more than his gut, and fired.

A plasma bolt sizzled through a flailing tentacle, hit Stone in the arm, and severed the limb mid-bicep. He kept coming.

Jones flexed all over, cursing himself for whatever he did to end up here—in this cave, on this planet, on whatever side of the universe this was.

He tried getting back to his feet. His leg burned. There was a hole in his suit. His O_2 level was plummeting from six hours, down and down it dropped.

He managed to stand, but the inside of what had been his good leg felt like streaks of lightning cascading over his muscles from left to right, bottom to top, and back. He hobbled forward and fired again.

Blue energy completely dissolved another black limb.

He howled and fired again.

It tore into Stone's gut. Red ash floated from the wound, followed by tumbling hunks of cauterized intestine. Stone's marionette of a body bore down on Jones.

Jones lifted his aim as he limped. Tears streamed from his eyes, a mixture of exhaustion, hate, and love for the man his captain once was.

He fired again.

He was going to die. Yes. But these things weren't going to use his captain to do it.

The shot melted Stone's helmet and tore a hole from his chin through the back of his head. His remaining tentacles waved wildly.

Jones skirted left, around Stone's corpse. He ground his teeth as each step ratcheted his agony higher and higher.

He moved past Hendrix, as his limbs detached. Squids crawled over his body. Some dug into the holes, ripping away flesh with their pincers; some attacked tentacles; but most continued their charge after Jones.

Red letters flashed in his HUD: *Suit Breech, Emergency Action Required.*

He pushed forward, ignoring the claw-clack against stone, ignoring the sounds of things digging into his once-friends and tearing them to pieces.

His heart pounded in his ears. The sides of his face were hot. He wanted to puke. He felt like blood was streaming from his nose, ears, and eyes. It was. It ran from his pincer bite, leaving a trail behind him that excited each squid that crossed it. Shocks and spasms traveled from his legs into his gut, into his chest.

Jones looked ahead into what felt like an infinite darkness and knew this was the end. It was as far as he was going to go. It was the farthest for any human on this mission, and he hoped no others would follow. Maybe they would find a way to seal the wormhole on the other side? But by God, no other human should be forced to deal with this Hell-planet.

He was about to drop to his knees, to resign himself to the ripping and tearing he knew was coming only feet behind him, when he noticed another light ahead. Another door was opening.

It made no sense, but neither did any part of this planet. He pushed himself toward it.

The light grew brighter, brighter than anything he'd seen since the other side of the wormhole. It illuminated every squid, beast, and corpse in the corridor. He heard a hiss and then a squeal from the monsters on his heels.

Was that it? Was light the thing that scared them the most and drove them back? Simple, bright, white light? He felt so dumb and then didn't care. He rejoiced in the sounds of their pain as he tried to bury his and drive himself forward.

In his mind, his salvation lay ahead. It was a place where there was clean, breathable air. Maybe there were intelligent creatures in there who had learned to deal with the monsters on this planet, and they were reaching out to save him. It had to be.

He inched closer and closer into the brightness. His legs barely moved. His lungs burned as acid found its way up into his helmet. He tasted blood and the bitter flavor of death. But he kept moving until there was nothing around him but light.

Blackness. Pain in every millimeter of his flesh. Jones saw, but it was more of a vision than from his eyes. His eyes didn't work. They collapsed inward into pulp. His muscles, bones, organs, compacted into a space no wider than a single human hair and as long as a skyscraper.

His flesh crumpled as it twisted around steel, titanium, copper, composite plastics, and carbon fibers. They wove around the strings of flesh that were once Stone, Hendrix, Diaz, and Samuels.

The massive crimson wormhole continued to flow into itself, unknowing and uncaring, a monolith surrounded by the armada of USSF ships. Expelled from its center drifted a mile of raw elements that once composed the USSF Crow.

Love Is Cold

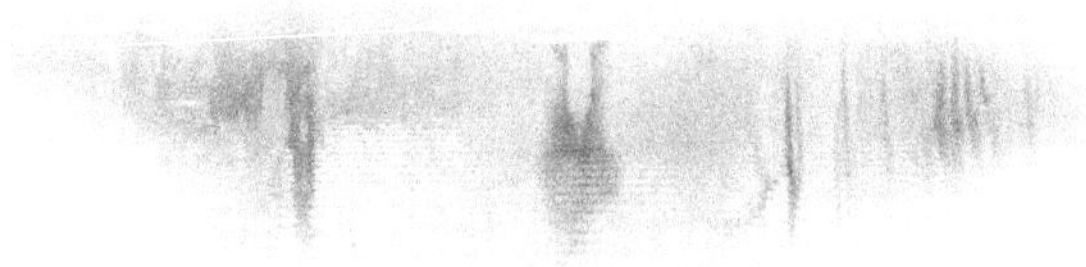

"**W**ELL, WHERE ARE THEY?" Sarah gazed across the tan grass, empty campsite, and barren fire pit. Evergreens encircled the small meadow on three sides, a shallow stream and then more trees on the fourth. The surrounding mountains, snow-capped and ready for winter, looked down on them like the rim of a bowl.

"It's still early, isn't it?" Mitch glanced at his watch: *5:13 p.m.* "I mean, it isn't quite night."

She rolled her eyes. Her brother was always the optimist. "Weren't we all supposed to leave right after school?"

"They said they had to go back home and get something. Darcy forgot her special pad or something. Jim said she'd kill him if he didn't take her."

"Huh. Well, as long as she doesn't get distracted and start TikTokin g... But yeah, she was a total bitch last time she didn't sleep well."

Sarah set her backpack down beside the circle of rocks that made the fire ring and rubbed her hands together. The sun was ready to touch the mountains; the brisk day was about to turn into a cold evening.

Mitch set his bag beside Sarah's. "I guess I'll gather some firewood. You want to start on the tents?"

"Sure."

He slid his hatchet free from the side of his bag and headed into the trees. Sarah watched the sun drift ever closer to the western mountain. A cold breeze blew one of her brown curls across her face, somewhat tickling, somewhat chilling. A blanket of clouds marched across the sky, pink on one side, dark purple on the other. It was definitely going to be a cold night.

Sarah detached her tent from her bag and unrolled the dense nylon on the dry grass. She unfolded the poles and laid them out on the ground, and as much as she wanted to avoid it, her thoughts went to yesterday morning, to Andy.

She had stood at her locker, trigonometry book in hand, a dumb expression on her face. Her jaw hung open, and her heart was on the floor, Andy's heel stomping it into the commercial-grade linoleum.

"I need space." He shook his head as he said it, and she could read his mind as if his thoughts were tattooed on his forehead. He was bored with her. She'd done practically everything he'd asked, and they'd had fun together, but now he was bored. He wanted someone new.

As much as she wanted to pick up her heart and run, the anger growing in her stomach kept her grounded. It said: "How dare he?" and "He deserves what he gets." "He'll never find someone better."

She thought of swinging her trig book up and giving him a bloody nose but settled for saying, "Okay. I could probably use some space too."

That rearranged his expression from almost sincere to puzzled.

Her eyes burned. The tears were coming, but she couldn't let them. Not yet. She grabbed her notebook and her calculator, hardened her face and ground her teeth together, then shut her locker. She was down the hall and around the corner when the dam broke. She made it into trig, sat at her desk, and buried her head in her arms.

That was when Mitch dropped into the seat beside her and told her about the Halloween camping trip he and Jim were taking. Sometimes she hated having a twin, always in her business, always nosing in with her friends and her private moments. Other times, it was the best thing in her life. It was having someone who knew you inside and out and knew the exact moment you needed a break from the rest of the world. It was having someone willing to sacrifice their *guys' weekend trip* to include you and make you feel better, even let you invite his best friend's sister, your best friend, so you weren't the only girl there.

Sarah chuckled to herself as she slid the final pole through her tent's nylon loops. An image of Mitch's puppy-dog stare came to mind from Darcy's visit the other day. He had been practically in love with Darcy since the third grade. Sarah wondered for a second if he might have invited her along just to get Darcy there. Normally, she wouldn't have put it past him. She secured the last pole and remembered his dour look in the classroom—no, this time it was genuine.

She rolled out Mitch's tent several feet from her own, slid in the poles, and gathered the stakes and hammer. She pushed the first steel L into the dirt, raised the hammer, and heard a whistling sound from somewhere near the stream.

It was a weird sound, and she glanced over to see what may have caused it. The noise replayed in her mind, something between a man's whistle and a bird call but hollow, as if caught by the wind and restrained.

The stream babbled on. The woods beyond it were darker than last she looked, almost black in the fading daylight. The setting sun hovered halfway down the ridge, and as her gaze swept the circle of trees on her side, the whistle returned.

"Over there?" she mumbled to herself. She stared into the darkness opposite the stream. It had to be over there, but she wasn't sure. This time the sound was light; it felt like air, like it was all around her. She shook her head, and as she turned back toward her stakes, she saw a shimmer in the gloom from the corner of her eye.

"Hello?" She stood and walked to the edge of the stream. "Jim? Darcy? Is that you guys?" There was only blackness beneath those trees. A faded path stretched from the stream to the shadows, and Sarah noticed a pattern of stones along the dirt every dozen feet or so. She somehow knew it was an ancient trail—something she wanted no part of.

Cold rippled down Sarah's arms. Someone was over there, whether she could see them or not. Someone was watching her from within the distant obscurity. At that moment, she really wanted Mitch there. She really wanted her twin.

She backed away from the water, and wind blew across her neck. She felt her heart racing inside her chest. The smell of the stream—damp earth and crisp moisture—rose in her nose but with a mildewed scent that reminded her of something rotten.

She turned, and a shock bolted up her system. Mitch stood right in front of her; he stared into the same darkness.

"Jesus Christ, Mitch!" She shoved him, knocking a pile of firewood from his arms. She pressed the hammer against his chest until he took it. "For that shit, you can hammer in the stakes."

"Shit. Sorry."

Sarah stomped in a circle around the fire pit, catching her breath. She forced her eyes to avoid the stream and anything beyond. Instead, she examined the clearing, which looked untouched by man other than the ring of stones. She kneeled between the pile of wood and the ring and started building the fire.

"Why this place?" She laid a small ball of dryer lint from her pocket in the center of the ring and gently placed small twigs above it. "We've never been out here before. How'd you hear about it?"

Mitch banged in a stake then said, "It was Jim's idea. Said he'd heard it was a cool place. Said there was a story behind it that would be perfect for Halloween."

She set a circle of sticks up like a tepee over the smaller twigs and lint, then she glanced at the dipping sun. It was almost behind the mountain.

"Well, he's going to miss the chance if they don't get here." She tried to sound spiteful, as if they should miss out for their tardiness, but as soon as she said it, she knew her frustration was because she wanted them there. She wanted more people, more security around her.

She drew a Zippo from her pocket and lit the dryer lint. It blazed, catching the small, dry sticks above it almost instantly. The flames rose, and Sarah held her hands over the tepee as yellow tendrils licked and climbed their way up.

"He'll be here. He was pretty excited about the whole thing—especially after I said *you* were coming."

"He doesn't have a *thing* for me, does he?"

"No— I don't know... He better not." He started on another stake.

"Damn right. I'm just here to stare at the stars and relax."

"Same here..."

A stick cracked in the woods behind them, and they both turned.

"What's up motherfuckers!" Darcy shouted through the trees. "We're here, bitches!" She stepped into the dry grass, strutting as if she was on stage or recording one of her TikToks.

An unstoppable grin spread across Mitch's face as he rose and took her in. Her jeans were skintight, sparkling from every pocket. Her jacket was slender and stylish, this year's line for the distinguished skier. Her pulled-back hair and oversized sunglasses completed her camping chic ensemble.

Sarah rose, gave the fire another glance—it was in full blaze—and she met her friend with a hug. She realized Darcy's back was bare. "Where's your stuff?"

Darcy frowned and pointed to the woods. Jim came through the trees wearing two camping packs, a sideways hat, and unzipping his coat.

"Holy Christ!" He dropped both bags and unzipped his jacket. "Never again, Darcy."

"Oh, stop—we made a deal."

He shook his head and looked at the sky then glanced through the side of his eye at Sarah. "Yeah, I guess so, but…"

"But nothing." Darcy spotted the fire and ushered Sarah toward it. "Put up the tents," she barked at her brother and turned her attention to Sarah. "He has been such a little bitch today."

Sarah chuckled and sat by the fire, Darcy at her side.

The sun slipped from sight and dragged any remaining bit of the day's warmth with it. The fire flicked and popped, calling them in as if it knew it was the only giver of heat, light, and safety.

"Shit, girl." Darcy held her hands up to the fire. She glanced at the woodpile. "They're going to need to get more wood. I want it hot."

Sarah chuckled again. She smiled at Darcy, grateful she was there, and thought this was going to be the night she needed.

The fire crackled on. The tents were set up. The sky became darker and darker as every celestial body was hidden behind an endless cover of clouds.

Mitch brought out premade quesadillas, which he fried on a small skillet and distributed to the group. Darcy pulled a bottle of whiskey from her bag, courtesy of her father's liquor cabinet, and passed it around. Sarah took a quesadilla and skipped the booze. When their dinner was done, Jim sent around a Tupperware container of brownies.

Sarah picked out one of the treats with a crunchy edge and passed the others on. She took a bite and shivered, then tossed a stick on the fire.

"So, are you ready to spill?" Mitch took the container, a brownie, then turned to Jim. "What's the deal here?"

"You mean this place?" He set the Tupperware down beside him. He scanned the barely-visible circle of woods around them, pausing across the stream where the old trail would have been. He smirked. "Sure, I guess I can tell the story now. I doubt any of you would leave in the dark, even if you wanted to."

"What?" Sarah stopped mid-bite.

"Joking... It's just not a nice story—what supposedly happened here, I mean."

Darcy stared at her brother, repeating, "What?"

Jim held up his hands. "It's Halloween, isn't it? We're in the woods—shouldn't we have a ghost story?"

Darcy rolled her eyes. She tapped on her phone—*No Service*; it was out of habit more than anything. It read *11:45 p.m.*

"Go on..." She took a swig from the bottle and sent it around again.

Again, Sarah passed on the bottle. She took another bite of her brownie, and the fire seemed to grow brighter.

"Okay," Jim said. "It's like this.

"Halloween night, 150 years ago. Back then, there was no state, right? Before Montana joined the union. This was just wide-open land for trappers and miners and Indians. Well, over there..."

He paused and pointed into the darkness, to the other side of the stream.

"In those woods was a young trapper. You know, back then you didn't go to school 'til you were twenty-five like today. You worked as soon as you were able to. Well, this guy, he was maybe eighteen, and he lived in those woods with his young wife. And just like working, you got married young too—she was only fifteen or sixteen, maybe."

"And what?" Darcy interrupted. "He hacked her up one All Hallows' Eve?"

"No." He looked into her eyes and waited.

The fire popped. The cold wind chilled every inch of Sarah's body. She took another bite, and the crackle of the flames sounded with a rhythm of a far-off place. They beat like some ancient drum in a circle of men and beasts that were up to something. She didn't know what, but for a moment, she wanted to kill the fire. To smother it away so she wouldn't have to hear that awful sound.

"Something killed them both," Jim said.

Darcy leaned back, her lips pursed. She drank from the bottle.

"You see," he went on, "It was an exceptionally cold fall that year. And just like we sometimes get snow on Halloween, they did too. Only this year, it wasn't a sprinkle; it was *feet*. On the twenty-eighth, it was a foot. Twenty-ninth, a foot. Thirtieth, a foot—and as excited as the trapper was to hunt game in the snow, they hadn't built up their log pile for the winter yet, and it was getting cold in that tiny cabin. So when the thirty-first came, and the snow kept falling, they were getting worried."

As if on cue, white flakes began to drift across the campsite. One landed on Sarah's nose and gave her another chill. She swallowed her last crumb and reached for the container for another. Jim passed it over, pointing up at the falling flakes.

"Perfect," he said. "So, that Halloween night, they huddled next to a tiny fire, the trapper afraid to add too much wood because they may run out. But the wife, she wanted it warmer."

"Damn right," Darcy said. She grabbed a stick from the waning woodpile and tossed it into the fire.

Jim nodded. "So they fought. She wanted to burn the little bit of wood they had left; he wanted to save it. Finally, she threw it all in, and they were warm—for a while.

"You know how when it's really cold, like super cold, fire seems to burn faster? Well, that's what happened. By midnight, it had burned down to ash, and they had nothing left. The trapper knew that if he didn't do something, they were going to freeze to death in that tiny cabin, so he took his ax and a lantern, and he went out into the storm."

The snow fell heavier. The flakes grew larger. It patted against the tents and sizzled on the fire. Sarah took a bite and looked at the dwindling pile of wood. Only a few pieces left, no way there was enough to last the night. The logs sizzled and cracked, sizzled and cracked, that damned song again. They needed more wood. Someone needed to go get it.

"So what happened?" Mitch said. "He freeze out there?"

"He didn't come back," Jim said. "The wife bundled herself up tight, but it wasn't enough. She decided that he was just being lazy out there, and she went to look for him." He pointed across the stream, to the woods again. "Turns out, he went snow blind and got lost. He built a fire right by those trees and stayed there until dawn, when the storm lifted.

"The next day, he came back, and she was gone. He looked all around for her—couldn't find her."

"God, that's horrible," Sarah said. "She must have frozen in the woods."

"Well, there's more. When spring came, and everything started melting, he was out here." He pointed at the stream. "He found her. Frozen solid.

"She had walked right past him in the storm, fallen through the ice, and froze to death not a hundred feet from her husband."

Sarah looked toward the water. Its babble seemed to rise above the crackle of the fire, and inside the sound of rushing water and torrent against rock, she heard the faint sound of screaming. She felt eyes on her, cold invisible eyes that pierced through the darkness and chilled her all over.

"Let's go," Sarah said.

"What?" There was laughter in Mitch's voice. "You're not serious. That was just a story."

Darcy took a swig and leaned against Sarah. "Don't worry, sweetie." Her voice was all slurs now. "I'll keep you warm if you need me to."

"Tell her it's just a story," Mitch said.

Jim shook his head. "No, it happened. The good thing, though," he pointed again. "People say her ghost stays on that side of the water. It can't cross the stream unless it's invited."

"Let's go." Sarah stood. The world spun around her. Embers from the fire seemed to dance in the night. They drifted up and swirled in the falling flakes, a ballet of orange and white specks. The crackle, the pat of the snow, the rush of the water, all seemed to play for the dancing specks and drive them to their beat. It was rushed. It had a purpose. It called to her to come see the water, all while the back of her mind told her to run away.

"What's wrong with me?" She slumped back to the ground. She looked at the crumbs in her hands. "Was there something *in* these?"

Jim looked sheepish for the first time that night. "Well, Mitch said you needed a little pick-me-up."

"Fucker!" She'd smoked pot before, but only a little. This was nothing like that. It rolled over her in waves that alternated between the beauty of the fire to the call of the water, to the sound of—but that couldn't be real. The scream in the water swelled, *Help me!*

"I'm not going anywhere in the dark, Sarah," Mitch said. "I'm sorry you're having a bad trip, but those woods at night—that's a bad idea."

"Fucker," she repeated. She stood again and wobbled forward and back. "I'll go by myself then."

She turned toward the woods, and her foot caught on something. She stumbled forward and fell into the grass. Stiff stalks poked into her hands. Her face scraped against something sharp, and snow tapped against the back of her head.

"Sarah!" Darcy jumped up and stumbled to her side. "Come on, girl." She guided Sarah to her tent. "Why don't you lay down for a bit."

"Yeah…" Sarah let her friend guide her. She crawled into her tent and laid on her back. She reached to close the zipper, but her hand missed. Through the crack, she saw the fire. She saw Jim grinning. She saw the bottle passed around and Mitch drinking.

Sarah's eyes closed, and the music returned. The rhythm, the rushing, the scream. Her eyes cracked open, and her brother and friends were dancing by the fire. Snow drifted down like fat flakes of confetti.

Was it New Year's Eve? Had she missed months?

Her lids pulled shut. The scream was even louder. She opened her eyes to a strange, slanted view of Mitch and Darcy, naked, writhing. She blinked, and behind them was Andy.

"Andy?" Sarah muttered and reached. Her eyes fell shut. When they opened again, Mitch and Darcy held hunting knives dripping with blood. Jim was on the ground. A woman stood behind them whom Sarah didn't know. Her hair was long and black, tangled, and her stare pierced through the gap in the tent and into Sarah.

Her lids closed. She forced them open.

Behind the woman was a man. He gripped an ax in his hand and raised it over his head.

"No…" The word barely escaped her mouth, and she fell back into blackness.

Cold against her back and face. Something moved below her. Her hair pulled. Freezing, freezing, freezing.

Sarah's eyes shot open. Frigid water rushed over her face, her chest, her legs. She screamed, and water ran into her mouth. It was gritty and tasted of dirt. It smelled of death and mildew. She shoved against the ground, a layer of smooth, slimy rocks in mud that sloshed in her hands and gave no grip. She waved her arms and tried to sit up.

A weight pressed onto her chest, then it was two.

She looked up through the water, her eyes numbing from the cold. A woman stared down at her. She was pale, her eyes white and clouded, her skin cracked and splitting away from her face.

Sarah shook and flailed her arms at the woman. If she could strike her, she could get away. But her hands passed through the air as if there was no one there at all, only a cold mist where the woman should have been.

Her face, her hands, her legs, numbed then burned from the cold. She closed her eyes and coughed. She opened them and saw Darcy. Darcy was holding her down in the water. Mitch was behind her, grinning.

She blinked. It was the black-haired woman and the strange man. Blinked again. Her brother and her friend.

She sucked water into her lungs. It chilled her from the inside. Her lungs clenched, and she coughed it out. She rocked upward, just getting her lips above the rushing stream, and she sucked in a mouthful of air.

Darcy pushed her down. The woman pushed her down. Every muscle in her body flexed and seized.

Pressure on her stomach, something else. Through the numbness, pain. She looked down. The knife in Mitch's hand was in her belly. The icy stream carried away streaks of red.

She screamed and flexed, but her mouth failed to reach the surface. Water rushed into her lungs again. She coughed and seized, coughed and seized.

Sarah opened her eyes, and she was no longer in the water. The night was a gloomy mist. The snow had stopped, and a light fog stretched from one end of the clearing to the other.

Yellow light flickered in the distance. The fog broke, and Sarah could see it was the campfire. Darcy and Mitch sat in each other's arms. They stared at her.

"Guys?" Sarah walked toward them. Her legs moved, but she wasn't going anywhere. She looked down. She was on the other side of the stream.

In the water was a snow-topped lump frozen against the rocks. She looked closer and saw her jacket, her pants, her face.

It Stretches

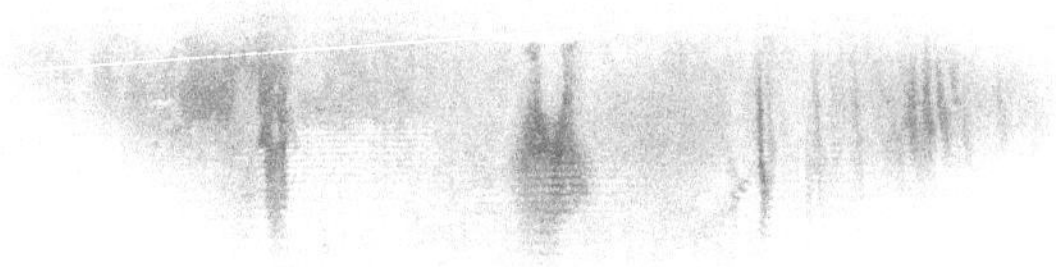

IT STARTED AS A numb, rubbery section of skin at the tip of Joan's left index finger. She poked and pulled at it a little at her desk while checking email but didn't give it much thought. It had been a busy Monday, and her immediate conclusion was maybe it was a callus or she had been stung by something Sunday while planting flowers at Grandma's house and just hadn't noticed at the time. Surely, the sensation would go away over the next few days.

She was just too tired to deal with it.

Friday had been a late night with Renny. That man could drink—and took you with him—and once they got back to his place, he was like the Energizer bunny. Joan had been worried she would chafe if she didn't slow him down here and there, and when he wanted round after round after she was ready to call it a night, she began to wonder if she needed to check his bathroom for blue pills and cocaine.

Saturday, she needed a late morning, and though her head ached beyond belief, she found herself dragged to brunch with Marlene and Sasha from the office. The watered-down mimosas helped her head a little, but after brunch turned to shopping, to pedicures, to happy hour, to Custer Falls's one and only poor excuse for a nightclub, she was on the edge of passing out before her feet hit her front door.

Sunday, there was no getting away from lunch with Grandma; the woman was more of a mother than her own. And when she said she needed help with the weeds she couldn't reach, Joan wanted to vomit right there on the dining room table at the thought of being hunched over in the dirt, sweating out two days' worth of liquor.

But she did it. And she smiled. And she brought home a plate of beans and chicken and potato wedges, which were still in the fridge as she walked her way out of the office. She didn't want to cook, though—even the thought of reheating a plate of leftovers was daunting—and decided that takeout would work so much better.

She got home around six, a bottle of wine in her left hand and a plastic bag of Chinese food in her right. She set both on the coffee table (no need to take them any farther than where they'd be consumed) and put her bag on the couch. No sooner had she dropped into the sea of overstuffed leather when Mr. Fluffers, her orange, tiger-striped tabby cat, came out of the bedroom whining.

Joan pursed her lips and made kissing noises *hello*. She opened the bag of takeout, placing the plastic utensils and packets of soy sauce on the table and using the bag as a placemat below her styrofoam container of Mongolian beef, fried rice, and two egg rolls.

Fluffy-Butt, as Joan affectionately called him, leaped over the back of the couch and crawled into her lap as she sank her fork into what should have been her first bite of rice.

"Not now, man. I need to eat."

He rammed his head into her chin, purring, his thick coat brushing against and itching her bottom lip.

"Really?"

He meowed loudly, and she huffed, dropping her fork into the takeout container and rubbing him from nose to tail. He rammed his head into her chin so hard she had to lean back. He purred and drooled, and Joan couldn't help but think of the cat she lost when she was eight.

Whiskers—at eight, that was the most thought-provoking name she could come up with—was a drooler. He drooled on her bed, the couch, her lap, anywhere and everywhere. Mom had even left rags around the house, one in each room, to make sure it could always be cleaned up quickly. She prided herself on a tidy house, and Whiskers wasn't going to change that.

When Whiskers went missing, Joan secretly suspected her mother had something to do with it. The complaints about the litter box, the drool rags, the frustration at an animal that shot across the house at night keeping her awake, all seemed to be a constant until Whiskers just disappeared one day. None of them expected to hear a month later (Joan several years later) that the culprit was actually a ten-year-old, budding serial killer next door named Edward Lawrence.

The thought gave her shivers, even as Mr. Fluffers rubbed his warm body against her chest.

Whiskers had deserved better. She would make Fluffy-Butt want for nothing as her subconscious constantly reminded her she never knew when the cat's last day would be—or her own, for that matter.

She gave the feline a hug and carried him as she went into the kitchen. She set him down beside his water bowl, fetched a packet of Sheba, and peeled back the foil. He rubbed and nuzzled his way in as she dumped it onto a plate.

"Easy, Fluff. Have I ever not let you have it?"

She shook her head and dropped the trash in the can then rinsed her hands. Most of the time, the smell of wet cat food didn't bother her, but when she was eating, having the scent on her hands could turn her stomach.

Joan's eyes ran across her meal as she sat back down, now with a corkscrew and wine glass. She knew it was getting cold, but after the thoughts of Whiskers and little Eddy Lawrence had passed through her mind, she would need a sip or two before doing anything else.

The bottle popped as the cork came free, and Joan shook her head at the momentary depressing thought of having to drink it alone. She set down the cork, still attached to the corkscrew, and an image passed by of Jason stroking her back and then slamming the door when he moved out. She held the glass and poured, and it was nearly full when she realized the problem had gotten worse with her hand.

"What is that?"

She held her left hand, fingers splayed, in front of her face. Both her index and middle fingers were now numb, but more than that, they looked different. Their hues were darker, as if they'd been dipped in her merlot, and their tips looked oddly extended. It didn't make any sense, but her fingertips had to be close to an inch longer than they were this morning.

Panic shot through Joan's mind. The immediate thought was that she had cancer. She didn't know what kind of cancer could make your fingers grow, but Nana (her other grandmother) had died last month of cancer, so this had to be it. Her fingers had tumors, right? Maybe the tips of her bones, they looked longer now... It made a little sense.

She grabbed the glass with her right and took several large gulps, her eyes glued to her poor, wounded fingers. Whatever this was, she needed some help handling it, even if all she had at the moment was liquid courage.

Joan decided she would finish her glass of wine and eat. Maybe she'd call Marian later tonight after her shift was over and see if she could come by and commiserate. If her fingers didn't look better by morning, she'd head to Urgent Care and call in late for work.

With her mind made up and a plan in place, she gulped down the rest of her glass and poured another. She scooped a forkful of rice, and as she chewed on it, she flipped on the television and scanned through the options on Netflix.

She scrolled past recommendations of *Real Housewives* clones and made-for-streaming rip-offs of last year's action thrillers, settling on a new-to-her horror of some kind. The name was generic enough, *It Stretches*, but there was something about the imagery of the cover art that pulled her in. Maybe it was the girl who somewhat resembled herself; maybe it was the weird-looking, demonic world behind her. It had a campy and B-budget aesthetic, but it also had a familiarity to it. There was a dreamlike quality that seemed to fit her state of mind, reaching from the television into her living room.

She just had to know more.

She clicked play and set down the remote. The movie started, and she raised her glass to it, toasting to a more relaxing evening than her day had been, even if she had to focus on ignoring the weirdness in her fingers, and she drank.

After what seemed like a dozen logos and intros, the thing finally started. On the screen, a woman sat on a couch, a plate of food and a glass of wine on the coffee table in front of her. The camera panned around the room, showing that she was watching TV, and as the woman scooped her food and took a bite, Joan felt an irresistible urge to do the same.

It was like she was in that character's mind (or it was in hers).

She chewed her Mongolian beef. The woman chewed something vague—the camera angle didn't allow Joan to see quite what it was, but that feeling of familiarity returned—almost like she was watching this woman through her own eyes, not through the lens of TV.

Her head grew light, her body, the room, fading into the background.

She took another bite, and so did the woman. She was about done chewing and ready to pick up her wine, and the thought crossed her mind that this was another Netflix dud, despite the sense she was somehow part of this show, more than watching, knowing this other place like she knew her own.

A knock came from the door on TV.

It was the last thing Rachel wanted to deal with after her day. She was finally home and settled on the couch, and now someone was at her door—probably to sell her something.

Rachel looked through the peephole.

A man wearing a gray jumpsuit stood outside her apartment door. She didn't recognize his face, though she could only see half of it. The bulb beside her door was out again, and the corridor's lighting sucked. It was like the complex wanted her to get raped.

A chill ran over her body, and Rachel had to lean away from the door. It was like something frozen had blown toward her, and her instinctual response was to run.

She shook her head. Maybe there was some creep factor to a guy outside her darkened door at seven o'clock at night, but it didn't mean she needed to run and hide. And as much as she complained about the lighting being rape-ready, she thought her complex was generally a safe place. It wasn't like it had ever happened there—that she knew of.

She felt silly, foolish for the urge in her chest that told her not to answer. But she did.

"Who is it?"

"Uh," the guy on the other side started but seemed flustered. "I'm Hector. I'm supposed to change out your smoke detectors. The ones you have've been recalled, so I got a replacement here."

Smoke detectors? Rachel tried to think. She didn't remember hearing anything about a smoke detector problem.

He shuffled his feet. "There was supposed to be a note in your mailbox yesterday about it."

Had she checked the mail yesterday? Not today, she knew that.

"It's late. I think you should come back tomorrow." The cold feeling increased, numbing her fingers. She shook her hand, but it didn't abate. "You know, during regular hours."

"I really can't. They say it's a liability, and it has to get done today. Sorry."

She studied him through the peephole. Hector swayed back and forth. She could see a pair of round objects in his hands.

This didn't feel right. She was nervous, a feeling of something terrible barreling toward her, but she was sure she was just overreacting. It was like her mother was hovering over her shoulder, whispering that every man wanted to hold her down and have his way with her. The guy was clutching two smoke detectors in his hands—he had to be legitimate.

But still...

An idea came to her. "Let me see your license."

He stood there for a moment then, as if he suddenly understood, he dug it out of his pocket. She chained the door and cracked it.

"Let me see."

He slid it through to her, and she shut the door. She didn't recognize the image from around the complex, but what did that prove? The name said Hector, so he wasn't lying about that.

Rachel snapped a photo of it with her phone and uploaded it to Facebook with the caption, "Letting this guy into my apartment to do maintenance."

She waited for the post to upload and made sure his image, name, and address were all legible then unchained and opened the door.

"You're on my Facebook now for everyone to see, just so you know." She held out the ID.

Hector nodded and took the license. "I get it, man. It's cool." He slid it back into his wallet and came inside carrying a three-stair step stool.

Rachel backed away and sat on the couch. The door clicked shut, and as she watched Hector unfold the stool under her living room's detector, she thought she should be feeling a little better about it. If the guy was actually going to do the work, she was safe. Right?

He climbed to the top and unhooked the smoke/carbon monoxide detector. He fumbled the new ones in his grip as he realized he was going to need both hands to remove the wiring clip connecting the old one to the apartment's fire alarm system.

"Shit," Hector mumbled and glanced sheepishly at Rachel. "Sorry."

She smirked, and he climbed down, leaving the old device hanging from its wiring. He set the new ones on the edge of the couch and climbed back up to deal with the problem.

That was when Rachel felt an unrelenting terror emerge from her core.

There was a tingle in her limbs, and she looked down at herself—at her hands. Her fingers were as red as her wine and seemed not only longer than they should have been but growing. How could her fingers be growing?

They waved in the air like snakes as they extended, and aches shot up her arms. It was like muscle cramps combined with a shearing, slicing pain. Her nails pinched together and rounded, forming claws, and she didn't know what she could do other than scream.

The sound belted from her mouth and nearly knocked Hector off his step. He turned his head, and seeing the wavy tips of her fingers—now pointed at him—his first reaction was to smile. She was playing a joke on him—had to be.

But the expression on her face wasn't a joke. The things, which first looked like plastic pointers she had stuck on the ends of her fingers, were waving like live snakes, not stiff or floppy rubber. Whatever that was, it wasn't natural. And it wanted him.

He could feel that, and fear gripped his chest.

He shuffled to back away and tumbled off the step stool.

Hector thudded onto the carpet, his head knocking the drywall under the counter and denting the beige plaster. "What the shit is that?" He scooted away like a startled animal.

Tears wet Rachel's cheeks. She wished she could wipe them away but didn't want her fingers anywhere near her face.

"I..." she blubbered. "I don't know."

Red fingers, now several feet long, clawed at the floor and jerked Rachel from the couch. They dragged her along the ground toward Hector, and she screamed as the carpet ran across her knees, burning.

"Fuck!" Hector scrambled toward the door.

Rachel's palm and the top of her arm had turned red. She was tossed side to side like a ragdoll as her fingers raced toward the maintenance man.

Hector grabbed the knob. He gurgled as blood splashed then ran down the white door.

Joan's eyes jerked open. She was facing her ceiling, dimly lit by the Roku's screensaver. The darkened living room was quiet aside from a distant, wet, smacking sound.

She had fallen asleep, that was for sure, but was it the wine or was the movie that bad? The wine glass on the coffee table was half-full, her styrofoam dinner half-eaten.

Joan pulled herself up, and her hand seemed caught on something. She looked toward the warm area on her lap, and Mr. Fluffers had her fingers in his mouth. But he wasn't doing what it looked like. She had to have been seeing it wrong, her dreams not completely faded from her thoughts.

She couldn't see his face. He was on her lap, pointed toward her feet, but she could swear he was gnawing on her fingers. His head bobbed up and down, and that sound… But it couldn't be. She felt nothing, and he would never do that. She'd heard stories of old cat ladies dying and their cats eating their faces—hadn't every cat owner? But she couldn't believe Fluffy-Butt would do that to her, especially not during a nap. He'd probably found something—God forbid, a mouse—and climbed on her lap to eat it. And… he was on her hand, which had fallen asleep.

That made sense, didn't it?

She pulled her hand away, expecting pins and needles. It came, dragging Mr. Fluffers and turning him to face her.

A jolt of electricity shot through Joan. A scream perched on her lips, ready but not sure if it was time to explode.

Her finger was indeed inside the cat's mouth, but the cat's jaws were not moving. Its body writhed back and forth, the wet, sloppy noise of something sliding against meat slipping between her finger and the cat's lips.

Her eyes adjusted to the sight.

Fluffer's eyes were still, glazed over, and whatever red, numb thing that was on her finger was inside him, doing what? She couldn't imagine right now.

Joan shrieked and jumped from the couch, arm out, the flight center of her brain trying desperately to shoo away the danger at her arm's end.

Her foot was all pins and needles, and she caught it on the coffee table then sank through the air. Something solid thunked the back of her head, and Fluffers, blurry, slapped onto the carpet beside her head, her finger (redder than before) still in his mouth.

It was like the TV turned completely off, though that wasn't quite it. In the midst of her living room's blackness, she sank deeper than the floor, warm, wet, soothing sleep consuming her.

There was a knock at the door.

Joan opened her eyes to a room way too bright, and her eyeballs ached at the intrusion.

Another knock.

The curtains were drawn, all the windows covered, but the pain—the pain was like staring into the sun. She had to close her eyes and cover her face.

"Joan? Are you in there?" It was a familiar female voice on the other side of the door. Her words reverberated against the hard hallway walls.

"Joan?" Another female, also familiar.

There was a jingle (keys?), and the door lock crackled and scraped. Someone was coming inside.

The knob turned, and Joan heard them come in. More than *heard*, she knew they were opening the door, knew a warm wind was blowing through the alcove beyond, knew it was Marlene and Sasha, and Sasha was wearing her Thursday jeans. She could tell Marlene's blood was rushing through her veins, nearly in a panic, and Sasha was wearing a pad, her period early. She didn't know how she knew these things and didn't care because, even through the cover of her fingers over her face and her sealed eyelids, her eyes ached so badly.

She moaned as her friends neared. It was a sharp, stabbing pain in the center of her pupils and a heaving, throbbing sensation on the back of her eyeballs. She wondered if it would hurt more or less to rip the things from their sockets.

"Joan!" Marlene kneeled on the floor beside her. "What happened? Are you hurt?"

"Bright," Joan moaned.

Marlene looked around the room. To her, it was a gloomy, boxed-in space. She wondered if someone had drugged Joan. She couldn't imagine a simple hangover bothering her this much—it was noon for Chrissake, and Joan was a hangover pro. But here she was on her back, covering her face like a vampire, and—was that blood on her hands?

"Sasha." Marlene pointed at the windows. "The blinds—under the curtains—close those, please?"

Sasha pinched her lips together and went to the windows. She lowered the blinds while wondering if they would have to call an ambulance. She'd never seen Joan so sick. The woman was like a rock. Last to stop drinking, first to start, last to want to go home at the end of the night. She was like a force of nature. But here she was on the floor, and the idea that something had taken her down like this was world-rattling.

Behind both the closed blinds and the blackout curtains, the room was like night. Sasha stumbled to the other two and caught a glint from the cat's bowl on the kitchen counter. She wondered where the cat was; she always loved to give Mr. Fluffers a squeeze when she came by.

"Joan, the blinds are shut," Marlene said. "Try opening your eyes. Otherwise, I feel like we're going to need to call 911."

"No," Joan groaned. "No ambulance." The idea alone of flashing lights and sirens pained her.

Her eyes fluttered as she tested the darkness. It still felt bright, still drove pain into her retinas, but it wasn't as bad.

"Good." Marlene smiled. "I was getting worried. Are you having a migraine day today? I didn't know you got migraines."

Sasha stood behind Marlene, thinking she should have thought of migraines herself. Of course, pain and light sensitivity were a thing for migraine sufferers. But what do you do to help people with migraines?

Marlene could see Joan's eyes—open now—but in the darkness, seeing anything else was a battle. "What can we do for you?"

"You didn't come to work," Sasha chimed in. "We were worried about you."

"Noth—nothing..." Joan's words were weak. "You should go."

As Joan achingly looked around the room, she couldn't believe she had spent the whole night on the floor. And where was Fluffy-Butt? That little attention whore was always front and center when visitors came over. That meant all the free pets he could get. But—a flash of memory returned. Mr. Fluffers, that sound, falling down. What the hell had happened?

"Joan?" Sasha said.

But before Joan could even think about responding, her eyes exploded in pain. It made no sense. The room was dark, but the stabbing sensation had spiked in a way she couldn't have imagined if she hadn't experienced it. It was like her eyeballs were attacking her, like they were growing thorns inside their sockets and digging into her skull.

"Get them out!" was all she could muster. Because at this point, there was no stopping it, no fighting the pain other than removing the orbs from her head. That would do it. That could make the pain stop for good.

"Get what out?" Marlene said. "I don't have any migraine meds, dear."

She looked up at Sasha. "I think she needs the hospital."

"It's a good thing we came." Sasha took the phone from her pocket and started entering her passcode.

"We'll get you help," but there was a helplessness in Marlene's voice. She could do nothing but talk, and it showed.

Sasha had entered the last digit, and her screen began to change when blood shot from Marlene's back and sprayed across Sasha's face. It dripped from her chin onto her phone, and confusion set into Sasha as she wondered why this hot, dark rain was falling inside Joan's apartment.

A weak groan passed from Marlene's lips, muffled by a long, snake-like appendage filling her mouth that was once Joan's hand. Tendrils dug through the back of her head and out into the darkened room. Tendrils ran down her throat and into her lungs. They punched upward, cracking through her skull and into her brain, where they dug and clutched at meaty tissue and devoured it.

Sasha's phone slipped from her hand and thudded to the carpet. She froze, trying to decide if it was better to run or scream. She was unable to finish the thought let alone make the decision.

Joan rose without standing. It was a fluid levitation above the ground, her weight held up by hundreds of things that were no longer her legs but something else. She had changed into something—she didn't know what—but beyond the returning pain in her eyes, she was glad for whatever she was becoming. She felt Marlene's brain and lungs swallowed into her limbs, and the rising fullness satiated a hunger she didn't know she had. The sway of a hundred appendages below her felt like a dance, like the twirling she had often done as a child in her ballerina outfit, a pink leotard and shiny shoes. There was something about it that lifted her thoughts and brought what felt like a smile to her face.

In reality, there was no more face to smile. Dozens of tendrils hung from her transforming skull—slimy, wavering things that spread across what had been her forehead and drooped over her cheekbones. Only her misshapen mouth and eyes remained, hiding under the cover of her new limbs and stretching from their previous perches into melting extensions of tentacled flesh.

Sasha gasped. The new gulp of air was like a shot of energy reminding her she was alive, and if she wanted to remain so, she'd better do something.

She watched her friend's body crumple in on itself, contorting, imploding, pulled toward the draping limbs, the hanging flesh that should have been her other friend.

Sasha's thoughts flashed from her inability to help Marlene to what Joan had become to a fear of screaming. That might bring the monster's attention to her. So, instead, she spun and raced for the door.

A slimy fluttering sound followed Sasha. It was wet and, even over the carpet, seemed to slosh and slurp as it closed in behind her. She set a hand on the knob and twisted. Light broke through the gap as the door spread wide, and a shrieking scream sounded behind her.

Sasha didn't look back—she'd seen enough already. She burst through the door and sprinted to the stairs, to the parking lot, to her car. She jumped inside, thanking God she had driven and not Marlene, and started the engine.

She was at the apartment complex's entrance when she finally took a breath. Cars passed by on 12th Avenue toward their lunch hour meals and rushed back to their jobs. Her fingers trembled as she fought to decide what to do next. Call the police? Go home and crawl under the covers?

Did it matter? She was alive!

She was just realizing she had lost her phone when there was a thump from the car's rear. Sasha spun in her seat, and through the rear window, she saw the impossible. Joan was shoving her car forward.

Traffic whipped by at forty-five miles per hour, and Joan was pushing Sasha's car into the torrent of steel.

"No!" She pushed harder on the brakes.

The car moved anyway. And faster.

It was thrust so fast her tires stained the asphalt drive with black lines.

There was screeching and crunching, glass shattering across the avenue, and Sasha's face met the grill of a Peterbilt hauling a trailer of lumber.

Joan returned to her apartment in a daze. The blinding light of day felt like a wedge being driven into her skull. Even the darkness of her home didn't make the pain relent.

She shuffled past the living room, ignoring the enticing smell of the half corpse beside the couch. She went into the kitchen, her mind on the cupboard over the microwave, on the leftover pills from her root canal last month. Those had to be able to stop the pain in her eyes.

She reached for the cabinet handle, and a wave of agony knocked her to the ground. She screamed and covered her eyes.

It didn't help. It seemed nothing would, unless...

It took less than a minute. She reached under the veil of dangling tendrils, ready to pluck out the bothersome orbs, but the pain stopped. She pressed inside to feel what had happened, and long, white strands stretched down from the cavities the organs once inhabited.

She sighed. She practically squealed. She stood up in relief and floated from the kitchen above a swarm of undulated tentacles, expanding and contracting as they carried her forward, her mind on the meal she had left in the living room.

Joan sank to the ground, her tendrils wrapping, digging, consuming. She thought back to the Netflix movie, how good that maintenance man tasted; to her collapse, and she realized it must have been a dream. A vision? Her future shape guiding her to where she was going?

She brushed it off. Did it matter?

She wondered if she should visit Renny tonight.

Cody Was Here

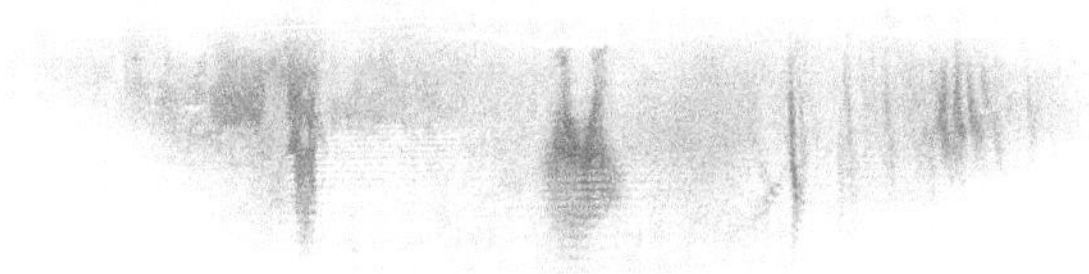

AN UNEXPLAINED ALLURE PULLED Summer and Gavin to the creek bank the day they moved in. It pulled them from the small A-frame where Mom unpacked bags, putting away the few things they had been able to take as they stole away in the night a week prior. Only the things they could carry. Only the important things they couldn't live without and remembered to grab in the haste of the moment.

Summer had wept just about that entire week, only pausing as they stopped to sleep in fleabag motels and to force food into her body at Mom's request.

She had understood the situation. She'd heard the screaming and fighting and seen the bruises in the mornings after Dad's drinking got the best of him. She'd never expected that it would have come to this, though. Her meager twelve years had not prepared her for life on the run.

Gavin was less aware. He was asleep when it all happened, then carried to the car and laid down in the back. He awoke the next morning, the Ford Escort wagon a few hundred miles from home, his biggest concern being if they could stop at McDonald's for pancakes.

It would have been easy for Summer to dismiss him; that's what every-one else did. He was a ten-year-old kid, born missing part of his brain and, while not formally diagnosed, suspected of having schizophrenia on top of other disorders. But she knew better. It was kind of one of those miracle things—like how they say a blind person hears extra well—the parts of his brain he possessed compensated for the missing pieces—mostly. If you didn't know about his condition, you'd just assume he was a regular, happy ten-year-old with some impulse control issues. And while neither Mom nor Summer told him what had actually happened to Dad, he was content believing they were taking a little vacation without him.

Neither Summer nor Mom wanted to correct him. It was like an unspoken decision they had agreed upon. *Let it last—let him have that a little bit longer.*

It was after a few nights in the A-frame, on a day when Summer and Gavin were again planning to spend most of their daylight hours down at the creek, that they first met Cody. While Gavin didn't question it, the fact another kid would be there struck Summer as a little odd. There were no other houses around the A-frame, just miles of forest. It was something of an exempt structure, a ninety-nine-year lease inside thousands of acres of Custer Falls National Forest.

Summer was walking the eighth of a mile from the house to the creek alone that day. She had wanted to finish reading a chapter of *Harry Potter and the Sorcerer's Stone*. The wave of wands and the drama of it all hovered in her mind as she neared the water and heard Gavin talking.

She passed it off as him playing and chatting to himself at first. He did that sometimes. And then she heard Cody and sped up.

When she reached the water's edge, she was surprised to see a pleasant-looking kid, maybe ten, like Gavin, dressed in jeans and a white T-shirt. His dark hair was slicked back, and he smiled as their eyes met.

She glanced down at Gavin, his hands deep in mud. "What's going on?"

"Looking for skipping stones." He didn't look up. He raised a two-inch rock and shook it beneath the water to clean it off, then held it high to examine it.

"No," the new kid said. "Bottom's too rough." He was right. The top of the stone had been worn smooth, but the bottom was craggy and lopsided.

"Hmm." Gavin tossed it into the water. *Bloop.*

"Who are you?" Summer tried for her nicest *what-are-you-doing-here* tone. It was hard to muster. It wasn't that she was opposed to making new friends, but she and Gavin weren't supposed to be talking to anybody. They were supposed to be "laying low," as Mom called it. The last thing she wanted was for them to be separated—that's what Mom said would happen. She saw blood on Mom's hands, her hands, strobing blue lights, the men with badges cuffing her, dragging her and Gavin into separate cars to separate foster homes, to—she saw herself in an institution, white, padded walls and... She trembled at the thought. Anything could happen if they didn't follow the rules.

She needed to get rid of this kid before he knew too much and got them caught.

"Cody." The new boy nodded as he said it. He smiled at her again. As much as she needed him to go, the expression was endearing in a way she didn't quite understand. She didn't want him to go.

She gritted her teeth together. "You're not supposed to be here, Cody. It's private property."

He grinned. "You're crazy. These woods aren't private." He pointed at the path to the A-frame. "The house isn't even yours. You're renting it for your vacation, aren't you?" His eyes begged her to prove him wrong, a friendly bet to see who was right.

A shiver ran down the center of her back. How did he know that? She was about to ask and stopped herself—she didn't want to sound paranoid or make them look suspicious. And then, *Of course, Gavin told him that. Had to be.*

"Well, either way, we aren't supposed to play with strangers." She reached toward her brother. "Gavin, come on."

"It's all right." Cody threw up his hands. "I'll go." He started onto the path that followed the creek to the right. He walked about ten yards with a playful stride and turned back. "How about tomorrow?"

Summer frowned. "No. We can't play with strangers."

Cody hemmed and hawed for a moment. There was an eagerness in his sounds and a look of contemplation—the look of a child solving the mysteries of the universe to get Mom to allow one more cookie from the jar. "What if I wasn't a stranger? What if you knew me?"

"What?" That didn't make any sense. Either you knew someone or you didn't. "What are you talking about?"

He grinned. "Before you go to bed tonight, look in the closet. Look in my red box."

Summer turned to Gavin and back to Cody. Her tongue was poised with questions. *How do you know what's in my closet? Have you been in my house? What red box?*

But Cody was gone. The creek water rippled in the distance.

Summer looked up the path and didn't see him. She assumed he had ducked around a patch of brambles and run off, but there was a feeling that told her that wasn't right. He obviously didn't just disappear, but...

It didn't matter.

Summer sat beside Gavin. They dug into the mud together and made a pile of stones to skip. It wasn't long before they'd forgotten about Cody altogether. In fact, it was bedtime before any thought of the boy returned.

No one said a word at dinner. Mom had made spaghetti with plain sauce—not even any meatballs. Summer thought about complaining but didn't. It was the look in Mom's eyes, a glassy redness from crying that looked tired—so tired. She got the feeling it was all Mom could do to boil the noodles, and if there had been one more step involved, they wouldn't have had this.

When Mom was picking up the plates, it occurred to Summer that she had barely tasted the meal. She couldn't imagine why, but her belly still felt empty.

Rightly so. She didn't deserve to eat.

Mom retreated to her pillow and blanket on the sofa. The television played some British detective show that flared with static like clockwork every nine seconds. Summer and Gavin climbed the narrow stairs up to the loft.

She picked up her book and crashed on their bed. It released a gust of air that smelled of must that briefly overpowered the lingering scent of pasta sauce, then faded.

Gavin opened his book of word searches and sat at the foot. Those usually calmed him, but this time, he just shuffled through the pages, unable to decide where to start.

Summer had just flipped the book open, zeroing in on the paragraph's start and ready for more of Harry's misadventures when, over the page's top, she spied the beckoning closet a few feet away.

Before you go to bed tonight, look in the closet. Look in my red box.

That was dumb. She returned to her book, her bookmark, a holographic scene from Mount Rushmore showing the mountain before and after the sculptures, shone at her. A tiny string dangled over her fingers and tickled.

What the hell was that kid talking about? She thought. *He was trying to screw with me. There's nothing...*

She looked at the page: *Chapter Five.* The words blurred and mingled with one another. P and T swung like a line dance. T and H switched places with EE, and they switched back again.

She turned to Gavin. He huffed, staring at the outside of his book.

Summer closed Harry Potter. There was no holding her back. The idea was drilling through her thoughts relentlessly from that yellow, louvered door. No matter how she tried to ignore it, it wasn't going anywhere until she looked. She had to prove that kid wrong.

Before you go to bed tonight, look in the closet. Look in my red box.

"Okay." She set the book on the bed and walked two steps to the closet door. "I open it, and I find no red box, and it's all over. Just a dumb kid playing a trick on me."

She reached for the knob and felt the return of that chill she'd felt by the creek. Only stronger. It spread over her shoulders and raised the hairs on her arms. It grabbed onto her belly and tightened around it, and she wasn't sure she could keep dinner down, however little of it she had eaten.

Her fingers hovered over the closet's brass knob. They didn't want to close, didn't want to touch it. There was a repulsion there. Magnets came to mind, the way two north poles pushed away from each other. She laughed at herself. It was fake, but she did it. Her fingers weren't magnetic. She just needed to grab it and—she wondered if she had looked in this closet before.

She remembered running up the stairs when they had first gotten there. Mom had spent ten minutes trying to get the door open, something about how the landlord hadn't left the keys in the right place, so she had to jimmy the lock. Once it was open, Mom pointed at the stairs and said, "Upstairs is yours," and the next thing she knew, her face was buried in the pillow, soaking it with tears. There was no dinner that night, only leftover snacks from the road. Doritos, beef jerky, candy bars, bottled water. She nibbled. But she didn't open the closet. The smell of the entire place was dust and mothballs, and opening that closet would have been just one more thing to spread that smell until Mom opened the windows the next day and aired the place out. But even then, she didn't look inside.

"Dumb," she mumbled and seized the knob. It was cold under her fingers. "Dumb." She cranked it counterclockwise and pulled.

A wave of musty odor. Dust motes dancing.

The top half was filled with clothes packed tightly together. The bottom held a half dozen shelves with sheets, blankets, and towels. She let go of a heavy breath. *No red box.*

Of course there was no red box. That kid was just messing with her.

"What's that?" Gavin asked. He stood and came to the closet, setting his word search book on the bed.

"Just a dumb closet." Summer leaned in and spread the hangers apart. A green silk blouse. A yellow pair of slim pants. Another blouse, this one white with a slightly ruffled collar. There was a feeling as she sifted through the garments, a sad one as if these belonged to someone who could no longer wear them. One after the other, the feeling mounted that she could be looking at a rack in a vintage clothing shop, a sign above that read *1960s*, but no—this was a house, and the woman who used to wear these was surely... dead.

Another chill, this one around her hips, cooling her legs, not stopping until it reached her toes.

"Look." She hadn't even noticed Gavin was sitting on the floor at the base of the closet, digging through the bottom shelf.

In his hands, he held a red wooden box.

Cody leaned over the edge of the creek. The rush of cold water washed most of the blood from his fingers, but some of it was more stubborn. It clung under his nails. It fought to remain as stains in the creases of his hands.

"Cody!" Dad called from the path home. "Get over here, boy!"

He took another look at his hands. The shiny wetness and the dimming light of dusk made the details hard to read, but he thought he'd gotten it all—or enough that Dad wouldn't notice.

"Coming!" He picked up his red box and made sure the clasp was tight, then hid it behind the first branch of a bramble patch beside the path.

He'd made it two paces toward home before Dad stepped in his way, scowling down at him.

"Didn't you hear me calling you?"

"I yelled back. Said I was comin'."

Dad swallowed, doubting himself, wondering if he could have heard the boy and it not registered. He lifted the beer in his right hand and took a swig. It didn't matter if the boy called back or not; he wasn't home when he was supposed to be. You couldn't trust kids to be out in these woods alone... not here... not now.

He leaned over his son and swatted him on the rump.

"Ow!" Cody looked up, shocked, tears in the corners of his eyes.

"Don't fake cry with me, boy. Get home."

Cody took off, a smirk on his face.

Dad scanned up and down the path, across the water, and into the trees. A cold, late-summer wind blew over his neck, and gooseflesh bunched on his arms.

He wondered if he'd gotten there in time, if the boy was safe or a lost cause. Only time would tell.

The scent of roast beef was thick within the A-frame's walls. The reheated pot sat on the stove, drenching the small house in a fog of humidity that, on any other day, would have made it feel like home. Today, it was a mixture of grief and anxiety, a sultry overlap of what was lost and what could have been.

Cody and Dad sat in the kitchen and ate, not a word passed between them. Not a question about Mom. Nothing about the small shack downstream. Not a whimper from the crawlspace below their feet.

After Dad put the dishes in the sink, walked Cody into the living room, and chained him to the floor, he found his shotgun and sat by the wall. He lit a cigarette and waited.

Full dark swelled around the cabin, and there was just a moment when it was so quiet that both the boy and his father drifted off. But as the witching hour came, Cody screamed, yanking the chains tight.

"Don't," Summer snapped at Gavin, his finger hovering over the red box's clasp. It was too late.

He flipped open the box, and Summer stepped back. She didn't know what she expected to see, not after her head was flooded with scenes from what must have been another life. Dead things? The small and mummified bodies of forest creatures that Cody had been *playing* with, had had to wash his hands in the creek to clean the blood from his fingers? Or news clippings of his mother's death, maybe just a notice she was *missing*? Possibly some other maniacal object that she had no way of imagining?

Inside the walls of the creaky wooden container was only one thing: a folded piece of pink paper.

It was pale, faded from time, but even so, it seemed unlike a thing Summer expected a boy to collect. There was nothing printed that she could see, and she wondered what devious things could be drawn or inscribed beneath the folds. But as Gavin lifted the page and began to unfold it, her heart jumped into her throat.

"No." She snatched the object from Gavin's hand and retreated to the bed.

"Hey!" He jumped to his feet and followed.

She didn't understand the compulsion other than a protective need to keep it away from him. There was something folded within that sheet of rose-colored parchment, and she was desperate to keep it away from Gavin. It was not something he should have—not something he should be near. But simultaneously, she needed to know what it was. She needed to hold it in her hands and find out what was so important that Cody would have hidden it here. What was the reason behind the chains in the living room?

It came to her as an undoubtedly true conclusion that, yes, those were Cody's memories, that whatever had happened those many years ago had been real and somehow projected into her mind. It didn't make any sense, but she knew these things as facts. It didn't matter that a boy of ten would not have been around in the sixties and still here this afternoon—the word ghost the furthest thing from her mind. What she knew was his father was a bastard who had chained him up. His mother had been missing. And whatever was on this paper was a key to it all, and she had to know the answer.

"No!" Gavin yelled back. He jumped at Summer, arms flailing as she moved, and then fingers grasped at her hands and tore her digits back to get to the paper.

A sudden rage took over. Summer grabbed her brother by the head and pushed him back. She rolled over the bed and stood on the other side, holding the page aloft.

He growled and perched himself on the mattress. He looked for a brief moment as if he was about to speak, and he leaped.

She raised her other arm to block him. Her hand went into his mouth, and he clamped down as his legs wrapped her waist. His momentum thrust them both into the wall.

There was a thump and then stars. Her fingers screamed as he bit down, but instead of objecting, her mind was focused on the approaching floor and then blackness. A cloudy sensation of fatigue clawed into her mind. She was able to open her eyes just once.

She saw Gavin rip through the paper, leaving shreds in his wake. He jumped to his feet and ran from the room, a very old key in his hand.

Cody's face was as pale as the full moon. His eyes, turned white, bulged from their sockets as blood streamed from his ears, drawing a scarlet line to his chin.

Dad screamed back.

Cody charged across the room. He stumbled as he moved, but his run was faster than any runner Dad had ever seen. Within a breath, he was a foot from his father, the only thing restraining the swipes of his long, yellowed nails being the length of his chain.

Cody screamed again, this time with words neither of them knew. But someone did. The one who put them in his head.

"Let me go!" It was a man's voice coming from Cody, a deep, rumbling tone that sent shivers through Dad's limbs and squeezed his bladder tight. "Let me go!"

"Get out of my son!" Dad screamed back.

Cody blew a heavy breath over the space between them. It smelled of rot, of months of wet, moldy decay and rank, swampy earth.

"This is mine now," the thing commanded from inside the boy.

"Let him go!"

"Daddy?" It was Cody's voice now, whimpering. "Please let us go, Daddy. Please?"

Dad pointed the shotgun at Cody's face. Tears rushed down his cheeks.

"Don't do that, Daddy." The boy rammed his fingers into his eyes, twisted, and ripped them from their sockets.

"Oh, God." Dad trembled, the gun shaking in his grip.

Cody held the ruined orbs toward his father. "Let me do it?" He dropped the organs to the floor, and as one hand seized his jaw and yanked it downward, his other dove into his mouth.

"No..." Dad slumped against the floor.

There was a crunching sound as Cody's hand twisted between his jaws. Blood ran over his lips in a trail that ended at his elbow before pouring like a faucet onto the floor.

Hot red splashed onto Dad's knees. He could taste his son's blood as it hovered over the air between them.

The crunching went on. Then slurping. The sound of suction against a wet object that refused to move.

As Cody pulled his hand from his mouth, bloody bone trickled to the floor. As his fist escaped his jaws, it clenched a handful of purplish-gray tissue.

It took Dad a moment to understand what his son was holding. The entire house seemed like it had been dragged into another dimension, and what he was seeing seemed to fit that, not the real world he knew. He was in a place of monster and madness, not a house in the woods where he and his family were supposed to enjoy a relaxing retreat. But whether real or demented, the sight, its lines, the place where it had been ripped from, formed the conclusion for him. As much as he wished to deny it, he could not deny what Cody was holding: a child-size fistful of his own brains.

Dad vomited without regard to where he was or what he was doing. Partially digested roast beef, carrots, and potatoes tumbled from his lips, over his chin, onto his shotgun, and down to the floor. It took several seconds for him to realize it had happened, and all he could do then was rotate the barrel and place it into his mouth as his son's empty eye sockets watched him.

I'm sorry, he thought, but his lips didn't move. And he was—for letting this happen, for bringing them to this place, for leaving Mom alone with him, and—the boards below them creaked; a scratching sound from the crawlspace.

He reached for the trigger. He felt the cold blue steel against his finger, and an invisible hand clamped onto his digit and ripped it backward. The bones in his hands cracked as each finger rolled in reverse, folding over the rear of his wrist. Some portion of his mind pictured Bugs Bunny cracking his joints before a show where he pretended to be the symphony's conductor—only white pain ripped that away, and blood sprouted from his hands in fountains.

The gun clunked against the floor.

Dad flew backward into the wall.

Cody giggled.

The door opened, and Mom walked in, skin grayed and her cheek ripped from the right corner of her mouth to the rear of her jaw.

She wagged her finger at him the way she used to scold Cody and grabbed his ankle. Cody's chains dropped to the floor, and he grabbed the other ankle, giggling again.

They dragged Dad out the back door.

When Summer opened her eyes, the first thing she saw was the darkness that filled her window. The first thing she felt was agony in her right hand.

She held it up. Her fingers were covered in dried blood, and the first two were split open with giant gashes, as if someone had tried to unpeel them from the first knuckle to the second.

"What?" She cried and tried to orient herself to what had happened. Where was Mom? She needed a bandage—stitches—Gavin—that key.

"Mom?" she moaned.

There was no response. Her heaving breaths brought in scents of rot, blood, and sulfur.

"Mom!"

She waited a minute. Still nothing.

Summer worked herself onto her feet, and her skull ached like it had been cracked open. Pain from the back of her head to her eyes came in throbbing punches. Her teeth shrieked as if they were about to shatter and dribble from her lips.

"Mom!" she cried and stumbled to the stairs. She forced herself to pause at the edge so she didn't lose her balance and—

As she looked down the narrow steps, she felt her body leaning, rocking forward under the pressure of either her own lightheadedness or some invisible force—she didn't know which. She grabbed the railing as she tilted. She twisted, falling, but kept her grip. Her feet slipped and thumped against treads, sliding (pulled?) downward. Her body wanted to go; it jerked, and her hand came free of the handrail.

Thuds rocked her rear. Her ankle rolled beneath her sliding core, and she toppled forward. All she could do was hope as the bottom floor soared at her face.

When Summer opened her eyes, her lips, her cheeks, and her hair were wading in a pool of blood. She moved her head to rippling crimson, and her nose cracked. A shock jolted through her nerves. She was amazed to find all she could do was whimper.

Summer pulled herself up, her hair matted in gore, dragging it over her clothes, dripping ropes of redness across her arms and legs.

"Mom!" she cried.

Still no response.

She crawled on hands and knees to the couch where Mom slept. The covers were pulled back, half on the floor. The TV was a wall of static. She squinted past the television and saw the back door was open.

"Gavin?"

There was little to do beyond weep as she tried to understand. Her head, her face, her fingers, all raging bundles of pain. Her mom was supposed to be there. She was supposed to make everything okay—to fix it all. (But she hadn't fixed it with Dad, had she?) Gavin was gone, and as she looked at Mom's indentation in the cushions, she realized there was a line of blood where Mom laid her head.

"God..." She trembled.

What the hell was... And her mind went to Cody.

This was all his fault. Whatever had driven Gavin to knock her down—the key—they had only found it because of Cody. Whatever had happened to Mom, it was because of Gavin, because of Cody. But Gavin couldn't have moved Mom, she was too heavy. She must have followed him, trying to stop him... and that key...

What was that key?

It didn't matter right now. It was Mom and Gavin that mattered, and she had to find them.

She glared at the darkness beyond the open door, then stumbled to the kitchen. No flashlight, but she did find matches. Into her pocket. She searched for candles; there were none.

She looked into the night once again. Light or not, she had to go.

"Mom!" Summer's voice lay flat over the night air. It was lonely against the near silence, with only the distant sound of the creek to offer some reassurance that she wasn't the sole living thing in the world.

There was no response. Summer didn't expect there to be, but hope necessitated the call. If only Mom would answer. If she were nearby and could help figure this all out, it would mean the rock of hopelessness forming in her stomach was misdirected, and Mom could search for Gavin instead of her doing it alone.

But no. Her absence, the blood, the open door, it all meant this was her job, no matter her hesitation or how bad she ached.

Summer ventured out onto the path to the creek. The night chill blew across her body, and she wrapped her arms around her chest.

"Ow!" her left hand touched her right. The skinless section of finger raged with pain.

There may have been a trail to lead her, to make sure she was actually following them and not just going for a stroll to the creek, but she didn't even look down. She knew this was the direction. Because that was where Cody was.

Cody… was he a ghost? Some demon, monster, alien? She wished she knew. What she was sure of was he was somehow behind all of this. He'd done something to his family all those years ago, and now he wanted to do the same to hers.

She couldn't let him. She shook her head in disgust, the image of his empty eye sockets reoccurring in her mind. She would not let him take everything she had left.

Not after Dad.

The memory came rushing back—she just couldn't keep it away.

She was supposed to be sleeping. She had been sent to bed like any other night. She'd brushed her teeth and gotten between the sheets. Tonight, though, instead of closing her eyes and drifting off to thoughts of taming trolls and unicorns and having lasagna dinner with Garfield, she sneaked under her covers with her book and a flashlight.

She was halfway through the chapter when the yelling started.

"Will you keep it down," Mom said. "You're going to wake the kids."

"Fuck them!" Dad was definitely drunk again. "This is my house. I pay the bills. I can yell AS LOUD AS I WANT!"

Someone walked past Summer's door, and shadows crossed the crack below.

"Get back here," Dad said. Another set of shadows.

Mom, muffled now, maybe in the living room, "Why don't you just leave? Go see that whore!"

He smacked her. It would have been an indistinct sound had Summer not heard it a thousand times before.

"Just go!"

Another smack.

Tears dripped on her book, salty wetness over some spell Harry was failing to cast.

Mom cried.

"I'm not leaving *my* house."

Shuffling sounds. Something thumped.

"Get off of me! Let go!"

Another smack.

Things blurred in Summer's mind. She saw the hallway outside her room. She saw Dad's hands on Mom's throat. She saw blood.

It was everywhere. It was on her hands and soaking her pajamas. It stuck to her skin and slithered under her fingernails.

And Dad looked at her. Shock and fear. He was afraid... of her. How was *Dad* afraid of *her*?

A knife tumbled from her hands and clattered against the floor.

There were so many tears. In the car, in the motels, in the little A-frame, now on the path to the creek. They were never-ending. Was that all life was? Was that all she could ever hope for, an endless string of sadness throughout her years?

She remembered the flash between relief and horror in Mom's eyes as Dad fell quiet. Summer could do that again if she had to. She'd find Mom and, if only for a moment, would help her have that relief.

She reached the creek and stopped inches from the water. The babbling caress of the shoreline teased her. It mocked her. It was an immutable sound, a part of the immortal landscape, unconcerned with her short-lived desires and problems. But as she looked at the edge, saw where her and Gavin's footprints had pressed into the mud and rock, she saw something more. The dark of night was on the water, but the roll of waves, the splash against the land, was darker than it should have been.

She crouched and looked closer—it wasn't just the darkness of night. The creek was not water. It was blood.

Summer shuddered, and panic filled her chest. She tripped over her own feet and fell backward onto her rear.

"Whoa!" She scooted away, petrified she would get some of it on her. There was a creeping sensation that it was poison, and even a drop could somehow infect her.

She shook her head. "Mom!"

Where could they go? They had to have come this way, but they weren't—

A memory. When Cody had gone, he was following the creek to the right. What if they went that way?

She didn't want to go the wrong way—to get lost—

"Mom?"

—but it was the only clue she had.

Summer climbed to her feet and started following the path along the bank. She watched the blood with a mindful eye. It was just blood, sure, but something warned her to keep away. Not to let it near her.

There was a moment when she glanced and her heart jumped. She could have sworn she saw—but she couldn't have—Gavin floating, standing over the river of blood. She turned again, but he was gone.

Brambles and bushes rustled as the breeze blew into Summer's face. Somewhere deep in the night, safe from the reach of whatever thing was causing her dread, she heard an owl hoot. The dirt under her feet crunched as she walked.

She'd gone a dozen paces when Mom screamed.

It was sharp and cut across the creek, slamming into Summer like a bullet. She spun and saw her, Mom. Her arms flailed. Her eyes bled. Her skin was pale in the darkness. And she was being dragged by Gavin and Cody by her hair.

"Mom!" Summer's heart pounded. She looked left and right, wondering how they got over there. There was no bridge or downed tree to cross.

She had no choice.

Every inch of Summer's flesh rose in goosebumps as she set her foot in the river of blood. It was warm, seeping into her pants and crawling up her legs.

She whimpered as she moved.

Mom screamed again. They dragged her between a pair of trees where a shack stood, and they disappeared inside it.

"Mom!" Summer moved faster. The water rose over her knees and up to her hips. Waves crashed into her, splashing drops of blood onto her face and hair. She tasted a drop as it fell into her mouth—its salty iron gave her chills, even in the hot stream. Shivers down her arms.

She pinched her mouth shut, but she knew it was too late. Whatever germ or evil was in that river was inside her now. But maybe Mom could fix it? She just had to get to Mom.

"Mom!" She climbed the bank and hurried into the trees. Sheets of blood ran from her legs, soaking the grass and shrubs on the shoreline.

She sprinted to the shack.

The door was closed, and the key extended from the lock.

The ten-by-ten shack was a place Summer would never have tried to enter any other day. Its rough, wooden walls and bare, shingled roof were weathered and rotten. Weeds grew up the corner, hooking into the moldering fibers and returning the structure to the forest.

A skinny door hung crooked inside its frame, and there was a single, dirt-coated window on the shack's side. Summer was sure that through the mold and rot she could see a face. It was nearly human, but not, something like a skull with holes where its nose should have been. Its eyes were pure black, and she thought she could see horns above its ears. Surrounding the image were words Summer couldn't read.

She whined as she stared at the knob. She needed to go in there. For Mom. For Gavin. But there was a radiance coming from that door she couldn't deny. It was hot, like the blood in the creek. It was heavy, pressing through her clothes and into her skin. And it was bad. It was the sensation she felt on test days when she walked into school knowing she hadn't studied. It was the fear that pushed her under her covers when Dad was yelling. It was the heavy dread of knowing she had doomed her family when Mom rushed her to the car after washing off the blood.

She didn't want to go in, but she had to.

Mom howled. Her voice was pained, muffled through the wood and somehow wet by the saturation of blood in the air.

Summer whimpered and seized the knob. The door squealed as it opened, and a wall of humidity slammed into her. It was salty and smelled of iron, and as it touched her skin, she felt instantly wet.

She saw a dark, wooden interior; narrow tables lined the opposite wall, workbenches soaked in thick, sticky blood. There was a flicker coming from somewhere inside, but she couldn't see it, couldn't see Mom or Gavin.

"Hello?"

"Summer!" It was Mom. She was in there, and she needed help.

"Mom..." She swallowed her fear and jumped inside.

The door slammed behind Summer, and the shack went dark. From the left, a flicker lit the room, and Summer felt like she had been transported to another place. The walls were deep red, soaked in blood. The ceiling opened to a night sky, but there were no stars; there were flames racing across the sky and forming shapes. A blazing eye looked down upon her.

"Mom!" Trembling, she stepped deeper into the shack.

A fire sat on the floor, but instead of burning wood, it was composed of bones. Around the flames were the bodies of three people, long dead, their corpses aging like mummies. Beside them, she saw Mom, her eyes smashed into her sockets and blood running down her face. There was a skull, horned and black, sitting atop some kind of demonic totem pole. And in the far corners' gloom, visible only when the flames flicked at their highest, were two glowing faces.

They seemed to have no eyes, or none that reflected through the murk. Only red shined. It covered their cheeks and dabbed the tips of their noses. It created an arc across their foreheads, marked with the same letters that had been on the door.

Summer stared from one shadowed figure (Gavin) to the other (Cody) and crept toward Mom. She kneeled beside her and took her hand.

"Mom?"

Mom didn't answer at first. She gasped through deep breaths. Her bloodied hands rested on her knees as she sat cross-legged at the fire. Her head turned slowly toward Summer, then picked up speed, and as she did, her chest heaved faster and faster. Air rushed in and out as if she was preparing for something.

As her eyeless face stared deep into Summer's gaze, a laugh burst from Mom's mouth. As her head leaned back, her cheeks ripped open from the corners of her mouth to the back of her jaw. And she laughed louder.

Fear raced deeper through Summer with each belt of mirth. She tumbled backward onto the cluttered, grimy floor and pushed herself away from this crazed person who had been her mother. The woman who had looked upon her and smiled when she was little. Had taught her a thousand things through lessons and a thousand kindnesses through life. She had been the single best light in her world, even through the bitterness of the last week, and—she couldn't believe this—she was gone, replaced by some sort of cackling thing. And as Summer retreated, the boys in the corners came toward her.

She didn't know what this was, but that thing by the fire was no longer her mother. Blood gushed from its eyes, and blackened teeth ruptured its gums, sprinkling white ones down her chin and into the blaze. A darkness radiated from her body, riding on the wind with her laughter, grabbing onto Summer and shaking, screaming, "You're ours now."

Summer yelped as she rotated, sprang to her feet, and sprinted to the door. She seized the knob and turned and pulled.

It wouldn't open.

"Let me out!"

She yanked, but it wouldn't give. It was a wall of stone, not a simple slab of wood.

Gavin giggled. Cody giggled.

They passed the fire, raising their arms and reaching toward Summer.

Summer screamed. She yanked on the door again. It refused to move.

She watched her brother and the other boy closing in. Their bodies seeped onto the ground, waves of blood flooding from their insides and their clothes as if they had been in that creek. Their fingers grasped, and their mouths opened, revealing the cavernous interiors of their heads.

The panic was electric. It shot into Summer's legs and jerked her forward. If the door wouldn't open, something else would.

She climbed onto the closest workbench and met glances with the eye in the flaming clouds. She grabbed the top of the shack's wall—it was true, it had no roof—and hoisted herself upward. She tugged and climbed.

Hands seized her feet, grabbing, pulling her back into the shack. She kicked them away and rolled over the top of the wall, slamming onto the ground outside.

Something poked her ribs, but she ignored it and rushed away from the shack on hands and knees. She climbed to her feet and ran.

She was in a forest of black trees with black leaves. Black dirt that was stained in dark orange (blood) for as far as she could see. Bones and shards of bone lay scattered across the land.

Summer stopped as she realized this place was nowhere near her A-frame. It didn't look like she was even on the same planet any longer.

"Help!" she bellowed into the wilderness.

She was answered with crashing trees and the ground shaking. Both parted with a deafening eruption of black leaves and soil that filled the air like fog. Then, a beast broke through, leaving Summer breathless and frozen at its indescribable horror.

She closed her eyes, clenching her teeth, her body trembling.

She saw the blood on her hands, the knife, and her father's dead body. What could she do other than wait for death and accept it? She was sure now she was in Hell. It was where she was supposed to be. She should just let it happen.

The noise was like a crashing train. It vibrated the ground as the monster neared.

She only wished she could have helped Gavin. She wished she could have saved Mom.

Heat washed over her. It was coming from that thing; it had to be.

She was ready for it to take her or eat her or whatever it was going to do. What she didn't expect was something to grab her from behind and pull her.

Summer opened her eyes. It was Gavin. It wasn't, but it was. He was malformed and disgusting, but something about him was different—his essence had changed, and he was dragging her back toward the shack.

"Gavin?"

He didn't answer—didn't have time to. The beast from below ground was moving in, and Cody was climbing the wall from inside the shack. She did the only thing she could, what came naturally; she took Gavin by the hand and ran along with him.

She tried to lead them away into the woods, but Gavin refused. He guided her back toward the shack as if it was the only way. It didn't make sense—or did it?

She saw it.

There it was, gleaming in the lock, reflecting the fire in the sky: the key. It hit Summer like a wall; that was the way back. It had been the way here, and now it was the way back.

They reached within ten feet of the shack when Cody lunged and grabbed Gavin by the arm. Gavin shook him, but Cody pulled himself closer and bit into Gavin's shoulder.

Blood ran. Something else seeped from Gavin's wound, a black sludge that only made sense when looking at his distorted face under this demonic sky.

Gavin screamed, and Summer pulled.

The monster swiped with hands the size of cars and lifted Gavin and Cody into its grip. It tried for Summer, and Summer went the only place within reach—she grabbed the knob and turned and leaped through the door.

Summer ached all over. She dreamed of Hell and paying for her sins with blood and pain. When her eyes opened, and the sun shone down through the trees, it was like a miracle—until she saw where she was.

On the ground beside the shack. The key in her hand. Mom and Gavin gone.

It took everything she had to stand and even more to try the door. It opened, but all it held was a dirt-floored old room that had once been someone's little shop in the woods.

She screamed. She cried. She looked at her finger as it throbbed in pain, and she wondered if anything would ever be okay again.

It wouldn't. Without Mom, without Gavin, even without Dad, she was truly alone. But as the day moved on, after trying the door a dozen more times, she understood she had to go back to the A-frame.

Summer stayed at the A-frame for a week. She lasted as long as the food did. She bandaged her finger the best she could, and she tried the key a hundred more times. But once the food was gone and it sunk in that the shack was not going to open on that place again, she understood she had to move on.

It was a lonely morning when she searched the house, found her mom's keys, and started the Escort wagon. She took her copy of Harry Potter, Gavin's word search, and not much more. She didn't want anything else that would remind her of that place.

That life was over. She started a new one when she ran out of gas in Custer Falls.

The Trophy

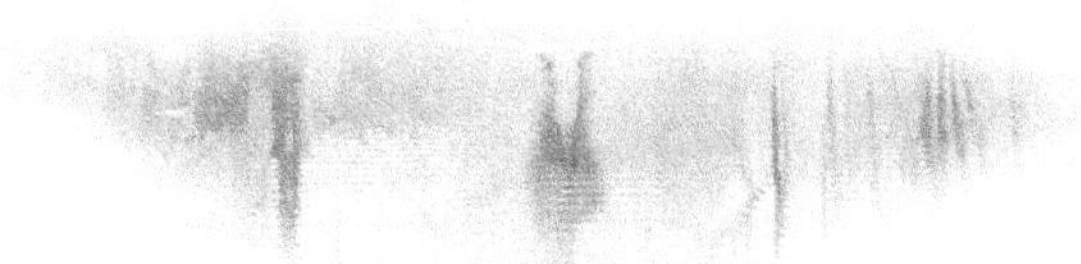

FRANKLIN JONES MIGHT HAVE been drunker than he was on most nights, but that didn't mean the aliens weren't real.

He stared into their bulbous, pink faces, their quad-eyes bright and their smiles deceptively wide, and wondered if they really meant what they'd said. Frank wasn't one to take things at face value. He knew everyone had a motive, everyone had a plan, and everyone was ready to cover their own asses at a moment's notice. So when they said they'd reward him beyond his wildest dreams, he was by nature a bit skeptical.

They examined each other in a moment of thought while the Milky Way hung above, the white noise of the waterfall upstream gently hushing the crackle of Frank's campfire. The residual salty taste of his hot dog dinner and the smell of burning pine reassured him his senses were too sharp for this to be a dream, even with the rolling sensation of drunkenness and the pile of Bud Lite cans.

If only Lil was here, he thought. Lil would have known what to do, and she wouldn't have hesitated. She would have known the second those bastards touched an alien toe on planet Earth whether to let buckshot loose into their faces or smoke a joint with them and say, "Welcome to Earth."

He was pretty damned sure they wanted something out of him—no being would come all this way across the universe just to hand out rewards. But if it was some advice they wanted about his homeworld—the best place to pick huckleberries in northwest Montana, or directions to the White House—or his oh-so-delicious kidneys, he couldn't be sure.

"You know what, fellas…," he started. His intention had been to tell them this wasn't a good time for him to leave the planet, but Frank found himself switching gears mid-sentence. "I'll go with you."

Why not? Lil had left him. That was the whole reason he'd come to Custer Falls—to be alone with a case of domestic piss-water, camp, and swallow his frustration at being dumped. He was mostly there.

"I'll just need to bring that." He pointed at the remaining pair of six-packs peeking through the ice in his open jockey box. "Or do you have beer up there?"

Frank couldn't quite place how he'd gotten where he was. There hadn't been a transporter beam with flashing lights and a swirl of silver sparkles, or a bright white light carrying him away—not that he could remember anyway. But he was in a different place, that he was sure of. And he needed another drink.

There was darkness all around him, but he didn't feel like it was *on* him. He could see his jeans, his red flannel, his six-packs—one in each hand. But the floor, the walls, the ceiling—assuming he was inside—he couldn't see any of it. He couldn't even see his own feet.

Other people began to light up around him. A woman in a long, yellow sun dress. A man in a stained, white tank top. A teenager with a black Marshmello T-shirt. A woman in a business suit. At least a dozen others. They each stood in their own column of light, looking at each other with no visible ground between them and no explanation of what was happening.

Some began shouting. "Who are you people?" "Where are we?" "Where'd the aliens go?"

The Marshmello kid called, "What happened to my bong?"

Frank chuckled at the last one. It reminded him...

He set one six-pack between his feet and pulled a can loose from the other. Frank popped it open and chugged. He'd become very thirsty in the last few minutes and wasn't exactly sure why. Frank also noticed his buzz had dropped from, "I can't even make it to the car," to, "I can handle my shit," and that wasn't right.

He downed the can and tossed it into the blackness as he opened another. It wasn't until he was guzzling the second one that he realized he hadn't heard a sound.

Frank looked in the direction he'd tossed the can, at where the ground should have been. There should have been some glimmer, a small one at least. Even in this darkness, that can should have picked up the ambient light from him and reflected something back.

It didn't.

He frowned. It didn't make sense, but it didn't matter. He continued to tune out the others and finished his beer. This time, though, when he tossed it, he watched.

The can drifted from his hand into an infinite darkness. It traveled down as it left him, not bouncing away, but neither did it impact anything. He saw it pass beyond where the floor should have been and then pass from sight.

Frank's heart skipped a beat. What the fuck had he just watched? A chill crawled over him. As he looked at the nothingness surrounding them, the thought became concrete...that it wasn't just blackness. That *was* actually nothing...

The throbbing in his chest drove him to pop open another can. He chugged, waiting for the dulling coolness to entrench his mind, but instead, he found his mind clearing. The beer had done nothing. His drunkenness had faded to a two-beer buzz.

Frank popped another open and tipped it up. He squeezed the empty can under his arm, terrified to see what might happen if he tossed it. With each rise and fall of his Adam's apple, he felt his buzz fade further.

He'd barely swallowed the last drop, when screams of fear encircled him.

It was like the lights switched on but only for the surrounding fifty feet of altitude. The ceiling was still black, and there were no walls around the twenty or so people Frank could see. But below each person now, the situation became a bit clearer, and Frank was about to shit himself.

Everyone he could see, including himself, stood in the middle of their own two-foot-wide platform. It was black and round, over an abyss like the top of some skyscraper pylon. He stared, wide-eyed. The round structures went down and down, disappearing into the nothing.

Frank was overcome with an immediate need to sit. His legs wobbled, numb. If he was sitting, he couldn't fall. Right?

He lowered himself slowly. Dizziness flooded his brain, and he fought to keep himself vertical, plum, as straight as he could maintain while moving.

A shriek to his right. A woman thumped as her chest slammed against the platform, her legs swinging over the side. Blood flooded over her lip and chin. She grabbed for the edge, and it slipped away from her fingers.

"Jesus!" Frank felt himself tipping to the right as he watched her darken and enter the nothing. She grasped at empty air with bloody fingers, and fright shot through him like lightning. He shuffled back, now squatting over his second six-pack.

Frank listened through the rabble of the others. Maybe he'd hear her hit something? Maybe she'd land on a net and bounce and shout that she was okay?

Her voice faded to silence. It took way too long to do so.

Fuck, he needed a beer. Needed it to do its job.

He tuned out the rest. Frank took his sixer from below him and, with every ounce of focus, placed his ass against the base of the platform. He crossed his legs and tented his arms behind him.

Frank's head swelled with pressure. His fingers shook against his rest. He wanted to open a beer but feared he might tumble backward without his arm propping him up.

Frank looked at the others.

Many had taken the same approach as him, sitting on their platforms. The kid in the Marshmello T-shirt sat on the edge, his legs dangling over. Frank's dizziness grew looking at that asshole.

The woman in the sundress held her knees to her chest, face buried. Frank thought he could hear her whimper.

Stained Tank Top Guy was on his hands and knees, peering over the edge. Frank shook his head. That was no way to sit. He imagined the guy slipping and cartwheeling ahead.

After a minute, Frank's heart slowed enough that his body wasn't shaking along with it. He tilted upright and opened a beer. A few others turned and stared.

"Please, God, Jesus, Mohammad, whoever the fuck's up there, let this work?" Frank drank and spit. Liquid dribbled from his chin. Clear, tasteless liquid. "Fucking water?" He threw the can into the nothing. The few watching him tracked it as it fell, making not a single sound.

"What is going on?" the woman in the business suit shouted.

Frank was ready to find out himself. Whatever this was, he was growing more and more sure the reward of something beyond his wildest dreams wasn't going to cut it.

"Humans," a voice bellowed from somewhere above. It crackled, sounding hoarse and somewhat wet simultaneously. "We shall now begin."

"What the hell?" Frank muttered. He scanned the others. Each looked up to find the voice, then around as they failed.

"We have a great gift for your race," the voice continued, "but only one may receive it. Win the contest, and it shall be yours."

"How about you fuckers just send me home instead?" Frank yelled.

"Let us out!" the sundress woman cried.

"I don't want to play," an accountant-looking guy said on Frank's left.

There was no answer from the alien.

A rumble descended from above. It was deep, shaking every atom of Frank's body.

Frank's fellow contestants shouted. "What's that?" "Do you hear it?" "What are they doing?"

Frank felt his gut tighten. He thought he knew what it was. His heart raced as he looked up, then down, then up again.

The rumble grew louder. The platform below Frank shook with it, reverberating up his spine.

"Oh no!" someone cried.

The ceiling showed itself. It wasn't that the room had become lighter, that some part of the gloom had lifted.

No, the ceiling was lowering over them.

Frank's lips twitched as he watched, gauging how much time was left in his miserable excuse for a life. How much longer did he have to miss Lil, to regret not spending time with his kid in South Dakota, who he'd always said was too far away to visit. He could have visited her this weekend. That time would have been better spent than this.

"It's going to kill us!" Sundress said.

"It'll smash us flat!" a guy in camo shouted.

"What do we do? Anyone know what to do?" Business Suit said.

Ten feet, Frank guessed. That was all the space between himself and becoming a meat pancake. He fumbled with the cans. Why couldn't he at least die with a single beer? What kind of sick shit was this, to make him face his maker sober?

Six feet. The few who had been left standing were now seated. Eyes scanned up and down. They looked into the abyss and judged the ceiling.

"It's a trick. It has to be." "Do we jump? Maybe there's a net, and we just can't see it?" "Maybe the roof's soft and won't kill us?"

Dirty Tank Top stood and felt along the ceiling. He punched it, cussing and bringing down bloodied knuckles.

Four feet. Someone jumped. They screamed as they fell, the others watching, listening for a safe landing. None came.

Three feet. Another jumper. Another. Screams filled the immense empty space. Another.

An idea occurred to Frank. He took off his flannel and lay on his belly.

Howls of pain came from somewhere. Frank didn't try to see. Too little time.

Frank extended his arms, the end of one sleeve in each. He lowered himself over the platform's edge, stretching his flannel around the opposite side, the way he'd seen old lumberjacks climb trees using a strap to hold onto the trunk.

Some screams faded into the nothing below. Some soared as the ceiling pressed the top of Frank's head, pushing him downward.

"Hold, goddammit, hold," he commanded his flannel. It was just a ten-dollar piece of cotton, a stupid Walmart knock-off of an Eddie Bauer shirt—and right now, it was all that stood between life and plummeting to his death. He wished he'd bought better clothes. He wished he'd spent money for once in his life on something that would have mattered.

His fists clenched with everything he had. The fabric stretched. The sounds of tiny threads popping stung his ears.

A scream to his right. He looked this time.

Sundress was being crushed by the ceiling. Too scared to jump, no plan to hold on, she was lying flat against the platform, and it was crushing her like a hydraulic press.

Cracks came from her ribs. Her scream stopped, but her arms flailed. Was there no air left in her lungs? Frank wanted to look away, but something held his face still. The sides of her dress flooded with crimson, then poked outward. Shards of red bone ripped through, and her limbs stilled.

"God...," Frank mumbled.

The ceiling crushed her neck, ripping the top of her head from her throat and jaw, leaving it dangling over the side.

There was a pop over Frank's head, and beer exploded outward, raining over him. It stank of stale suds, which he wouldn't have minded, if only it didn't taste like water. Just fucking water.

A scream from his left.

Stained Tank Top hung from his platform from the tips of his fingers. Fingers that were now being crushed. The ceiling flattened the ends of eight digits, their skin and bone jutting outward in a burst of pulp, ripping his hands free. Tank Top drifted down into the black. Only, he was done screaming. He watched the darkness come, his hands outward, spraying blood into the nothing as he fell.

"Fuck!" Frank yelled.

There was a break in the rumble, in the screaming.

"Hello?" someone called.

Frank couldn't see who it was. They must have been on the other side of his pylon. "Yeah!"

"What do we do?" the other voice said. It sounded like a man, but its fear didn't allow for an answer.

Frank was already moving downward. His fingers ached in their muscles and burned in their joints. And he had no idea how long his Walmart shirt would hold his weight. The best he could figure, that bottomless pit couldn't be truly bottomless, and he needed to get down before he fell down.

"I'm going to the bottom," Frank answered.

"All the way down there?"

Frank didn't answer. He had enough to deal with without answering dumb-ass questions.

As Frank descended, the pillar he hung from grew rougher. Vertical grooves bulged from the surface, which at first reminded him of corduroy, but the lower he went, the thicker they became. He could no longer see the pillar and could barely see the top. Frank felt with his feet, and when his hands brushed the sides, the grooves were growing wider...and wetter.

The other voice had kept going for a while. Once the guy—he guessed at this point—had figured out he wasn't alone, he wouldn't shut up for a good twenty minutes. After Frank had successfully ignored the initial barrage, he'd gotten a lot less chatty, except for the occasional commentary: "This is really high." "What do you think's at the bottom?" "God, my arms are tired." "How did you get off the pillar?"

The sound of a drip tickled Frank's ears. It was quiet, not even registering at first. When it did, the shock ran up and down his spine like a pinball. He nearly dropped his sleeves, he was so happy. Just that little sound was all it took. A drop of water hitting something and singing, "There's something down here!"

"You hear that?" Frank asked. It was the first time he'd initiated a conversation, and for God's sake, he needed to know that sound wasn't just him losing his mind. "Hear it?"

"Hear what?" There was a moment of nothing, then...*drip*.

Frank found himself hurrying. He leaned in, dropped the shirt down, and walked his body lower. Again, and again.

Drip.

It was the most fantastic sound ever.

"I heard it!" the other guy shouted.

Frank found himself moving down faster and faster. The drip became louder, and the sound of tearing fabric arose from his flannel, and he kept moving. The idea flashed in his mind that he needed to slow. The flannel could rip.

No, he argued, we're almost to the ground. If it rips, so what? But what if it wasn't the ground?

Another flash, but this time an image. A drop of water collided with a ledge, just a small extension of the strange pillar he was moving down. The ledge collected the water and shuttled it to the side, dropping it again into another infinite abyss.

Frank froze. Was this part a trick too? Another mind game from these goddamn aliens, like the amazing-lowering-ceiling? To see who would kill themselves racing to the floor?

Fuck that. He wasn't going to fall for it. Though, they did say only one of them could win.

He continued down, hastily but under more control. The shirt whined less, and while he still refused to look down into the blackness, he let himself hope the dripping sound was salvation.

"Almost there!" the guy shouted. "I hear it."

Good. You see first if it's a ledge or a pond or a dripping vat of acid we're racing toward.

"I'm—" The guy's words halted, replaced with the sound of retching and a much larger splash than the drip.

"You okay?" Frank ventured a look down to his right. He spotted shiny movement.

Something was down there, not just a ledge.

"Ya...yeah." Splashing. "I just got sick."

Why the hell was he getting sick? "Is it safe?"

"I think so."

Frank let himself drop faster. He glanced down. It was like a lake. Black liquid with white ripples, shining peaks of tiny waves from some unknown and unseeable light source.

A little further, his foot splashed through a few inches of wetness, setting down on a solid floor. His arms were on fire. His fingers threatened to never work again and curled in on themselves, cramping from the repeated strain.

A smell filled Frank's nose, a thick, pungent odor that seemed to cling to his lungs as it traveled down into his chest. It was like a spoiled fridge, old meat that was moldy and rancid. It reminded him of the time the cabinet under his sink flooded, and it took him a few days to realize it. By the time he looked, there were three mouse traps with crushed mice, their furry bodies gnarled in fungus and decomposition.

Frank wanted to puke. He looked around—nothing but water—and the thought of his puke floating back into him made him gag.

That was when he noticed the sounds. Smacking and slurping, like something wet inside a garbage bag and someone licking and loving it.

What the hell was going on down here? He really needed a beer.

With a flash, red light bathed as far as he could see. The initial brightness forced his eyes shut. When he opened them, fear shot through his veins, standing his hair on end.

The bodies of the fallen littered the wet ground. Arms broken, legs twisted in inhuman angles. Some were in pieces, shattered and turned to pulp from the impact. But worse than that, in the harsh red glow, they wriggled with movement as things tore into them.

Beasts the size of bears, at least six he could see, tusks and mandibles ripping and slashing. They gorged and snorted, and Frank pissed himself where he stood.

One was close. At the base of the next pillar, it stabbed what Frank now recognized as the remains of Stained Tank Top. It jerked its head, and a chunk of skin and fat soared through the air and slapped Frank on the arm. The creature's gaze followed its meal. It looked up with a single cluster of black eyes and met Frank's stare.

Fuck, no. His entire body shook. His heart pounded in his ears.

The thing turned and took a step toward him. It lumbered, lifting its foot to walk, massive spikes on its feet breaching the water's surface and sinking again. It was coming for him. It wanted him next.

Frank stared back at the five, six, seven black eyes, merged and pulsing; they resembled goo-filled sacks. Some kind of flaps hung from its head. First, they simply swung with its steps, but as it neared, Frank saw appendages hanging below them. They were like tiny two-fingered arms with shiny claws.

A scream echoed from around Frank's pillar. It was somewhat in the direction of his climbing friend, but now with the lights, with these things surrounding him, he wasn't sure which way was which.

"Monsters! They're fucking monsters!" It was the guy. Splashes. Feet slamming into the liquid floor. He was running.

The thing in front of Frank glanced at the noise, and Frank froze. He held his breath. His heart pounded. The beast sprung from its stance, like a lion or jaguar, around the side of the pillar. Every other beast leaped in the same direction.

The man screamed, "No! Get away! No."

There was splashing. Tromping through the strange liquid.

Frank turned and leaned beyond the pillar. He saw the man and recognized him from the top of the platforms. The guy wore a white button-up shirt, stained from whatever liquid was seeping from the pillars, and a pair of suit pants that looked black in the red light. There must have been a dozen creatures chasing him.

One of the beasts launched into the air, and Frank heard himself gasp. It landed on the man's back, its long claws splitting the flesh and hooking into ribs and pelvis. He was like a toy to it. The man crumpled under the weight onto his knees, then his face splashed into the murk. A bubbling scream echoed in the giant space, and three other monsters seized his arms and a leg.

They sunk their pincers into his limbs and pulled, like some alien tug of war.

The man gurgled and coughed. He spat as if to scream again, but as his limbs tore free, it turned into a watery wail.

Fuck! Frank backed away. He lifted his feet slowly, careful not to splash, not to make any sounds at all. His eyes refused to leave the beasts.

Blood arced through the air as they rent and tore, and Frank just knew that if his eyes left them, they'd know. He had this strange knowledge—they were performing for him. They wanted him scared. They wanted him terrified. If he were to show them he was no longer interested, they'd revolt and come right for him.

Three beasts grabbed the opposite ends of the torn limbs and tugged against their predecessors. Two more monsters sank their mouths into the remaining leg and split it along its length, leaving bone and gushing blood to sprout from his hip.

Something hard thumped Frank's back. A jolt ran through his system, and he spun. He knew it would be one of them, or something worse. He pictured fangs and pincers, bloody claws and breath smelling of decay.

It was a pillar.

A small laugh leaked from his lips. He heard a splash in the water behind him.

"No," he mumbled. He'd fucked up. He'd looked away. He'd laughed, and they knew he was there and ready for the taking.

Frank didn't chance turning and looking. He pushed himself off the column and ran.

No more cautionary steps. Each stride plunged his feet into the murk and thrust him forward. Water splashed and dripped back down. It tinkled against the surface of the black pool, like rain against a calm lake on a misty winter day. It screamed his location. It called to the beasts yet to follow, saying, "The meal's over here! Come and get it!" but Frank had no other choice. His control was gone. His fight was gone. All that was left was flight.

Splash-thump, splash-thump. Pairs of footfalls crashed into the pond behind him. Frank pumped his legs and forced himself faster. His sore hands, clenched into fists, raced forward and back in a madman's swing. He pushed with the knowledge that he was already dead—they just hadn't reached him yet.

Frank called into the distance, howling like a beast. Air rushed in and out of his lungs. He felt the damp, soiled atmosphere brush over his cheeks as he cut through the forest of pillars.

Until the world shifted.

Step after step, he felt the liquid's depth shallow. He was rising from it. Frank passed the last pillar. A bank of red fog lay ahead, but the splashing was still back there. He heard it right behind him, felt hot breath on his heels. Frank searched the fog and wanted to cry, spotting what looked like a door ahead.

Was that the end of this test? Was that where he'd enter and get his reward? For an instant, he saw himself going through it, slipping the monster's grasp, and being given the greatest gift. It would be one that no other human had achieved. It would be the most important accomplishment of his life. And with that thought, he decided he wasn't these things' next meal. He was going to make it.

Frank grunted and forced his legs to move faster, harder. He was getting closer, maybe within ten feet, and slammed his shoes into the dry ground, his wet soles sloshing.

Six feet left. Frank raised his hand toward the door. He was going to make it. But the *splash-thump* of the thing behind him had dried to simply *thump-thump*, *thump-thump*, and it was ever so close.

Another stride. Frank could taste the freedom. He could feel his safety just ahead. His reach extended. The beast's gallop went silent.

Frank's hand touched the door. It slid open, its movement making less noise than the gust of fresh, clean air rushing from the other side.

He'd done it. He'd made it. One more step.

Burning pain burst from Frank's leg. He toppled through the door, screaming, trying to understand what was happening. His face hit the floor. Hard, cool, slick like steel, it smashed into his skin. He felt a crack in his cheekbone and tested blood.

A sound like growling from behind him. He tried to crawl away but couldn't. Frank was caught on something, half in and half out of the doorway. He rolled to his right. Overcome with a wall of burning pain, he saw the monster's pincers deep in his leg. Blood streamed along the beast's points from the depths of Frank's upper thigh. It yanked on him, jerked, and he hopped two inches toward it.

"No!" Frank saw what would happen if he didn't get away. He saw himself ripped to shreds. His mind flashed to the attack on that guy. Two beasts fighting over hunks of flesh, like angry dogs with a toy.

He couldn't be that, not when he was so close.

Frank lifted his other leg and slammed his foot into the door frame. He pushed, trying to pry his limb from the monster. If he could shove hard enough, it might relent. It might get tired and let him go.

"Leave me alone!" he screeched and fought.

It didn't. It clamped down and pulled harder.

He heard ripping. The sound of his flesh being torn echoed inside his ears. It was foreign at first, a strange noise, like wet paper tearing in the distance. And then everything was in the distance.

Blood poured from him. His mind tired, nothing left to give as his body drained. The room was darkening. The growl of the beast lessening.

He felt himself slip, and reality jolted back to him. No. Frank looked down and saw the gashes in his flesh, deep in his muscle, white femur shining back at him.

"Fuck!" He thrust harder with his free leg.

There was a wet crack. Frank pushed himself free. He rolled away from the door and heard the faint *thump-thump* slipping away.

The pain in Frank's leg had gone. He looked down and saw his entire limb was missing. A short, fleshy stump protruded in its place. It extended just a few inches from his crotch, out of his shredded and stained pants.

He rocked forward and sat. "What the fuck!" Frank stared where his appendage should have been. He still felt it. It felt cold, like it had been out of the covers, and he needed to bundle it back up. Despite the feeling, his eyes demanded it was gone.

He reached hesitantly down and touched the end of the stump. Shivers flew down his spine as his finger made contact.

"What did you do?" Frank screamed.

"We saved your life   for the time being." It was the pink alien. He stood behind Frank, staring down with all four of his eyes blinking in sync. His grin was just as wide as it had been when this all started. "You would have bled to death had we not intervened."

Frank looked at the nub again. The ripping noise, the sound of his flesh being torn, it resonated in his mind. He trembled.

"Don't worry," the alien said. He leaned down, and before Frank could protest, he slid a metallic cup over the stump. "You won. And this will help."

As the alien withdrew a step, the cup tightened over Frank's stump. It felt tingly and just a bit itchy. It extended several inches, then turned and extended several more. Once it had grown to nearly the length of his other leg, it turned, growing a few more inches before stopping.

Frank couldn't believe what he was seeing. It was like some sci-fi show based on a really cool book he would never have had the time to read. The alien's cup had become a prosthetic leg, and as he thought about moving it, it moved for him. A robot leg?

Relief flooded through Frank. He was going to get the prize. He'd go down in the history books. He was going to be famous.

"Now come this way." The alien turned and walked toward a door on the opposite side of the room.

Frank swiveled his new robotic foot. He expected to hear gears and pistons whir, but it was silent. *Well, goddamn.* He stood and rocked back and forth, figuring out how to balance. It was amazing. In just seconds, he was walking, following the alien through the other door.

Like the first room, the ceiling of this new space was out of sight. Frank gazed into the infinite black above and tried to keep pace with the pink alien.

"So, do I get the reward now? Or, can I celebrate with a beer?" Frank wouldn't admit it to his new friend, but at this point, he would almost take a beer over his prize.

"Just ahead." The alien didn't look back.

When Frank's gaze rejoined the ground, they were approaching something resembling a stage. On it were at least a dozen objects, each shaped the same—a four-foot-tall, twisted, tree-looking design but in different colors.

"What are those?" He walked up to the side of the stage and had a closer look. There was a red one, a brown one, a blue one, even a green one. Frank examined the surface of one of the objects, and he felt a tingle at the back of his neck. Something didn't feel right about these things.

Bumps and lines ran across what he now thought might have been a sculpture. It was smooth, then rippled, the circles and layers of multiple materials pressed into a trunk and spreading limbs.

Frank looked at the next one. It was blue. He saw variations in the color. In some places were spots of white, small flecks of red.

No, whatever this was, it was *not* good.

A feeling shifted in his gut. It warned, then screamed after it felt he wasn't listening. "Get out of here!" it said. "Forget the prize! Turn your ass around and get the fuck out!"

He took a step backward. His new leg didn't listen. It remained stiff, and he nearly tripped.

"This way," the alien said.

Frank held his ground. "Wait. What are these?"

"They're winners." The words left the pink alien's mouth with the condescension of an older child lecturing his bratty younger sibling.

"Winners...?" Frank gazed at the next one. Was that smoothness...

skin? Were those layers... organs? Spots...bones? "Fuck!"

The alien gazed down at him curiously.

What was left in Frank's stomach hurled onto the floor. He tried to move, to back away from the alien, but his leg didn't respond. Frank tried and failed again. It wasn't that it wouldn't obey him; the thing was stuck, as if it were sealed against the floor.

"Let go of me!"

The alien made a sound. It was almost like a chuckle, except a high-pitched noise whistled through the sides of its head.

"This way," the alien repeated. He walked toward the end of the stage.

Frank felt himself being pulled. He skated across the floor. Something dragged him behind the pink bastard. "Let go of me!"

At the end of the stage, there was a solid black box the height of a man. It split down the center and opened. Inside, Frank watched what could have been a mold for the objects on stage. A negative shape, silver tunnels, branches, a trunk. It all collapsed into the outer shell, sucking itself in, the silver form melting into the box.

"Inside." The alien gestured, sweeping his arm toward the container.

"Fuck no," Frank shouted. "I'm not going in there. I'm not a piece of..." His mind raced, fear clouding his thoughts. All he could imagine was those walls closing in, the silver insides crushing his bones, his flesh, clamping him into the shape of some alien tree-trophy-whatever. The word shined like neon. "Clay. I'm not here for you to mold me."

Frank was dragged, his feet scraping the ground. His arms flailed. He was being pulled forward by an invisible force, and as much as he fought, he just kept moving. Frank was going inside the forge, whether he wanted to or not.

He thought of his home. He should have stayed home. Why did he go camping? Because of Lil. God, Lil... He wished he was with her instead of here. Anywhere but here.

Frank pressed harder into the ground with the tip of his functional foot. It slid, the sole skipping across the smooth metallic floor.

"Stop! Please!"

He slid closer and closer, and as he reached a few feet from the chamber, he noticed what was on its floor. But it couldn't be. Could it?

In the middle of the silver space, on the shiny, polished floor, was a single can of beer.

Frank burst with laughter. It was silly, crazy, then maniacal. It took over his entire body, shuddering through him. Frank stopped fighting. He leaned forward, his gut in pain from the clench of his hysterics. By the time he realized it, he was standing inside the box.

Tears ran down his cheeks.

The box closed. He watched the smug look on the alien's face as the enclosure sealed, and Frank could do nothing but laugh.

There was a deafening clunk. The box locked, ready. Frank picked up the beer and looked at it.

He stopped laughing.

On The Run
One

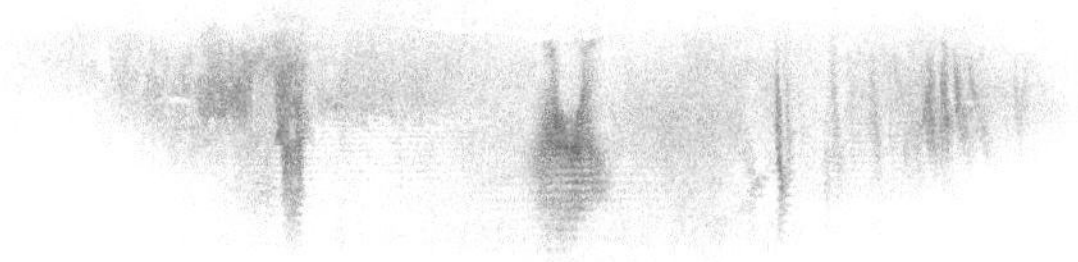

TAYLOR HAD SLOWED THE bleeding from the entrance wound, but the bullet's exit was harder to seal. She pressed the frayed cloth under Jacob's leg, watching it soak even as she tightened the strip of ripped T-shirt around his thigh.

There had to be a nicked vessel in there. The bleeding was too slow to be severed and too fast for just an open wound. She was no doctor, not even a nurse, but back in another life, she was a Girl Scout with a merit badge for first aid. She hoped that would be enough.

The crew had fled the job over an hour ago with no sirens behind them. It should have been a good haul—if only the entire thing hadn't gone pear-shaped in the last two minutes.

There they were, bags of jewelry in their hands, ready to dash, and some wannabe hero with a concealed nine had to go John Wick on them. Mike and Maria, dead. Jacob, a shot through the leg. Then Little Stevie—fuck, she didn't even want to replay that back in her mind—the man let loose with the shotgun. The salesman, a hole in his face from front to back and his head lolled as he dropped. The mom and baby in the corner, there was so little left they could have shared a kid-sized coffin. The Wick-imitator, not a limb remaining. The only reason Stevie stopped shooting was his magazine went dry, then Big Steve hauled him out the front door.

God, it was a cluster fuck.

Taylor had never been so glad she was the driver, though making the rest of them wait for Jacob to limp his ass to the van almost got her shot.

They were down to six. And she only trusted herself and Jacob.

Now, Big Steve, fifty-six, drove, his fists twisting, strangling the steering wheel as the miles flew past. His wife, Loretta, also fifty-six, sat in the passenger seat, tapping at the armrests ceaselessly. Little Stevie, twenty-three, spun a hunting knife in his palm behind his father, staring at the cars that passed in the fast lane and flinching every time he saw a passenger he wanted to play with. Honey, twenty-four, whose name Taylor was pretty sure was chosen when she started stripping at fifteen, played with her golden hair, tracing it down the neckline of her halter top and into her cleavage, then out, then did it all over again.

It was a confined space of pent-up energy and rage with the little bit of loot they were able to get away with stuffed under the center console's grimy junk. A map from Utah dated 1997. A yellowed owner's manual for the brown 1995 Ford passenger van. A registration (forged) under the name of Steven Offgood of Pierre, South Dakota.

None of the front passengers ventured a look back. At this point, none cared if Jacob made it or not. His loss just meant a slightly higher cut of the few gems they'd gotten away with, a small stash Big Steve said they'd go through once they reached the cabin in western Montana, where they'd planned to lay low for two weeks before moving on.

Taylor wasn't sure Jacob would make it two weeks. She wasn't sure he'd make it to the cabin at this point, not if they drove the whole way through the state without stopping like Big Steve had said.

She needed water, a sewing kit, and a basic first aid kit at a minimum, and Steve had refused to stop every time she'd asked. They passed Rapid City, and the answer was *No*. They passed Gillette and again, it was *No*. They'd gone through Sheridan, Crow Agency, and Hardin, and every time it was *No, No,* and *No*. When they neared Billings, and Taylor could see the fuel gauge hanging near *E*, she begged, "I know we have to stop anyway. Just let me grab water and a first aid kit in the gas station."

Stevie turned in his seat as they pulled up to the pumps. He rotated his knife as he looked at the floor of the last row. Jacob's eyes were closed.

"You sure he isn't dead already?"

Taylor saw him as clearly as she had through the glass wall of the jewelry store. She saw the hunger in his eyes, the glossy sheen of corruption, and the grin that went with it. It was chilling in a way she hadn't encountered before. It was a craze, a bloodlust she thought only existed in movies and psychopaths like Bundy or Gacy. How the fuck did they get involved with such lunatics? She'd known this crew was on the edge, a little out there, but now—how had she let Jacob talk her into this—

She remembered last night, Jacob rubbing her belly, the bump not yet showing. They needed a nest egg, something to get them started on the next phase of their lives—that was why.

Taylor scowled at Stevie, but she didn't move her hand from the wound. She didn't want to chance releasing the pressure.

"Steve?" She really needed him to say yes.

The big man turned in his seat and looked her in the eye, judging, summing up her intent and ability. He turned to his wife. "Retta, see if you can find what she needs in there." Back to Taylor. "Dear, you're covered in blood. You can't go in there. You two neither." He pointed to Stevie and Honey. He got out and started pumping.

Taylor watched Loretta cross the lot and go inside, and she prayed they would have the supplies.

Hard-packed and refrozen snow crunched under knobby rubber as Melissa Cambridge stopped her quad at the top of the soft ridge. It was a good vantage point along the east pasture that let her gaze down at her daddy's herd. All thirty head of Angus were gathered around the two round feeders. The mothers-to-be were feisty today, pushing hard to get their shares of hay, their bellies stiff and ready to pop. She thought of the calving season's fast approach and smiled. The faces of those little guys always made her smile, and she doubted if it would be a whole two weeks before they started making their appearances.

She paused, wondering how many babies she'd seen on this ranch over the eighteen years before she left for college. She didn't know if she could count that high. She remembered Dad looking over them, all heart, concerned with each life, not just the dollars those babies represented. That was back when the fields were full—back when Dad was healthy and could manage them. Thirty head was the smallest she had ever seen the herd.

The smile dropped from her face.

"You have to help him... at least until the auction in the spring... then we can sell them all at once." There was sadness in Mom's voice that day. Mom knew what she was asking—asking Melissa to abandon her third year at Montana State, possibly ruining her entire college education if she wasn't able to make it back by fall. But Mom knew she wouldn't say no. That's why she called her and not Matt. Matt would have just told her to call the McGregors and have them all slaughtered—it would have added up to a quarter of the price, and a man dying from cancer needs

every dollar he can squeeze out.

She started the quad back up and headed toward the house. She saw herself riding this old thing, sitting between Dad's legs, the wind in her face, and loving every minute. She clenched hard on the handles.

Melissa rounded the copse of ponderosas that flanked the barn and parked beside the line of vehicles in the driveway: her old beater of a Honda, bought to simply run around Bozeman once she no longer had to live on campus; Dad's old F250, so rusted it was hard to tell where the corrosion ended and the brown paint began; and Mom's little Isuzu, which, remarkably, looked almost brand new when it was wet and glossy.

She brought the quad's key in her coat pocket—it was likely going to freeze tonight, and the last thing she wanted was to come out to a frozen starter in the morning—and she climbed the steps to the wooden porch that wrapped around the house.

The smell of stew was seeping through the cracks around the door, and a thousand memories hit Melissa before her hand touched the knob. Swinging on the corner bench with Matty, with Mom, with Dad, with Jeffry Lions, her prom date—and the day they had to take it down because it had become too splintered and too far gone to repair.

She saw herself hiding underneath the porch when all the cousins came over for Easter in '07, and she wondered how the hell she wasn't bitten by a black widow or brown recluse while she covered her mouth and held her breath to keep from being found.

She saw the smile on Dad's face as he stood in that door frame every day while she was walking up the driveway from the bus. Always. Rain, shine, snow, it didn't matter. And she knew it hurt him more than anything that she was missing college right now to be here. But with so little time and so little healthy lung left in his chest, she knew she was in the right place. When he died, she would be with him, not a hundred miles away. She wouldn't hear about it from a phone call. She would get to say goodbye.

School would wait.

She had to help take that swing down, she thought once again.

She wiped the tears from her eyes before going inside.

Two

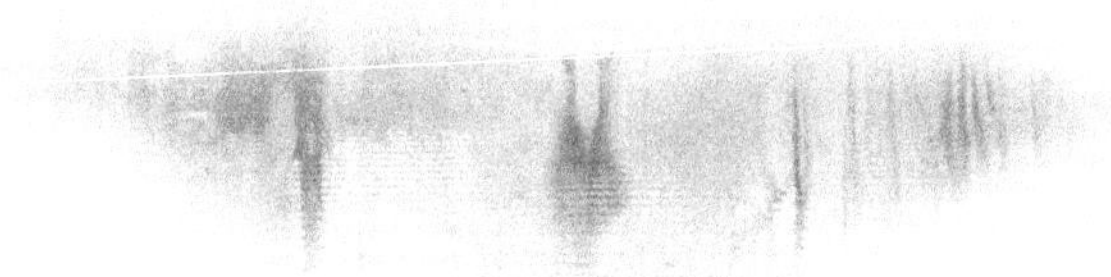

TAYLOR WAS FINALLY ABLE to sit and rest on the van's back row seat. Her hands were sore and caked in Jacob's blood, but he was bandaged, and, for now at least, the bleeding was under control.

He lay on the floor in front of her, eyes closed, passed out but still breathing. Taylor hoped he was dreaming something good, because the way things were going, they needed some kind of respite.

The sun was behind the mountains, and the back road Big Steve had taken them on was much rougher than the interstate had been. It was a squirrelly, two-lane drag that wove between ranches and hills. Potholes and patches shook the van every few minutes, and Taylor was amazed Jacob could sleep through it all.

Her eyes went from him to the mountains to the endless spaces filled with cows or pine. She imagined what it would be like living out here, away from the stresses and aggravations of living in the city. Having a nice, peaceful existence away from the scum she'd had to do this job with, away from the psychos in the seats in front of her. She unconsciously rubbed her belly and thought of kids playing in those fields without a care in the world. Hair fluttering in the breeze. Mud on their knees. Smiles on their faces. Living free of the concerns their parents had to face to keep food on the table and the wolves at bay.

That would be nice for her little one.

Maybe if the robbery had worked, they could have afforded something—not quite the size of these thousand-acre ranches, but something. But no. That wasn't how it turned out.

She thought of her childhood in the section eight complex, the threadbare sheets, the empty cupboards, the windows that never quite shut, and the dozens of times her apartment was robbed for the meager items they had. That was what her kid was destined for now. She and Jacob had tried and failed to do something to raise themselves from their hole, and now, she just didn't think there would ever be a way out. They may be on the run for who knew how long, and with his leg in the condition it was in, they were at the mercy of Big Steve and the gang for the time being.

It all seemed so hopeless.

Her gaze found a wooden ranch house down a long driveway, and sadness drenched her mind. It was a pleasant-looking home, not extravagant, and she wanted to weep that she would never be able to offer her baby something so *normal*.

That was when the engine sputtered and died.

"Goddammit!" Big Steve growled from the driver's seat. He fought with the wheel—the power steering having died along with the motor—and pulled the van over to the shoulder. Once the vehicle was stopped, he shook his head and opened the center console.

Taylor's stomach dropped. She knew what was in that console other than the loot. This wasn't good.

"What's going on?" She forced her voice to the front, disguising the fear that swelled within. They weren't at the safe house yet, far from it. They hadn't been spotted by the cops, but she knew the BOLOs were out. It was only a matter of time until they would be seen by the wrong person if they were stopped on the side of the road, even one as lonely as this.

And Big Steve was pulling his pistol from the console.

"Engine's dead." He gave his head another shake and turned to face the entire crew. "The light came on a while back, but I was hoping it would last the rest of the trip. But that's how shit rolls sometimes."

He looked each passenger in the eye, one at a time.

"We're going to push this thing into the next driveway, and then we'll have to *borrow* a new vehicle. Everyone out. Retta, you steer."

Honey opened the sliding door and jumped out. Stevie followed. Taylor glanced down at Jacob and stepped over him to join the others. As her foot touched the ground, her eyes traced the driveway ahead. It went to the house she had just been admiring. Big Steve's words rang in her ears: "We'll have to *borrow* a new vehicle." She saw the lights on, amber beacons behind closed, sheer curtains, and she wanted to cry. She knew the hell that was about to head that way.

"What about him?" Stevie said to Big Steve as he gestured toward Jacob. "He don't have to push?"

Big Steve's eyes went up and down the road. Still no cars in sight. "Just get back there."

Four sets of hands pressed against the back of the van, the Steves on the outside and the girls in the middle, and they pushed. It was like a wall at first, then slowly it gave way and rolled.

Taylor kept her gaze on the ground, not eager to be face to face with either Little Stevie or his girlfriend. The rocks glimmered in the fading light. Then there was dusty asphalt, cracked and pale, its paint faded to nearly nothing, then she felt the van turn and go over a bump (the driveway threshold), then a rumble (a cattle grate), and she saw the fence posts on either side of the path. The grade angled upward, and it was like they were pushing against a wall again.

"Retta, hit the brake!" Steve called up the side of the van, and it stopped cold. He was out of breath as he pointed up the long driveway to the vehicles in front of the house. "We can use that pickup to haul it the rest of the way. No need to kill ourselves over this."

But kill them for it, Taylor thought. A chill washed over her.

"Let's go," the big man motioned, and the five of them walked toward the ranch.

Melissa watched diced potatoes and carrots bob in the bowl she held over her lap. Dad was in his chair to her right, adjusting his oxygen tube so he wouldn't get any dinner on it. Mom walked in from the kitchen, sat on the couch between them, set her bowl on the coffee table, and held out a hand to each of them.

Dad took a hand and Melissa the other. He grumbled and wheezed and spoke, "Thank you, God, for this food..."

Melissa tuned out. The last thing she could do right now was listen to her father thank God while he struggled to breathe. He spoke in a guttural tone, phlegm vibrating with every syllable. She loved his strength, though she hated that he pushed on. *God really thinks a lot of you, doesn't he? Blessing a man with stage IV lung cancer and still expecting to be thanked.*

She clenched her eyes tight, holding back the tears.

"Amen," her father choked out. Mom repeated. Melissa couldn't force the word out.

Mom picked up Dad's tray and set it on his lap. She raised her bowl and grasped her spoon, and footfalls thudded in the kitchen. Then the bedroom hallway. Then the front door swung open, and in stepped a man.

Melissa stood, her soup crashing to the floor, and her bowl exploded on the hardwood. She felt the weight of the world collapsing in on her. Yes, she had heard those other steps, and she knew she was surrounded by the sound alone, but the sight of this man grabbed hold of her insides and held her in place.

He had to be six-six, a broad, brute of a man. His head was salt and pepper gray, but there wasn't an inch of him that could be mistaken for old or feeble. The stubble over his chin looked like it could sand down rust, and the darkness in his deep blue eyes pierced into Melissa's mind. It was all she could do to hold herself back from trembling.

Mom shrieked. Her head was on a pivot between Big Steve at the front door, the son and girlfriend strolling in from the kitchen, and Loretta and Taylor walking in from the bedroom hallway. All of them had guns. All but Taylor had a look on their faces that read danger, meanness, and death.

Melissa opened her mouth and started, "What do you—"

Steve lunged forward, his right arm swinging. There was a crack as the side of his pistol slammed into Melissa's jaw. A stream of blood drifted, following her down as she dropped.

"Bastard!" Dad flung open the drawer of the end table that held his oxygen machine. He withdrew a shiny .45 caliber pistol, not taking a single breath and moving as quickly as a man half his age.

A shot came from the kitchen. Dad's chest burst with a flower of crimson as his gun screamed. The flame reached across the table but flew wide, and splinters exploded from the door frame.

Another shot from the kitchen, and Dad coughed blood as his gun dropped.

"Terrance!" Mom reached for him, but she didn't get up. Her legs were frozen in place, and her heart pounded inside her chest, making her body feel hollow, like nothing but a container for the throbbing at her center. "Terry?"

Dad collapsed in on himself.

Melissa stood, and Big Steve slapped her hard with his free hand, tossing her back onto the couch. She saw Dad, blood streaming from his nose and his mouth, his eyes locked open but unfocused, and she knew he was gone—he was dead, not gone. He was no longer on this planet with her, and while she knew it was coming from that god damned disease, it wasn't supposed to happen yet. *Not now.* She was supposed to have time with him. She was supposed to make his last days count and tell him she loved him. Remind him that all those nasty things she'd said as a teen weren't meant—they were just the screams of a dumb kid who didn't understand that all he wanted was to give her the best he could, teach her the best he could.

But that time was gone now, erased from existence as if it was never even a possibility. As if that god that mocked him with his cancer had just laughed in his face, yanking that little bit of time away—it was never his, never hers, never a real thing other than inside her mind.

The front door slammed shut, and Big Steve towered over Melissa. "Where are the keys to the truck?"

Three

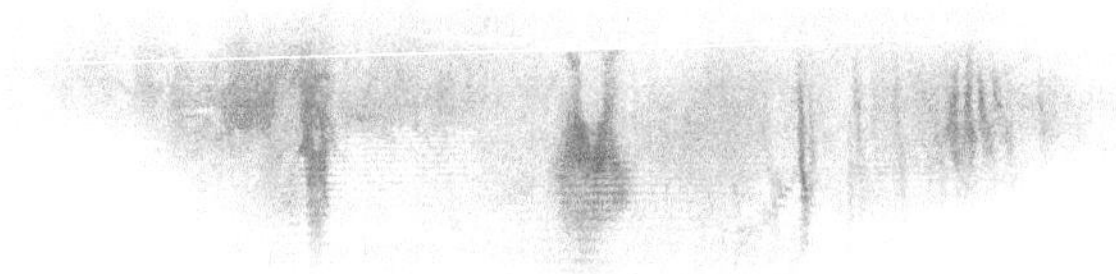

M ELISSA WEPT, GAGGING ON her own spit, sorrow, and rage, her hands duck taped and her back against the living room wall. Mom mirrored her, though her gaze was somewhere beyond now, off in some other place only she could see.

The female intruders had dragged Dad out the back door and came right back, making Melissa think they'd thrown him on the deck, just far enough that they wouldn't have to deal with him.

While the three women cleaned the inside, Big Steve and Stevie—

Steve had taken the time to introduce them all, which assured Melissa her and Mom's fates were sealed—

had taken Dad's truck to the road, towed their van onto the property, and hid it behind the barn. As soon as they came in, the girl Taylor rushed out and returned with her limping boyfriend. That one looked like the walking dead; he was so pale, and none of the rest cared—not the way they seemed to care about each other.

Melissa watched all this, her stomach bubbling with fear, eating itself as she tried to figure out what she and Mom and Dad had done to deserve this and how those bastards were going to end it. She guessed they needed another car, but it didn't seem like they liked the look of the Honda, the

Ford, or the Isuzu. But just as Stevie had suggested they take them all and follow one another, Big Steve grew stern and stormed outside, a cigarette in his hand.

Melissa wanted this to be over. She wanted them to just take whatever car they wanted and go—even if it meant death came quicker. The tears hadn't stopped streaming down her cheeks since that bastard Stevie had shot Dad, and she didn't think they would stop until she was gone too.

So might as well get it over with.

And she hated herself for thinking that. Especially with Mom right beside her.

Big Steve came back in. He glanced at his prisoners, then tossed his butt outside. He sat on the couch and surveyed the room, making sure everyone was watching him.

"Just got a text from Shamus. The robbery's all over the news over there. And they got our pictures from the gas station in Billings. They know we're headed west, and they're looking for us. So instead of going back out there to be the only ones on the road tonight and grabbing a hundred percent of every smokey's attention that we pass, we're going to settle in for the night."

"Shit." Stevie shook his head.

Big Steve pointed at him. "I don't want any shit from you." He waved his finger around the room. "From any of you. We're going to dig in, and we're going to rest. And hopefully, we can get back on the road tomorrow." He pointed at Melissa. "And as long as you keep your shit together, there's no reason you'd have to join old Dad out there."

She guessed this was him being caring but stern. She wanted to spit in his face and stomp on his nuts. Instead, she nodded. The thought of Mom was what she was holding onto now. She knew their names, sure, but it sounded like the news did too. Maybe if they played along, they *could* live through this. Maybe...

Through the course of the night, Melissa watched as the intruders helped themselves to the pot of stew, the dry goods, and once they found the basement freezer, about five pounds of frozen beef Dad had been trying to ration until after the auction. That freezer was full year-round when the ranch was booming, but with Dad's medical bills, they just didn't keep much after the slaughter anymore.

The criminals had gone through Mom's things and stolen the three pieces of jewelry she owned. They found Dad's rifles and his old Single Action Army revolver and added those to their piles of loot. They'd ransacked Melissa's room and took her laptop and tablet, both bought for school and the only things she owned that were of any value.

But none of that mattered if Mom lived; at least, that's what she kept telling herself. *For now*, was what she kept repeating in her mind as Mom somehow slept—the stress of shock maybe?

Jacob was stretched across the couch while Taylor ran her fingers through his hair and caressed his face. Big Steve and Loretta had locked themselves in Mom and Dad's room, and that was quiet now. Little Steve and Honey had taken Melissa's room, and Honey moaned through the walls.

Melissa pulled at her bonds, duck tape wrapped around her wrists behind her back and circling her ankles. She was pretty sure she'd yanked all the give she would get, and it was nowhere near enough. All that was left was the numbing in her fingers and the burning around her wrists, but she had to keep trying. She had to get Mom out if possible. As much as she wanted to think they might let her live if she cooperated, her gut told her it wasn't true. It was a fanciful dream.

So she pulled and twisted and didn't stop.

Terrance's corpse was stiff now. It still bled, though.

The night's frost was settling over his back as he lay face down on the porch. His lukewarm blood was slower—there wasn't much left—but it seeped through his wounds, filtered through his shirt, ran onto the deck boards, and dripped onto the red earth below. There, it was taken in like a fleeing family to shelter, sucked into the awaiting soil and slurped down below.

There was something that wanted it down there. There was something starving for it, deprived since the days when Terrance butchered the half-dozen cows he held back from the auction each year, kept to feed family and friends, their blood (unknowingly) appeasing the land that had made all of this possible—let him raise his family and keep them healthy—

But it was hungry now. Whether it was cow or human, it needed to be fed.

As the last drops fell and Terrance's wounds froze shut, as his body cemented itself to the deck boards with once-living adhesive, there was a rumble.

Mom's china clinked in its cabinet.

Melissa felt the house move below her.

Taylor looked up from Jacob and scanned the room. Her eyes settled on Melissa. "What was that?"

Melissa didn't answer. She held still, wondering the same question but not wanting to dignify this intruder with a response.

Taylor closed her eyes and shook her head. When she opened them, her face was coated in shame. "I'm sorry. Of course, you don't want to talk to me. I wish we weren't in your house right now. I wish—"

"Just go then," Melissa spat. "You already have my keys. Why not just leave and get out? Take your boyfriend to the hospital—he obviously needs it."

Taylor looked back into the hallway. A moan came from Melissa's room.

"They're looking for us. If I take him to a hospital, they'll arrest us. And Big Steve says there's a doctor where we're going." She gave another glance back and returned. "And... you don't want me to leave you alone with them."

"What? So you can protect us like you did my dad?"

"No, I just mean... I can try."

All Melissa could do was roll her eyes. It wasn't even intentional. It was a gut response to this woman's ridiculousness. She came in here with these thugs—sure, she had an injured boyfriend—but she wanted to pretend like she wasn't just as bad, just as responsible for what had happened to Dad?

Tears welled in Melissa's eyes as the image returned. It was like God had pressed pause as Dad's blood streaked through the air. She wanted to reach out and grab it and stuff it back into his body. She wanted to bandage and heal the wound. She wished so badly it could be taken back. But some things just can't be fixed.

She remembered almost twenty years ago, the first time she'd seen a calf come out stillborn. It just lay there on the ground in the snow, and she wished with everything inside her for its tiny heart—not much smaller than her own—to beat again. She wanted to see the baby move, to hear it cry and watch it stumble around on new, unpracticed legs. But it didn't. Whatever had stopped its heart couldn't be taken back.

It was a hard lesson, one that stuck with her. Some things can't be fixed.

"I'm sorry," Taylor repeated. Her eyes were back on Jacob, her fingers within the soft curls of his hair.

Taylor's other hand was on her belly, on her womb, and the image hit Melissa with the stunning clarity of exactly why Taylor wouldn't leave his side and why she wouldn't let them get taken to jail.

A whine of hinges that Melissa recognized well, and thudding footfalls came down the hallway. Stevie, covered in sweat and wearing only damp boxers, stopped at the edge of the room, surveying its four residents.

"You look like a sad group of fuckers." He smirked and continued to the kitchen. As he walked, his hand stroked his crotch and his gaze went up and down Melissa's body. He opened the refrigerator door and stood, leaning his midsection almost inside the thing while soaking in the coolness.

He sighed, then grabbed the orange juice jug, twisted off the cap, and guzzled. He dropped the cap on the floor and wandered back into the living room.

Melissa didn't like the way he lingered. His focus seemed locked on her, on her breasts. It was like she could read his thoughts, and there was a sickness inside him that wanted to drag her, still-tied, back into the room with himself and Honey.

She stared at the ground, praying something would hold him back.

The floor rumbled again.

Four

Bᴵɢ Sᴛᴇᴠᴇ sᴀᴛ ᴜᴘ in the bed, his pistol in hand. He touched Retta's shoulder and shook her.

"What?" She sucked in a gasp. She was always startled when she woke.

"Get up. Something's weird."

Neither had dressed down; it was a bad idea when they might have cops knocking on the door at any moment.

Steve stood and walked toward the bedroom door. His finger stroked the trigger as he strode.

"What do you mean *weird*?" Retta's feet hung from the mattress.

"Like—an earthquake or something."

"We are in Montana. Earthquakes happen."

"And SWAT trucks can rumble like earthquakes too." He peered through the bedroom window into the backyard's gloom.

She remembered the raid in Chicago so many years back—Tommy Cleaveland's head exploding when he tried to aim his revolver at that SWAT asshole. She tried to remember if there had been an earthquake. She wasn't sure. She *was* sure Tommy deserved to have his head split after raping her sister in that crack house bathroom two weeks prior, but not whether she heard a rumble.

"Okay." She pulled herself to her feet and picked up her own pistol from the old woman's nightstand.

Steve went to the door and leaned his head out. The hallway was dark, but he saw the living room clearly. That pain in the ass bitch Taylor was on the edge of the couch, and his dumbass son stood almost naked, a jug of orange juice swinging from his grip. He couldn't see the girl or the mother that lived here, but by the demeanor of the other two (specifically, the smirk on Little Stevie's face), he assumed the hostages were in their places.

It felt somewhat better to have a grasp on that room, but his pistol would stay in his grip until he'd looked out front and was sure.

Steve passed the next room. Door cracked, he saw Honey on the bed, naked, her legs spread wide. She was soaked in sweat and locked eyes with him. He kept moving as she grinned and stroked her breast.

When he reached the living room, all eyes except the sleeping old lady fell upon him. He scowled at the boy. "Put some goddamn clothes on, will you?"

Stevie cringed. He set the juice on the coffee table and headed toward the hallway. "What? What is it?"

"Just get dressed and get back here."

As Stevie darted into Melissa's room, Big Steve marched to the front window.

"And have Honey get dressed too!" He leaned against the pane and felt the night's cold on his forehead. His breath threatened to fog it up, and he wiped the dampness away as he searched the driveway.

There was no one in sight. The gloom was thick, with only faint moon rays finding their path to the ground through the hazy sky, but he was pretty sure there was no one out there. Still though, he didn't believe what he saw. There was something—he didn't know what, but there was something. Maybe someone was coming? Maybe they were at the street, at the end of the long driveway, with their lights off, preparing? He didn't know what was out there, but his gut said it was someone—and his gut was never wrong.

He shook his head.

It was true his gut was never wrong, but that didn't mean he always listened. The goddamn job today was a prime example of that. He knew there was going to be a problem before he walked into that store. He knew Stevie didn't have his head on right—Christ, did he ever?—but he brought him along anyway. He let Stevie do crowd control, and now he regretted it.

There weren't many things he regretted in life, not a job, a murder, a dollar spent on some frivolous piece of ass—shit, we were all walking corpses anyway, might as well spend it while you can—but he regretted this. That was his boy. He was a dumbass at times, yeah, but that piece of shit in the store nearly took him. He should have listened to his gut. Retta should have had the crowd. She would have found the gun on the guy, and they wouldn't be under an interstate manhunt right now. His boy wouldn't be inches from lockup.

He was sure they were out there. Somewhere.

His stomach was crawling. His palms were wet and itching. He had a dryness in his mouth.

It was only a matter of time before the shit hit the fan. He had to be ready.

Melissa watched her captors. They scurried around the house, peering through windows and clutching their guns. She didn't understand it.

She would have been amused by it had she not also felt something was off out there.

She wanted the cops. God, she wanted the cops to come in guns blazing and take out each and every one of these animals. For her father to have some justice. She glanced at Taylor, who had been posted at the kitchen window. The woman held a gun in one hand as the other held her belly—maybe that one could just go to jail? Maybe that would be okay?

But as much as she wanted the cops, she didn't think they were coming. That wasn't this feeling. She'd been pulled over for speeding. She was stopped once coming out of a bar in Bozeman, drunk and underage and praying not to get busted. This didn't feel like either of those times, and it didn't feel like a rescue, either.

This felt like a different kind of fear. It felt like the far side of the east pasture where Dad had buried that stillborn. It was where Dad had dug a hole with the backhoe and buried four carcasses the wolves had gotten to one year. It was the part of the pasture she and Matty refused to use when they played hide and seek or four-wheeler tag. It was never a smell, the thing you would think associated a place with death—Dad did a good job at burial; otherwise, critters would dig. The thing that kept them away was a cold feeling that brushed down her sides. It was a gnawing at her insides that pulled them this way and that and made the interior of her belly burn without eating a single pepper. There was something out there; though they could never see it, they felt it.

An image of that foul ground appeared in Melissa's mind as she watched the criminals squirm. She saw Dad nudge the carcasses with the rear of the backhoe's bucket, and the understanding hit her that what Dad was doing was not burying. It was not covering up something bad or rank. He wasn't getting rid of something he didn't want.

He was feeding the ground.

But no. That didn't make any sense. The ground was an inanimate thing. You don't feed it. But she couldn't shake that understanding any more than she could shake knowing that the woman in her kitchen was pregnant. These were facts. And as much as the far side of the east pasture told her what it was, the same sensation hit her now. The earth was here, outside those doors. These asshole criminals felt it—they may have interpreted it as cops, but it wasn't.

There was a sigh on Melissa's side: Mom. She was awake, her eyes shifting from door to window to window. She saw it in her mother's eyes as well. Mom knew it, too, and she wasn't scared of these men any longer. She was afraid of something else.

Honey stared through Melissa's bedroom window at the snow-skimmed parking area, the woodshed to the right, and the dilapidated highway in the distance. She didn't see anyone, but that alone didn't make things all right. Yeah, Big Steve had said cops, and the cops would have made the most likely group to be after them, but were they invisible?

The anticipation made her chest tight. Someone was out there, invisible or not. She knew it.

It was like her early days at The Marquis, the shitshow of a club outside Kansas City where she started stripping. Short for *The Marquis de Sade*, everyone knew if you paid a little extra, you could get just about whatever you wanted in one of their back rooms. It was a line she didn't want to cross when she was first hired, but her wants didn't play into how the customers felt. The reputation alone meant anyone walking through the door expected their wishes to be granted, even by the girls who would rather stay on the stage or earn a few extra bucks behind the bar.

It took less than a week for a bouncer, at the behest of the owner, to drag her into the back and throw her into a room with two guys looking to split her for the night. And the soundproofed walls ensured it didn't matter if she said yes or no.

She looked at those two, felt the sticky, perfumed air across her skin. It was the most vulnerable she had felt since she was twelve in Dad's shop and he'd been drinking all morning, skin mags in his tightened grip.

The bass thumped from the club's main room, and a tickle across her skin grew as the adrenaline spiked in her veins. She gazed at one leering grin and then the next. Her insides clenched as they grabbed her hands and her hips and forced her to her knees, and behind the fear of what would be left of her if she didn't go along with it was a sensation: what was surrounding her was more than just a pair of horny men—there was evil in the room. Real evil in the backs of their minds. It warned her that the word *No* from her lips would turn this from rape into much more—a beating they'd laugh through, blood and broken bones that might just... she didn't want to think about it.

It was better to play along. Keep them happy and keep that evil, that rage that wanted out of the back of their minds, at bay.

So she gave them a good time. And the next guy too. And so it went until she found her way out of that hell hole. But what she learned that night never left. She was tuned in now, and when there was evil on the horizon, she knew it was there. Shit, she'd felt it in Stevie, but she was able to control him for the most part. She'd felt it in Big Steve, but Loretta kept that in check, more or less—except when it was just the two of them, but those occasions helped buy some protection when Little Stevie got a little too rough with her.

As she looked outside, she felt that tingle, though. It prickled her skin and warned. Something bad was out there. Something evil. And more than staring out the window and waiting, she wanted to run.

When the next noise shook the house from the back, she knew she was right. They should have run.

Five

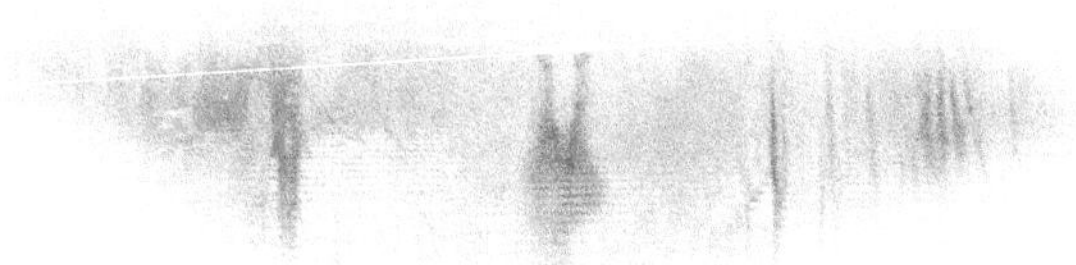

THERE WAS A RUMBLE below the house as it rose. It stretched from the moist earth below the deck, parting the bloodied soil that refused to freeze. It reached to the cracks between the boards, parted itself, and slipped through, finding a new home in what it had once seen as an obedient subject.

Not that it had any love for Terrance Cambridge. He was a human, a mortal, with no more value than the actions he completed for it. But as it soaked into his flesh through the broken and shredded skin, as it surged into Terrance's mouth and filled his orifice, then stomach, then lungs—as it found the cancer and seeped into the rotted, mutated tissue, it understood why it was being fed less, and it grew furious that something inside that house had taken away its means of sustenance.

Terrance Cambridge's meat crackled as he stood. The frozen strands of tissue tore from each other as his body moved under its control, yet the flesh obeyed, animated by it, driven by the final desecration, and it would not allow this to go unanswered.

Terrance/It took hold of the back door's knob and turned. When there was no movement, it raised a hand and—

Taylor screamed as a frozen, bloodied hand crashed through the door. The boom shook the house as shards of wood rained, and the door fell.

She backed away raising her gun, as what came through—it wasn't possible. It was the dead man. Not a live man, not like they had made a mistake and wrongly thought he was dead. This was a dead man, *dead*, frozen eyes leveling on her.

Ice clung to his hard, clouded pupils as they shifted. His hair clumped in mats of crystallized blood. His lips hung from his mouth like plump, purple sausages in need of a thaw, and his finger pointed at her, pale white nearing blue, and she knew this lifeless thing wanted the same for her.

That finger, that motion—it sent a realization through her mind that this was the last place on the planet she wanted to be. Even jail would have been better than this. She had more important priorities to consider than this ridiculous gang and the aftermath of their idiotic job. There was another life inside her that, if she died, would extinguish too. This, more than the thought of losing her own life, rocked every nerve in her being.

She shook. The gun tumbled from her trembling hand.

Taylor turned and ran.

Melissa spun at the noise, and her heart launched into her throat. What she was seeing didn't make sense. It was Dad. Dad was in the kitchen, moving toward Taylor, and then Taylor was screaming and running, and—but Dad was dead.

He moved after her, lumbering with the awkward footsteps of a stiff-legged, untrained being. His hands raised, and his mouth spread in a growling show of yellowed teeth and lips that cracked and split, breaking as his jaw widened beyond its full extent—and he didn't flinch at what should have been painful—should have made him scram as his cheeks split.

Terror rose inside Melissa. Fear of what was happening to her father. As if death wasn't bad enough, something was infecting him, and the pain and suffering it must be causing him—what it could do to her and Mom—turned her body to ice.

Worse than the breaking of frozen flesh was the sight of his gunshot wounds. They were gaping craters of red meat shedding crimson crystals onto the floor. Melissa saw into his lung, into the thing that should have spelled his death before these monsters came into their house, and her turning, tightening insides could take no more.

She puked.

Mom screamed.

The living room was flooded with criminals. Steve, Stevie, Loretta, Honey, Taylor, and on the couch, his eyes wide, Jacob—they seemed to appear all at once, and each that had one pointed their guns at Melissa's dead father.

"What the fuck?" Stevie screamed. His usual steady hand trembled as his eyes ran over the thing limping toward them from the kitchen.

"What's—" Honey fought to get it out. "That guy's dead!"

Big Steve didn't say anything. His gut rose inside his chest, but his grip was steady as he raised his pistol and aimed at the dead thing's center mass.

Everyone in the room knew the shot was coming, but they all shook as the bullet left the barrel, the flame crossed the room, and the *pop* rang in their ears.

"No!" Melissa shouted as a new hole ruptured her father's chest. She tried to believe it wasn't him, wasn't his soul in that thing, but the sight of the impact still caused her to jolt.

But the dead man didn't fall. Chunks of his frozen meat fell back, and others exploded forward, but he didn't fall. So Big Steve fired again.

More pieces of Terrance's tissues rained down, and Stevie, Honey, and Loretta each raised their guns and joined the firing squad.

Crumbs and hunks and splattery globs hit the floor. He kept walking closer, and they kept shooting. Their weapons clicked empty. Holes peppered the old man's corpse from thigh to head. A chasm parted the top of his skull. A window showed the kitchen through the back of his wide maw, and he kept walking.

Loretta fumbled for words and searched her pockets for another magazine. Jacob, whose mouth had hung open from a combination of shock and growing infectious fever, found a gun in his waist and raised it as the thing neared Taylor.

What none of them seemed to notice were the changing shapes of Terrance's lost pieces. When they had thudded to the floor, they were frozen chunks of protein. As they quickly warmed to room temperature, they melted into a slimy, gooey substance that was now inching toward the room's inhabitants, right on Terrance's heels.

"The fuck?" Stevie screamed. He found a second magazine in his pocket and opened fire. Big Steve fired right after him, and one bullet at a time cut through dead Terrance, slicing muscle and tendon, breaking bone, ripping through his head and neck and legs until Terrance toppled to the floor.

Melissa howled something between a scream and a cry as he slammed down in front of her. She pulled harder at her restraints and went nowhere. There was a burning need to get up and run, and her body shook, revolting at her inability to get it out of danger. Her mother nodded in a sequence of seizures, then her eyes fell closed, and her head lolled to the side.

The Steves' guns locked back empty again, and Stevie shouted, "Take that, motherfucker!"

But the movement he thought was just the body settling didn't stop. Yes, it was no longer walking. Yes, the bones and muscles were broken. But it still slid toward them by some unseen form of locomotion.

Terrance's arm separated along a series of gaping wounds in the forearm. Dark red goo leaked from the severed flesh, slid beneath it, and marched toward Honey's foot, dragging the dead man's hand behind it.

She screamed and ran down the hall.

The top half of Terrance's skull peeled loose to a slurping sound, and his brain slithered from his head, guided by strands of red slime that shot forward and dragged the brain and bone behind it. It wanted Loretta.

The corpse seemed to melt into slithering hunks of independent organs, muscles, and digits, and they all crawled toward criminals.

Melissa clamped her mouth shut, terrified to say a word. Not a sound. What if a single utterance caused those things to turn toward her?

A red string of sludge shot up onto the couch, dragging a finger behind it. Taylor screamed and shot, her bullets ripping holes into the sofa but missing the tiny, jittery target. She kicked at it, and it went nowhere, clinging to the cloth and then slapping against Jacob's leg.

Jacob dropped the gun and grabbed the finger, wrenching it away from himself. But as he lifted the digit, the string of goo didn't detach. It held onto his leg, crawling up his thigh, nearing the bandaged wound.

He threw it across the room, but the goo only stretched. It dove under his bandage, and he felt it digging into the open flesh of his wound. "Get it off!"

Taylor grabbed a small towel from the coffee table and tried to wipe his thigh clean. The grossness only seemed to multiply. It smeared and then bulked. It pushed deeper under his bandage, raising the cloth and cotton and pushing it away. At the same time, it slid from the towel onto her wrist and began slithering up her arm.

She screamed again and wiped frantically at herself.

Stevie took off down the hall after Honey.

Big Steve started stomping on the dismembered pieces of Terrance.

The skull cap crept toward Loretta.

Six

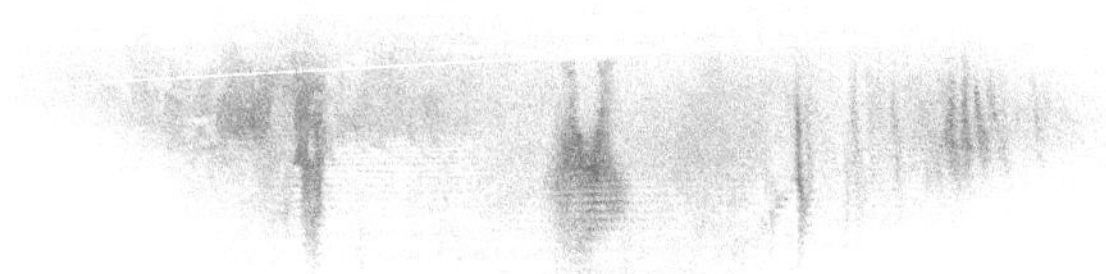

STEVE STOMPED AND BONE crunched. Red, gelatinous gunk squirted from below his boots, and then it wrapped around them.

He shook his foot, and it refused to let go. He scraped his boot on the floor, and a stringy clump attached to what was once Terrance's liver slapped onto his other foot and reeled itself toward him.

"Fuck!" The fear in Big Steve's brain was subconscious right now. At this moment, anger drove him, anger that this abomination was targeting his crew, his family. As hard as he fought to fling it away, it refused to let loose. There was an abstract fraction of a second where he heard a song in the back of his mind. Weird Al Yankovic sang *Gotta Boogie*, flicking his finger, unable to lose the hunk of disgusting dried snot, and Steve envisioned himself never being able to rid himself of this slime.

The top of Terrance's skull attached itself to Loretta's knee and climbed with fingers of red mucus. She screamed and ran to the front door. As her hand reached for the knob, the slimy bone sprung upward, sealing her mouth, and the goo dove inside her.

"Retta!" Steve ran toward her.

Her eyes rolled back into her head, and she dropped.

Steve grabbed the hunk of skull and pulled. It came loose but dragged a drooping line of crimson, which hung like a festoon from hell, thick and flowing like congealed blood.

"Retta!" Tears formed in his eyes as he saw her go pale, saw her tremble beside the door, saw the red nastiness begin to seep from her ears.

He dropped to his knees as Jacob stood.

Jacob's face was glowing red, his eyeballs swollen and ready to overflow their sockets. Red mucus dripped from his mouth and ran from his nose like a flu-infected child who didn't know how to blow. He leaned forward, and for the first time since they'd arrived at the ranch, Taylor was backing away from him, not just from fear for him but for herself.

His mouth opened, and Taylor's eyes brightened for a second as she expected him to speak, to say *Don't worry, I'm fine*. He didn't. He lunged at her, slime bubbling from every hole.

Taylor turned to run and tripped over her own feet. Her belly slammed onto the floor, her mind racing with terror—*that kind of impact could kill the baby*. She pushed up, and Jacob fell on her.

He clawed at her back, dragging himself up her body, teeth poised to chomp into her neck and rip until she stilled. Goo flooded over her back and washed up her body, around her waist, digging under her clothes.

"Jacob! Please!"

She pulled along the floor, not concerned with direction, just anywhere, away. She was moving toward Melissa.

Melissa had stopped trying to free herself. The thought had totally escaped her. She was watching in paralyzed fear. She was frozen in place, with nothing going through her mind but the screams inside her head and the sound of teeth chattering in her ears.

But it was no longer happening in the other half of the living room. It was now moving toward her. The madness, the unearthly evil in her home, was riding on the back of the pregnant woman, clawing at her, and it was nearly in her face.

She watched Taylor's eyes rise to look ahead. She saw the fear there, and she knew it wasn't just the fear for herself. She remembered watching the woman stroke her belly. She wasn't crawling to flee for her own life; she was fighting for that child.

Something snapped inside Melissa's thoughts. It was a rush that broke free, empowered by a hundred despicable things: these criminals in her house, the death of her father, the resurrection of his corpse, these inhuman creatures that belonged in the bowels of Hell, not in her living room. There was an overflow of feelings, a fountain of despair, rage, and worry, both for her mother and for that unborn child. But her body was bound, and all she could do with it was scream.

"No!" She projected every ounce of strength from within. "Leave her alone!"

Taylor kept crawling, but the thing on her back stopped moving up her. It looked at Melissa through Jacob's decaying eyes. The bulging balls deflated as if their walls gave way, and a burst of red slime gushed over his cheeks.

Melissa shoved herself backward, but she could go no further. What had she done? She'd focused the monster's attention on herself, and now it was going to come after her. Then it would go after Mom.

Jesus, what had she done?

But it didn't. It stood, rising from Taylor's back, and it turned toward Steve and Loretta. The layer of red slime on Taylor dripped away, and like a conscious pool, it slid across the floor toward Steve.

Taylor's face flooding with tears, she stopped beside Melissa and turned. They watched what happened to Steve and Loretta together.

Big Steve retreated along the floor until his back pressed against the coat rack and he couldn't force himself to flee from her any longer.

Loretta's eyes had popped. Red slime ran from her sockets, her ears, her nose, and her mouth, and she crawled along the floor, matching him in pace and direction.

He saw Jacob in nearly the same state, rounding the couch and getting closer.

How could this have happened to Steve? He was always a step ahead, always ready for the competition, whether that be cops or some punk wanting to take what was his. He'd always had the upper hand, either from wit or intuition or from his size. He *never* lost. So, how could this be happening?

His wife, the love of his life, moving over him like some ghoulish scavenger. Jacob, the weakest member of his crew, advancing to take him on. His son, fled. And the junk wrapping around his legs, seeping into his clothes.

That intuition spoke once more, definitely too late.

It said this was the end.

He felt the cold ooze crawl up his leg, inside his pants, as Retta leaned in as if to give him a final kiss. Her lips met his, and at once, goo shot into his groin and his anus. It poured down his throat and up into his nose.

He wanted to cough, piss, and shit as every cavity bulged inside. He wanted to scream but had no breath. He wanted to move, to run, to escape, but his muscles were frozen, drugged by whatever this was.

So, instead of any of that, he tried to enjoy the last embrace of his wife's lips as the red, mucus-like goo burned and ate his flesh.

Steve heard an engine start outside. He was half-relieved his son would escape. The other half of him hated that kid.

Seven

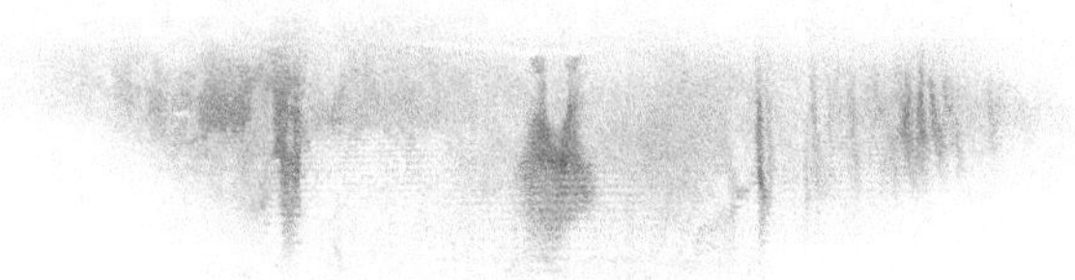

Taylor freed Melissa and her mother. They stood up to flee the living room. The strange thing was, once they were moving, the monsters no longer appeared to be a threat. The small pools of goo that Terrance had left after being shot had all melted into the cracks between the floor's wooden planks. By the front door and under the coat rack were no people and no monsters. There was a pond of red, gelatinous slime with small lumps that resembled the shapes of bones. But even those quickly sank into the crimson soup, and all of it descended into the floor.

The pool shrank and shallowed, lowering over the period of a minute. When it was gone, all that remained was a pinkish stain on the wood and a thick iron smell in the air.

Mom cried, and Melissa guided her to the kitchen. They sat, and Taylor fumbled over the cabinets and the stove and made Mom a cup of tea.

They sat for a long time. They wept, Melissa and Mom for Dad, Taylor for Jacob. After a while, Mom and Melissa forced Taylor to run before they called the police. They didn't know what they would say to them, but they knew they had to call. Melissa gave her the keys to the Honda with a warning: "Take care of that kid, and stay out of crime, or I'll come looking for you."

Taylor cried and agreed. Mom found the bag of heisted jewelry in her bedroom and made Taylor take it. It wasn't that much, but when they got somewhere to settle, it would get them started.

They all wept as the sun rose, and Taylor drove away.

Stevie shivered. The heater in Terrance's truck barely worked, and though Honey leaned on him, cuddling for warmth, she didn't make much of it.

He cursed as the sun came up behind them. He hated that he had to leave his dad behind. Big Steve was the only one who had ever stood up for him. He was rash and ill-tempered; he knew that. He was quick to cause trouble and make people want to fight. And Steve always had his back—but he didn't return the favor. Not once.

He liked to think Steve would have understood, but he knew that was bullshit. The man may have stood up for him, but his dad thought he was the biggest fuckup in the family and likely felt disgraced that he ran—or, he would have.

Stevie knew the old man was dead now. He didn't have to see it to know it happened.

But it would be okay. They had a vehicle, and he knew Shamus, the contact in Custer Falls. If they could just get there, it would all work out.

Stevie leaned back and breathed deeply, his eyes on the snow-capped mountains ahead. He held Honey tight, let his hand run over her leg, and grasped her hip.

They'd get through this.

The sign ahead read *Custer Falls 99 Miles*.

Acknowledgments

Thank you to my family for putting up with me. I say this in every book, and it bears repeating because they deserve it.

Thank you to Richard T. Ryan, who edited Chester's Cave, as well as the rest of Fedowar Holiday Horrors Vol. 1, where the story was initially published. Richard is a great editor and talented writer.

Thank you to Lyndsey Smith for including The Trophy in the first Fear Forge anthology. That story was so much fun, and I was honored to be a part of that book. If you haven't read that one, it's a really fun read, and Horrorsmith Publishing is one to watch.

Thank you, Heather Ann Larson, for your hard work on the bulk of this collection. You do an amazing job and I appreciate you.

Thank you, the readers, for picking up this book. I hope you had as much fun with it as I did.

About the Author

D.W. Hitz lives in Montana, where the inspiring scenery functions as a background character in his work. He is a lover of stories in all mediums. He enjoys writing in the genres of Horror, Supernatural/Paranormal Thriller, and Science Fiction/Fantasy.

Originally from Norfolk, VA, D.W. has degrees in Recording Arts and Web Design and Interactive Media. He has been a creative his entire life. This creativity has driven him in writing, music, and web design and development. He aspires to tell stories that thrill the heart and stimulate the imagination.

When not writing, D.W. enjoys spending time with his family, hiking, camping, and playing with the dogs.

Be sure to sign up for his newsletter today at www.DWHitz.com.

More from Fedowar Press

Bloodtooth by D.W. Hitz, a small-town coming of age horror compared to Needful Things crossed with A Nightmare on Elm Street with strong IT vibes:

After nightmares begin in the small town of Custer Falls, Montana, in 1992, it'll be thirty years before they end.

Available now from online bookstores or signed from Fedowar.com.

Uncanny Valley Days by C.J. Sampera

Rocked by grief and recurring apparitions of her dead brother, Olivia is losing her grip on reality and may have inadvertently invoked a cybernetic, serial-killing slasher demon. Or is it all in her head?

Available now from online bookstores.

Camp Slasher Lake: Volume One, winner of the 2023 Spatterpunk Award for Best Anthology.

A tribute to the glorious slasher movies of the 1980s, Volume 1.

Featuring stories from: John Adam Gosham, Gerri R. Gray, Patrick C. Harrison III, Carlton Herzog, D.W. Hitz, Derek Austin Johnson, J.D. Kellner, Brian McNatt, Nicholas Stella, & Vincent Wolfram

Available now from online bookstores or Fedowar.com.

Camp Slasher Lake: Volume Two

Another tribute to the glorious slasher movies of the 1980s, Volume 2.

Featuring stories from: Jay Bower, Justin Cawthorne, Kay Hanifen, D.W. Hitz, Brett Mitchell Kent, Aaron E. Lee, Kevin McHugh, Carl R. Moore, Daniel R. Robichaud, Darren Todd, & Mark Wheaton.

Available now from online bookstores or Fedowar.com.

Thank you for reading.